The Angels of our Better Beasts

FIRST EDITION

The Angels of Our Better Beasts © 2016 by Jerome Stueart
Cover artwork © 2016 by Erik Mohr
Cover design © 2016 by Samantha Beiko
Interior design © 2016 by Jared Shapiro

Distributed in Canada by
Publishers Group Canada
76 Stafford Street, Unit 300
Toronto, Ontario, M6J 2S1
Toll Free: 800-747-8147
e-mail: info@pgcbooks.ca

Distributed in the U.S. by
Consortium Book Sales & Distribution
34 Thirteenth Avenue, NE, Suite 101
Minneapolis, MN 55413
Phone: (612) 746-2600
e-mail: sales.orders@cbsd.com

Library and Archives Canada Cataloguing in Publication

Stueart, J. (Jerome), author
        The angels of our better beasts / Jerome Stueart.

Short stories.
Issued in print and electronic formats.
ISBN 978-1-77148-407-7 (paperback).--ISBN 978-1-77148-408-4 (pdf)

        I. Title.

PS8637.T865A8 2016   C813'.6   C2016-904209-X
                                            C2016-904210-3

CHIZINE PUBLICATIONS
Peterborough, Canada
www.chizinepub.com
info@chizinepub.com

Edited by Andrew Wilmot
Proofread by Ben Kinzett

Shelfie

A free eBook edition is available
with the purchase of this print book.

CLEARLY PRINT YOUR NAME ABOVE IN UPPER CASE

Instructions to claim your free eBook edition:
1. Download the Shelfie app for Android or iOS
2. Write your name in UPPER CASE above
3. Use the Shelfie app to submit a photo
4. Download your eBook to any device

Canada Council   Conseil des arts
for the Arts   du Canada

We acknowledge the support of the Canada Council for the Arts which last year invested $20.1 million in writing and publishing throughout Canada.

ONTARIO ARTS COUNCIL
CONSEIL DES ARTS DE L'ONTARIO

an Ontario government agency
un organisme du gouvernement de l'Ontario

Published with the generous assistance of the Ontario Arts Council.

Printed in Canada

JEROME STUEART

The Angels of our Better Beasts

C Z P
ChiZine Publications

I think I could turn and live with the animals,
they are so placid and self-contained;
I stand and look at them long and long.
They do not sweat and whine about their condition,
They do not lie awake in the dark and weep for their sins

—Walt Whitman

TABLE OF CONTENTS

Sam McGee Argues with His Box of ~ Authentic Ashes

*It is rumoured that Sam McGee once ran into a young man selling the authentic
ashes of Sam McGee, the cremated hero of "The Cremation of Sam McGee," by
Yukon poet Robert W. Service. Amused, he bought them, because how many
men could say they bought their own ashes?*

I was offered the chance to buy a piece of myself
the other day, and so I did. I came in a small bag,
which I found very saddening and undignified,
so I bought myself a nice hand-carved wooden box—
and I carefully sifted myself into it.

And I wondered, half in morbid amusement,
which part of myself I had purchased—the arms
of a road builder, the bad luck as a gold panner,
the sedate life of a married farmer, a churchgoer.
Was it the best parts of my life, or the worst?

I opened the box to examine myself up close—
to see what kind of man I was—the fine grain of me,
the coarseness, the smell of my life all burned up—

—when I was surprised to hear a voice come from the box—
like an excited street-corner barker. *"What a treasure you hold
in your hand! What a great life you have purchased!
A lucky man is he who holds the ashes of Sam McGee!"*

"Oh really," I chuckled. "Tell me about Sam McGee,
this treasure."

And, with a raucous, carnie shout, he quoted the poem—
the life story of Sam McGee, as written by Robert W. Service—
and unflattering, unmanly, untrue portrait of a Sam McGee
that never existed. It was just a name that Robert Service,
the damn Yukon poet, snatched up from the bank register
where he worked, needing a name to rhyme with Tennessee.

It was my name he snatched from that register I signed.
So I got to be the wimpy, whiny complainer, frozen solid
on a Christmas Day, stuffed into the boiler of a derelict
paddle wheeler, and brought back to life—briefly—in the heat
of the boiler fire. *"Since I left Plumtree down in Tennessee,
it's the first time I've been warm."*

"Stop!" I told the Ashes, as I had told every man, woman
and child I ever met, "That. Isn't. Sam McGee!"

The Ashes, however, disagreed. *"Why not?"*

"Because for one thing, I'm Sam McGee—and I'm from Ontario."

The Ashes drifted in thought for a moment. *"Who wants to be Sam McGee from
Ontario? It doesn't even rhyme."*

"It doesn't matter if it rhymes; it's the truth. I'm Sam McGee! I didn't take a
mushing trip on Christmas Day! I never whimpered about the cold! I was
never frozen solid! I was never stuffed in a boiler! I never came back to life!"

The Ashes said, *"Well, what did you do?"*

I was caught off guard, I'll admit. Always defending
myself against the fame of the false Sam McGee, saying
who I *wasn't*; what I *didn't* do; what *never* happened to me.
I hadn't really—practiced—my own biography. And I stuttered
some events I believed important in my own life, a beautiful,
settled, prosperous life with family and farm.

And the more I talked, the more I was tempted to embellish,
to make things rhyme—to swath a coat of brightly coloured paint
on the history of my life. But I didn't. I was true to my life,
every mundane thing.

But the Ashes, the true barker of the living world,
asked me, *"Wouldn't you rather be Sam McGee from Tennessee?"*
"No, I wouldn't," I said, and I was strong at first.

But the Ashes talked about immortality.
My name was on the tongues of bards across the world
and would be for hundreds of years. I was in the homes
of millions and millions of readers. I would be remembered
for a sort of Christmas Day resurrection,
the ability to withstand the fire,
to be renewed by it—
oh, the ashes got terribly metaphorical and metaphysical.

"No one knows of Sam McGee from Ontario—
and no one will. But you can choose to be
the Sam McGee of Robert W. Service and be
remembered forever—and isn't being remembered
more important than being true?"

I quivered, even shivered.
To have passed through this world making no mark
bigger than a few stories my children will remember—
compared to that of a life that entertained millions
in a story unlike any other—even untrue—
                              what would I do?

The Ashes, sensing victory, roared, *"What has the truth*
ever done for anyone? It's really not that catchy.
What you need is a good story."

"Story," the box whispered, *"is a light—*
whether it shines on you or burns you up,
it's still a light everyone can see.
And in this world of unnoticed billions,

there's a light shining on you, Sam McGee.
Deny Ontario, and be from Tennessee!"

And I thought of my life, and I thought of my wife, and I looked at my
ashen friend,
then "Here," said I with a sudden cry, "is the way this story will end."

I would be Sam McGee from Ontario,
but I would keep Sam McGee from Tennessee
on my bedside, dead, cremated, a reminder
that six billion people and their happiness was not
worth my name, a reminder that a good life didn't have
to be one that was recited on a stage, that bliss
didn't have to be shared like the morning news,
that I could allow Sam McGee from Tennessee
to rest in peace in a box forever. I didn't have to compete
with Sam McGee—
I just had to ignore him.

But sometimes, at night, I can hear the Ashes whisper through the
wooden lid.
In the dark, their voices say, *"it's not too late to become someone GREAT!"*

But I turn over in bed and smile.

These ashes are nothing special. Ashes say that to everyone.

‿ℓℓℓℓℓℓ‿Lemmings in the Third Year

I've always preferred my rodentia frozen, tagged, weighed, and placed in plastic bags; it unnerves me now to be interviewed by them. The lemmings, four of them, carry notebooks and an inkwell that looks like a dark blue candelabrum. They have followed me out onto the tundra, unsure why I am here. Since it is their job to observe me and ask questions, they approach so they won't miss the one vital piece of information for which they have been looking all along. But I'm not in a talkative mood.

The tundra is quiet. I would have expected that, really, back home in the real Ivvavik National Park, the real northern coast of the Yukon Territory. I would have expected the passive look of the Beaufort Sea as it gives in to blocky chunks of ice that grow in numbers like a scar forming on the water. I can still see the grass underneath a light snow. I expect that, too. The vastness of the Arctic is amazing, breathtaking, and all this you can read about in books, see on television specials, even visit.

"What are you thinking about, Kate?" one of them asks me, breaking the silence. They have scratchy, tiny voices—not like Alvin and the Chipmunks, but more like carnies operating a Ferris wheel for the sixth day in a row, people who smoke a lot. Lemmings chitter.

"I'm thinking about home," I tell them. I open the videophone that David gave me before we left. It was working when we first crashed, but it's not picking up a signal anymore. I am so *roaming* it's pathetic. You can't see it out there in the sky overlooking this flat, coastal plain, but there is a hole in midair that our plane came through, and it's completely invisible. It's only several hundred feet off the ground, we guess.

"Home is Las Vegas," one of them says.

I laugh. "Yeah. You guys would fit in well there, especially in a casino, or maybe even your own show." I wish I could mark the air with a dye—so I'd know where the window is. I pick up a stone and think about throwing stones up one after the other until one of them disappears, but that's several hundred feet. Couldn't make that if I tried. Besides, there's a chance that any window we came through has closed or moved on. That we are here for a long time. Like the ice freezing up behind you—we may be here until a lead opens in the air to take us back home, away from this land of speaking wildlife.

"She wants to go home," one of the females says. "She wants to give her research back to her people."

The wind batters my blue parka and drives black hair back into my face.

"No one," I laugh, "would believe our research right now. It wouldn't make a difference to them." They watch me punch the small buttons on the videophone. These phones are still so new; I don't know how to operate it like David would.

"Research is factual. It has to be believed," one of the males says.

"How can research be unbelievable?" a female asks.

I look up at the sky. From the sea to the mountains in the distance, it is all one flat colour.

"All right," I say, and put away my phone. I take a big breath. This is going to be a tough one. "It's time you learned about the scientific method."

I hear them behind me, scratching something on notepads. Every once in a while, there is a *glub* sound of a paw dipping into the ink and coming out again.

The day hadn't started off well. I have lived in a cabin for the last few months with two other scientists and a pilot who was trying to fix our plane. Except he had no parts. Because—*surprise!*—there were no stores for aviation spare parts in this place.

Dr. Claude Brulé, the lead scientist on this expedition, had abandoned science altogether for theatre. I no longer saw him in the cabin, as he now stayed with a polar bear that lived farther inland. The polar bears here were decidedly friendly and had a non-aggression pact with most of the animals, except the seals, but even that depended on times when the seals were selling the bears something and when they were not.

The bears were putting on a play for us. Actually, they were putting on a play before we got here, but Dr. Brulé had been helping them with direction since last week. He'd always had a fondness, he said, for Shakespeare.

Dr. Kitashima and I live in the cabin together. He is full Japanese, but speaks English much better than I speak Japanese. My father never spoke much of his own language around us girls, so I didn't pick up much. I did study Japanese in college a bit, but didn't speak it well enough to impress a native of Japan. Dr. Kitashima doesn't say so, but I know he'd rather I not speak any Japanese at all. He said I spoke it like a man.

Rather than abandon what we came here to do, Dr. Kitashima and I had been trying to conduct our experiments on *this* tundra. We had this belief—or I had, until today—that one day we would get back and that, in the meantime, science would be what would keep us sane. If we concentrated on our work, we would be able to think our way through this, figure out another way to get home. At least, he told me once, we would pass the time.

Our pilot, Ernest Stout, had a tent set up by the plane, but eventually, as winter set in, I knew that he would join us. His dog, River, had started to talk to him for the first time, and he didn't know what to do.

It's strange. I can't explain how strange it is. We had watched movies all our lives with talking animals; I had read books when I was child—*Watership Down*, fairy tales, *Charlotte's Web*—and none of them prepared us for all the animals talking. I haven't heard a mosquito yet, but I'm willing to bet that they have some language, too. The only reason that the bears, lemmings, ungulates, walruses, and birds (for the most part) speak English is because the bears learned it first, and they taught it to everyone else.

They all speak with a south-western twang.

"Do you mind if we continue our questioning?" one of the males asked me. They clambered on top of one of the huge wooden desks inside this cabin, dragging with much effort, their inkwell. At one point I had named them, but was so embarrassed about doing so that I refused to talk to them as individuals.

"I really have a lot to do," I lied. What is there to do in a place you can't escape? There were no research centres, no universities, no schools to get into, no professors to impress, no jobs to interview for. There were no other humans in this place that I'd seen, and the animals all acted as if we were the newest thing. For a while, we had many bird visitors—kittiwakes mostly—nosing around, wanting to know what kind of disturbance we would make to the environment.

I shuffled some papers on the desk, picked up my pen, and began writing a letter to my long-lost boyfriend David, whose worst nightmare had happened: he had lost me, just as he suspected he would.

He'd said, "If I let you go to the Arctic, do you promise to come back and get a degree here in Vegas?"

I couldn't have told him yes. I never wanted anyone to control my decisions, box me in. Well, now I had the whole world to move in, free and unencumbered by any other person but one bear biologist, one botanist, and one pilot.

Dear David, I am doing fine. How are you? I wrote.

"Will you be eating us soon?" one of the lemmings asked.

I looked up. Two of them were poised to write, one was approaching my elbow, and the other was aside the inkwell, looking horrified.

"I'm not going to eat you," I told them.

"But we're highly nutritious," one of them said.

"We have plenty of food." I gestured over to the back room, which housed a huge supply of seal and some vegetables that the bears traded for. "I'm not the big enemy this time."

"Do you enjoy eating lemmings?"

One of the females tapped his shoulder. "We know they do."

"We've never said that," I said.

"You enjoy meat?"

"I do eat meat, yes. But—"

"You will enjoy us. The bears like to dip us in gelled seal fat. I think that's what I would like. I've heard it is very tasty."

I shuddered. Researchers in the lemming community were basically sacrificial lambs. They came and did surveys to determine who would be their big predator in the fourth year, offering themselves as food after the data was delivered back to their community. All this data was compiled in the second and third year, and a major enemy was predicted. I'd never seen if this was effective; I'd heard from the bears it was not. According to them, the lemmings became paranoid by their own data and panicked in the third year, breeding like crazy to survive the coming "holocaust," making the fourth year a feast for all predators. It was a terrible, cyclical event, but it happened. Lemmings on our side of the window had spurts in population as well. It had never been a crisis, as far as I know.

But then, I'm not a lemming.

"I want to be cooked on that beautiful blue flame," one of the females said, pointing to our small gas hot plate, which we hadn't used in a while since we were running out of fuel and wanted to conserve for the nine-month winter ahead.

"You can't," I said coldly. I waved the pen at them threateningly. "We aren't going to use that very much anymore."

"But I get a request," she demanded.

"Sorry. I'm not even going to eat you. You might as well pick another subject to interview."

They were undeterred. "Did you come here specifically for lemmings?" a male asked.

Dr. Kitashima came in the door, and I felt as if I were saved. "Doctor," I said, "what have you heard?"

"Mr. Stout believes the landing gear is completely out of commission. Will not be able to fly the plane without it." He took off a stocking cap and placed it on another desk. He then went to the removable panel in the floor and grabbed a rake leaning against the wall and started to rake the coals beneath the wood, nestled down a few inches into the ground. It was not the best heater, but it worked.

I'd already heard some of that news yesterday. But I didn't want to believe it. I looked away, told myself that I could be as stoic and practical as the next scientist. I could make do with what we had, live a life here in the Arctic watching plays put on by bears, talking to doomed lemmings, shooing away nosy birds and foxes. I certainly didn't want to be the weak and emotional one on this expedition—the one who couldn't pull her weight. No reason to accuse me or fulfill their expectations.

"You have remained busy?" he asked.

"I've been working on reports," I said, sticking the letter to David underneath another pile of papers. I hope he didn't really listen to my voice—there was a catch in it. He smiled. "Good. That will pass the time."

He is short like me, and his face looks like a windshield after it's been broken. He seems much older than he actually is—I thought maybe fifty or so. Really no need for him to look as old as he does. Despite his sometimes annoying habit of treating me like his research assistant, I get along well with him.

"You have been talking to our friends," he said, indicating the lemmings.

"I don't really want to—" I started to say, but one of the lemmings interrupted.

"We are in the midst of an interview," he reminded me. "Did you come here for lemmings?" he asked again.

I ignored them, getting up and moving to where Dr. Kitashima stood. I started telling him how these lemmings were driving me batty.

"Are you perhaps avoiding the question?" one of them asked. "We've had that happen before." He turned to the others. "I would put, yes, she has come for lemmings."

"You can't put that!" I said. "I didn't confirm."

"You confirmed by your avoidance."

"That's not research," I told them.

"We hypothesized that many subjects lie and avoid. This just proves our hypothesis is a true one."

I blew up. "If all your data is skewed to answer your hypothesis, then why do research at all? Why not stay in your lab and make up whatever you want?"

They were quiet for a moment.

One of them said, "When data relies on the answers of individuals, isn't there always a margin for error due to the unreliability of interviews?"

"If they are unreliable, why would you do them?"

"How else will we collect data?"

"Look, I don't have all day to explain to you how research is done. But I'll tell you this: there are other ways to calculate threat in a closed system besides interviews. What am I saying?"

Interviews—we'd never *tried* interviews before now. No one—no animal—could tell us what they were thinking. And, come to think of it, if they had been able to, we would have solved a lot of mysteries regarding how animals communicate, what they are thinking. What a boon to science! 'Course, that's called anthropology.

I walked over to them. "Okay, what you are doing is more of a psychological survey. Now, that's not my field. But I do know this: surveys have a large margin of error, and that error margin rises when you are dealing with personal questions. You are asking predators if they are planning to eat you. Now let's think about this: Why would a predator tell you he was going to eat you?"

"They all tell us they will eat us."

"So how do you determine which one is the most threatening in a given year?"

"We go by intuition—in the way that the predators answer the questions."

"Intuition? That's not scientific."

"But it has been accurate for generations."

"Wait. You're telling me that the questions are a front—a disguise—for you to assess each predator through nonverbal cues?"

They conferred among themselves for a moment in lemming-speak—a high-pitched chittering. One of them looked up. "We cannot answer the question without skewing our results."

I was ready to throw something. "You are a walking, talking, *insult* to science!"

Dr. Kitashima swept the floor around me, asking me to lift my feet one at a time. "Perhaps this is opportunity."

"What opportunity?" I snapped.

"To spend time. Teach them about science. Real science. Help them see."

He swept the cabin methodically, in rows, until the dust was in one pile, and then, without another word, swept the pile out the door.

❧ ❧

That's why we are here now, the five of us, me and my team of protégés, approaching a snowy owl's nest on our bellies. In the distance, a snowy owl sits. It's a female, as they alone incubate the eggs. Males are usually out gathering food. This is about the distance that we need to be. She can probably see us, but that doesn't matter because my point will still come through.

"All right, let's stop here."

"Why don't we go up to her?" one of them says.

"We don't want to alter the results of observation. A scientist has to keep objective distance at all times. She doesn't want to influence the results of her research. Of course," I pause to remove a small rock from underneath me, "there is a theory that every observer has an effect on the thing she is observing. The Hawthorne Effect."

They scribble on a notepad and repeat, "Hawthorne Effect."

"But we're going to forget that," I say. "We are going to maintain our distance. The first thing you have to learn is how to observe." I look at the owl through my binoculars. She appears sedated.

"Okay, what is the owl doing?" I ask. "Observe her and tell me what you see."

They watch for a few seconds. A female says, "She is looking for us."

"What makes you say that?"

"She is looking straight at us."

I glance through the binoculars, "No, actually she looks like she's asleep."

"She is faking," they say.

"You don't know that. You have to go by what you can see."

"She is stalking us," they say.

"No, you're missing the point. You can't make up things—you can't interpret the data you don't have. You have to look at what she's doing and just write that down. Can we do that? Can you just write down what you see?"

19

They scribble for a few moments, looking up at the owl periodically, and then returning to scribbling. One of them even draws a nice picture of the owl.

"That's very good. See, now this guy over here has drawn a sketch to go with his observations. That's very cool, uh . . ." Suddenly I want to name them again. "Are you Luxor?" I ask.

"I'm Orleans," he says. I'm embarrassed because I named them after casinos. I wasn't feeling quite myself that day—a little excited, a little unprofessional. But now they were colleagues and not subjects, so it was different.

"Orleans, yeah. Okay, Orleans here has drawn a picture," I say again.

"It's a very nice picture," Mirage says. "Should we all draw pictures?"

"Well, pictures are nice." I prop myself up on an elbow. The wind whistles under my hood. "But not necessary. Just writing down notes of what you're observing is the important part."

Bellagio says, "She's awake! I saw her move."

"Good." I turn back and look through my binoculars. "All right. Now, look at what she's doing."

"She's cleaning herself," Mirage says.

"She is," I confirm. "Good, write that down." They proceed to write down this information.

"Why is this important? It doesn't tell us if she will eat us," Luxor says.

"Animal behaviour is an indication of their patterns, their habits. If we know the routine of this owl, we can then predict behaviour." I feel a bit like a professor instead of a graduate student.

"How long before we know if she will eat us?"

"Well, Mirage, you have to observe her over time. Like, a long time. Like, a really long time."

"A couple of days?" asks Bellagio.

"Well, some of these can last for months or years. Depends on funding."

"Funding?" they ask.

"Not important here," I say. "We have to watch this owl and find out what she's like, what she does, what her habits are. Habits don't lie like statements about your habits can."

"Like when we caught you lying," Luxor says.

"I wasn't lying," I sigh. "Okay, it's true, I came here to observe lemmings. I'm a biologist. I want to do this for a living. I was going to do just what we're doing now."

"Look at us through binoculars?" they ask.

"Yes, basically. Yes."

"What's basically?"

"That's not important."

"You would have snacked on us," Bellagio says.

I look back at the owl, and she has something in her mouth. It's a lemming.

"You guys better see this," I say.

They hum in chorus and breathe in, and then a world of scratching on notebooks.

"Well, we're done here," they say.

"What?" I look back as they start to leave. Bellagio has the audacity to cross over my back. "Where are you going? You're not done."

"We observed her eating a lemming. That answers our question." Luxor wipes his hands on his fur, smearing it with ink.

"You don't know how often she does that," I say to these science neophytes. "You don't know if the lemming was days old."

"But she was eating her. Clearly, she has the appetite and the habit." Bellagio turns to go.

Mirage stops. "But we don't know how often this owl does that, or if all the snowy owls follow her pattern. Kate is right. We have to stay and watch longer."

Good job! I think.

Orleans and Luxor are off, crossing the tundra. "I have a better idea," says Orleans, "we'll just ask her."

"That won't give you real data!" I call out after them. My words get lost in the wind. "This is not part of the scientific method! Wait!" But they are heedless.

"Men," I say.

"Males," Mirage and Bellagio say, but they aren't as upset as they need to be. They say it in a dreamy sense. "They *always* have such confidence."

"Listen," I tell them. "That's an owl. What's to stop her from eating them?"

Mirage titters. "Wouldn't it be wonderful to be swooped up by an owl? Feel that rush of excitement, even as the talons surround you!" She clasps her little paws in front and her eyes go wide.

I underestimated their death wish.

I stand up, brush off my coat, and walk quickly to catch up with the two others in my team. Back home in Las Vegas, I was in charge of the Mendor Lab. Diane Mendor really ran it, but when she got engaged, she became wrapped up in a lot of other things, and I just naturally took over. This feels like the lab all over again: a bunch of young grad students who think they know what they're doing, blustering right into a big pit. Live and learn.

Orleans and Luxor have scampered right up to the owl, but the owl is not reacting to them in the way I expect. She sees me, obviously, and this alarms her. Even though I'm shorter than the average human, there is no average here to work from, so I look tall. I've always wanted to be tall. Perhaps I stretch a little when we get up close to her. I've also only seen dead owls this close. I know a fellow student who's going into zoo science. She visited a whole owl sanctuary in California. Said they scratched a lot, and they were flighty. I wonder what owls here are like.

This one has her feathers ruffled, but she's not hissing. She's not moved off the nest, either, but I can't tell if she's upset or excited to see us.

"Hello," I say to her. "My name is Kate."

"Well, these *are* nice. Thank you very much, Kate," she says, eyeing my lemmings.

"They're not for eating," I say.

"We're here to ask questions," Luxor announces, pulling out his notebook.

"Ah, I already had a team asking questions. I told them everything I know," she says, but her tone is cheeky. She swivels around and pulls out a lemming from her nest. "You might recognize this one."

The lemmings chitter among themselves, some high-pitched squeaks, which are either terror or delight, or maybe both.

Mirage turns to me. "He was a colleague." But she states it as fact, without emotion. I haven't gotten used to facial expressions yet.

"The agreement, you know," says the owl.

"Of course," says Luxor.

I say, "What do you mean, 'the agreement'? These are my lemmings."

Orleans looks me square in the eye and damned if he didn't put his little paw on his hip. "You won't be eating us. You told us that."

"Well, I might. I might just get a hankering for lemming in the middle of the night," I say, with a little jealousy. "Listen," I turn to the owl, "these are my lemmings, and I'm training them to do things differently. So you can't eat them. They're experimental."

The owl blinks. "Dear, why do you want to change a good system?"

She knows. She knows the lemmings are basically naïve, and that their questions don't amount to anything. She's taking advantage of them.

She nestles her wings close. "Feel free to ask me any question you wish—for the agreement," she adds firmly. She doesn't look at me.

"Luxor, Orleans. You guys come home. I'll talk with you."

They aren't listening. Luxor has his notebook out, is flipping back through small pages. Orleans holds the inkwell and props it up between the two of them.

Luxor glances back at me to show me how this is done. "Now," he says, turning to the owl, "about how many lemmings do you eat in a given day?"

"About two," she says, without pause.

"And how large is your territory?" Luxor asks.

"It is squares forty-five to fifty-three on the *loo-tow* field."

Luxor beams, as much as a lemming can. "Well now, that's a large area. And you only eat two lemmings a day? Do you have a mate?"

"I do," says the owl.

"And how many lemmings does he eat?"

"He eats two a day as well, on average. Although, lately he has been flying off into other squares." She turns to her right. "He could be anywhere right now."

"Exactly," says Luxor. "And if you had to predict your appetite in say a year's time, would you say that you on average would eat the same amount of lemmings?"

The owl thinks, blinking, and then widens her eyes, little explosions of yellow. "Well, I don't know. Let me see. A year's time. Why, just thinking of that makes me terribly hungry. You know, anything can happen in a year's time."

Without warning, she lunges forward and gobbles up Orleans, slapping her beak against the inkwell. A squirt of red and inky black runs down her feathers. Luxor and the others are entranced. I move forward and grab the owl by her throat and place a hand around her legs, just above the talons—I don't want to be scraped. I squeeze until the owl's beak pops open. She must be in shock because she doesn't try to resist, and I turn her head toward the ground and shake her, trying to make her gag by pressing her throat. Nothing comes out; the owl has swallowed the lemming whole. But I know she can regurgitate. I've seen them do it. And with the size of Orleans, there should be a lot more ripping and tearing before she swallows. She's just trying to make a point.

So am I.

The lemmings are clapping behind me, and I can't tell if it's because of what I am doing to save Orleans, or if they are cheering for the "beautiful" death of their colleague.

The wings of the owl slide open like a fan, and she's big enough that when she flaps, she gets a lot of pull. I stand and she's flapping against my face and gagging.

"Cough him up," I say, like a gangster, but nothing is coming out.

The wind bites my face and ears, and I have the owl now shoved down toward her nest, hoping that by gravity something will expel. The wing cradles my face like a palm, reaching around my neck, quivering.

Finally, a body slips out of the owl onto the grass, covered in gunk. It's actually two bodies, and for a moment I don't know which lemming is Orleans, but they both appear still.

I push the gasping owl away from the nest. She squawks about "the agreement, the agreement."

I rub my eyes and begin wiping away the gunk to figure out who is who. I've seen small rodents mangled in traps before—traps that misfire, spring on a leg, clamp down on the body of a mouse, and by morning, the mouse hangs divided by the metal mesh. It's bothered me in the past, but not like this.

One of them is barely moving; I pick it up and see that it's Orleans, and I wrap him in my scarf and place him in the warmth of my pocket.

"We have to go back to the cabin," I tell them. I don't listen to their protests, and I don't check on the owl, even after I see her in my peripheral vision, stumbling out of her nest.

The cabin is full of scientists and a seven-foot-tall polar bear. All of them see me come in, and I go straight to the desk.

"Something happened," I say. My lemmings jump up on the desk. The cabin is warmer than outside, but you can still see everyone's breath. I think I catch concern in Dr. Brulé's eyes; he's reacting to something I'm giving off, something on my face.

"One of the lemmings," I tell them as I unwrap Orleans and lay him on the table. He's still. "Can I have the first aid kit?"

I've never patched up a rodent before—not a lemming, not a rat, not a mouse, not even the flying squirrels I studied in California. If they were injured, they died; if they were dead, we catalogued them. We put them in frozen bags until we were ready to take down notes. We thawed them a few days later along with all the other dead animals, and we wrote down how they died, where they died, how much they weighed. We sexed them, measured their molars to discern their age, and we put them in a large black garbage bag because we had everything important we needed from them.

Dr. Brulé helps me orient Orleans on the table, pulling his little arms to his sides. Dr. Kitashima stretches out the scarf like an operating blanket.

"We were interviewing a snowy owl, and then she ate him. He was moving fifteen minutes ago," I say to Brulé.

"He has some deep wounds," Dr. Kitashima says. Some of the gunk we wipe off keeps returning from the open beak marks near Orleans' tail. There are two cuts on either side of his face, too, and I can't tell if the blood is coming from his neck or his cheek. Cheek would be a flesh wound; neck would not.

Luxor, who rests his arm on a cup of water, says, "We have the data. This is what happens."

"Well," I tell him, "I didn't want to *let* it happen. I'm sorry."

I pull off some bandages and I cut a tiny square to wrap around his hind end—almost like a diaper. I'm thinking that if I can stop the bleeding, he'll be okay.

"Someone will have to go back and stay with the owl," Luxor says. "If we don't, she might get upset, and that will ruin all our data so far. This might spark a revenge cycle and increase her numbers of lemmings eaten per day. Revenge factors are difficult to measure."

Dr. Brulé gives me a look like he's doing the best he can, but it's not going to work. Neither of us has seen Orleans move. He's gone limp in my hands even as I raise his tail to wrap the bandage.

"If he's dead now," Bellagio says, "we can take him back as an offering to the owl, and maybe save the data."

I snap. "I'm not interested in saving the *data*! God, he's your colleague! You weren't even the envoy to the owls. You were *my* envoy." Dr. Kitashima can't feel any pulse at all. He has sensitive fingers, worked with small seedlings and plants all day. I've watched how tender he could be when growing things. "This wasn't going to happen," I say to Dr. Kitashima because I don't know to whom I'm supposed to say this. How I'm to account for this.

Both doctors stop for a moment, help me find my composure. They don't condemn me for my outburst. I respect that. Then Dr. Brulé takes out a syringe with a dose of stimulant in it. He injects this into the lemming, and we wait.

I remember my sister had a hamster when we were little. It escaped one day and ended up in the inner workings of the dryer. We found it when the smell from the dryer turned sour. She cried for days. I was stoic. I offered to buy her another hamster—a generous offer, I thought. She wouldn't speak to me, ran off to her room. I didn't understand why she was so upset. Later, she almost went into veterinary work; I went into biology. She owns two cats and a dog, a budgie, and several fish. I have no pets.

Orleans does not recover. "He was only in there for a few minutes," I say.

Dr. Brulé moves around to my side of the desk. "Owls have a narrow throat, Kate. He was probably crushed and suffocated in that amount of time. It's possible that there's a lot of internal damage. I don't know."

I look up at the ceiling. It's a high ceiling, made for bears to walk around in comfortably. The one here now simply watches. He fills up the room in my mind, like a supernatural being—if I believed in such things. Talking animals have that supernatural quality, the kind that makes me think I'm living in a fairy tale. I'm sure the bear doesn't understand the sanctity of life. I don't think I understand it anymore.

If animals talk, then they can't just be eaten as food anymore. They aren't any more a part of the food chain than humans are. If everything talks, where do you draw the line on feeling for them as individuals? God, I was slipping into subjectivity. They warn young graduate students about getting attached to the animals in the lab.

Don't name them. Don't pet them.

Don't ever let yourself get interviewed by them, either.

Luxor writes in his notebook. Bellagio and Mirage walk over to the body. Bellagio picks up the scarf ends and starts to drag the body off the desk. Inevitably it will fall on the floor with a heavy thump. It's all senseless. This whole place is senseless.

Mirage stops her. "Wait," she says, and goes over to the body and looks down at Orleans' face. She sniffs his face, and then backs up and looks at his ink-stained body. She traces her hands across the stains as if she is reading the last marks. He's become a notebook himself, I think. She says, in the quietest voice—I can barely hear her at all—"He had very good penmanship."

I want to scream, but Dr. Kitashima speaks instead. "How long did you work with Orleans?"

Mirage looks up at him slowly. "We catalogued data and research in the libraries for a season. He had good penmanship there, too."

Luxor says, "He was brave."

"He was efficient," Bellagio says. "And he drew nice pictures."

Mirage stands up and walks over to the inkwell. A small notebook rests against it. It's obviously Orleans'; it has blood on it. "We have his notes," she says. She begins reading.

"Snowy Owls eat two lemmings per day. She doesn't predict that she will be increasing or decreasing that amount. I believe, of course, that she's lying."

No one speaks. Mirage looks at all of us. Her small eyes, all pupil and dark, stare at each one of us in a glance. She closes the notebook and sets it against the inkwell, carefully, as if the weight of it will tip the inkwell over.

Luxor looks grave, and when he speaks, his voice seems loud. "I concur. I believe she's lying, too."

I notice that her fur is turning to its winter coat. Not all in one place, not like a white patch, but as if every tenth hair has changed to white. A subtle change, a gradual one. I look over at Orleans, now eternally brown, except for the ink scratches and a black, ink-stained front claw.

"It's a shame," Mirage says.

"Yes," Luxor agrees. "Kate should have let the owl finish. Now the data is skewed."

"No," Mirage says, "It's a shame anyway." She walks back to Luxor. "She was lying. You both knew that. Why do we trust data from lying subjects?"

"We've always known they lied. That's what makes it accurate."

She looks at me. "No," she says, "that makes it a waste of time." She steps down off the table onto a stack of books until she is on the floor, and Bellagio and finally Luxor follow her, down to the floor and out a small hole in the wall. Like a little procession, they leave. I think, there you go, Ms. Future Scientist, lead them away from this. She makes me want to smile, but I can't.

I take a paper towel and wrap Orleans in it, but I don't put it anywhere. I just sit at the desk for a while. Dr. Brulé makes tea for everyone. Dr. Kitashima opens a notebook and writes something I'll never read. The scratching sound of his pen makes my eyes blur, and I look up and see the great white mass of the polar bear looking down at me. I get shocked every time, thinking they will eat us. Can I really trust them when they look like this?

He just stares for a few moments, like I imagine God would stare—a god with big teeth and black gums, who makes me feel small and insignificant; a god that stares incomprehensibly, maybe unable to think of anything to say, of any excuse to give for such a mixed-up world. Here the whole natural drama plays itself out like it always has, except *now* I'm privy to all the voices, all the personalities, all the individualities of each player, each animal or bird that is stalked, chased, and killed. I get the privilege of talking with them over tea before it happens. I get to see their beautiful sketches of snowy owls.

That's either all wrong, or the way it should have been all along. I don't know which is better.

The bear leans over the desk and fills my vision with his face. He breathes through his nose at me, a puff of smoke. Bears believe you can read a person's thoughts in their breath—the breath that we see coming out of our mouths in the winter. Those are thoughts and feelings unexpressed, they think.

I sigh back as an answer, and my breath sneaks out as a flat line of smoke. He looks at it, closes his eyes, and moves away. I hope I said something right.

It's October now, and Luxor, Bellagio, and Mirage have gone back to their community of lemmings, not far from our cabin. They handed back their research—not only the research on which predator would be the most destructive, the most costly to their community, but also the recommendations they have based on the evaluation and gap analysis they conducted on their own research methods. Honourably, they have completed the mission of any scientist—human or lemming: they concluded their research, and it's up to the community to make decisions. Having returned, they stay in our cabin now.

"We would have sacrificed ourselves anyway," Luxor shrugs.

"This way we get to learn more about research," Bellagio says. They are all almost completely in their winter coats now. They line the railing on the cabin deck, and we look out onto the snow-swept plains, erased in the half-light of early winter, until they turn blue, merging with the frozen sea.

Mirage turns to me and asks the question I have been thinking about now for months: "What do you do, though, Kate, when you don't have a community to give your research to? We have no purpose for our research anymore. We can learn. But what does it do?"

I have a cup of coffee in my hand. I don't know where the coffee comes from—somewhere south of here. The bears trade for it. It's not the same as coffee from home—it's bitterer, a bit spicier, a darker flavour. But it's hot and it's good and it's my coffee now.

"You do it for yourself," I tell them.

She nods, hums a little, and then they chitter for a few moments. And then, soft as twilight, the darkness sweeps over us, silent, like a bird with black wings.

Heartbreak, Gospel, Shotgun, Fiddler, ~~~~~Werewolf, Chorus: Bluegrass

"What wondrous love is this that caused the lord of Bliss to bear the dreadful curse for my soul?"

—"Wondrous Love"

A werewolf has always been hiding in our gospel bluegrass band. I seem to be the only one who knows what you have to do when the moon is minutes from rising. Yes, if you're the bus driver, you have to be clever, you have to be fast, but eventually, because they are blinded by faith, you have to be the one who figures out how to save them. Because it's not just *his* curse anymore, not if you're all fleeing the same moon.

First, get out of there. Get Tommy and Amelia into the tour bus. Tear them away from the fans that wave their CDs to sign. The plastic bounces and reflects the setting sun like flashbulbs, but you have to ignore that. The fans crowd the bus. "We have to go," I tell them.

It's one of our nights.

Eric and Jimmy lead them away from the bus. The sun winks below the church roof. Behind me, in the heart of the bus, I can hear Amelia snapping the metal shackles on Tommy, pulling the leather straps. "Dadgummit, tell him to drive," he pleads. Even before we're on the highway, I can hear the straining, woeful sound of her fiddle, warming up, like a woman crying.

Second, get out of sight. I park the wide, monstrous Tinderbox tour bus outside of town, at a small hotel. I don't look back. I lock the bus—lock them both in there. It's a motel night for me and Eric and Jimmy and Wayne. Not so lucky for Amelia. I don't care about Tommy. I look back at the bus one more time before heading into the Sleepyland Motel. Pray to God she's okay for another night. 'Cause, at this point, Amelia's at the mercy of some moonlight, some leather straps, some metal clasps, and a god who thinks it's all too funny.

Here's the story, quickly, about how he got turned from a God-believin' missionary man into an achin', pitch-perfect bluegrass player after a dog bite. The way Tommy tells it is that he went to Romania when he was twenty and just beginning to play the banjo. He weren't no Earl Scruggs, but he had a lot of passion for playing, and went over to Romania to teach some kids how to play instruments—instruments they could make themselves out of boxes and rubber bands. He wasn't paid very much and he didn't have another job. But he believed in God, and that God would bless him someday. He did as much good as he could as a missionary and as a man.

He was out walking the streets of a little village outside Negrești-Oaș one night—which isn't a good thing to do, but he didn't know that—and he was praying, and he was praying, "God, what kind of difference am I really gonna make here? I'm just gluing together some instruments, and the children don't really have nothing to play. My real instrument—my banjo—well I could do more good with that if you blessed it. If I became big and famous playing the banjo then I could have the money to buy these kids some instruments." And he prayed and he prayed for God to bless him—to give him what he needed to be able to play. And wouldn't you know it, at that moment, a dog, a big black dog, came out of the night, right up to Tommy, and bit him on the hand. And he cursed that dog, and he shouted to God, why did you let this dog bite my hand? And the dog, sure enough, looked at him, cocked his head and said in a voice as human as you or me, "You don't have enough ache to play good bluegrass yet. But you will now."

Now Tommy didn't know that this dog was a werewolf, or that he too would become a werewolf every time the moon was full. Or that one day, he would kill one of those children he loved.

In the morning, I'm up early and outside to check. Because when you're the bus driver, you've got to be willing to do the dirty work—get the bus checked, keep it running or know where to take it, make the difficult calls when it breaks down, be willing to break the rules of physics to get them there on time. Check on the banjo and fiddle players locked in the trailer, keeping each other alive and killing each other. Watch over them like a blessed protecting angel if you have to.

The bus shines like a silver bullet in the morning sun. Clean. Cooling down. Texas, wide and flat, yawns and stretches out beyond it, a few miles north of Plainview.

Before I can get to the door of the bus, Amelia steps out looking like a sparrow tossed in a tornado, her body leaning over the edge of the step. She hangs on the door handle as if she might fall. Like always, I have a tube of her hand cream ready. Clovertree. Organic. Nothing else does the trick for her tired hands, her cramped elbows, her stiff shoulder—products of tireless playing all night long. I stumble to her that morning, as if to catch her.

"I got it." She looks up and smiles, wide, genuine—in love. She's been in love with him for seven years. She usually tells me, *He was a lot better tonight. I could feel it.* But this morning, she says nothing, no hopeful words. She's starting to realize that it's not going to change.

I decide then and there that I'm gonna shoot myself a bluegrass player. I'm going to shoot our star, Tommy Burdan. Set her free. Set us all free.

We should have shot Tommy a long time ago. Not these merciful, God-can-forgive-you Christians. They wouldn't hear of it. But I don't think it was their forgiveness or their Jesus slippin' in as much as it was their greed, pure and simple. "Capitalists," I whispered sometimes when I drove. They were only concerned with money. I'd never seen the books, but I knew they played some big concerts—upwards of 10,000 at most of 'em.

"Without him, we're nothing," Eric, the Dobro player says. He often rides shotgun, watching for fast food places where he could honour his love of french fries. "He writes the songs, he plays out the melodies, and he sings till your heart breaks. He's our ticket, yes sir."

Tinderbox is a five-piece bluegrass gospel band—banjos, guitars, fiddle, Dobro, bass—and they've had hits with their last seven albums. Lots of love and heartache and prayer and Jesus-walkin'-beside-you in their songs, and so churches love 'em. They can pack arenas and convention centres with the faithful who loved gospel bluegrass, but fill up festivals, too. My job was driving, connecting all the arena dots on the map across the South, the Midwest, the Prairies, up into middle Canada, and making sense of their touring schedule.

And saving all our asses when the moon was full.

If church groups knew what Tommy Burdan turned into on moonlit nights . . . what he tries to do—what he's done. It's our little secret. All of us, sworn to keep that secret. "Because the good we do in the world far outweighs the danger," Tommy says. "No one has to know. We keep it—we keep *me*—shackled in the Tinderbox and we don't have a problem at all. We lock up the devil. The devil won't destroy the good we're doing. We won't let him."

As long as we all agreed to never tell. That almost always worked.

But beautiful Amelia had to take the brunt of keeping us safe. She was the one to put up with it, to have to work extra hard to contain him; it was her that walked out of the shaking tour bus at night, and sometimes they looked at her differently, as if perhaps she didn't just play the fiddle to calm him—that maybe she did something else.

The only song that could contain him was "Wondrous Love," normally a four-part harmony sung by the guys, with Amelia's fiddle. But even if they could have sung it without Tommy, he wouldn't accept anything those nights but Amelia on the fiddle. So she, by herself, played that tune hours and hours on end, until the chords and the notes buried themselves in grooves on her face.

Tommy never remembered anything.

It was my job to go unlock the Box and take Tommy out.

We don't usually have much to say to each other, because I'm a bus driver, and, well, after someone sees you like this, it gets awkward.

I swear to you, it reminds me of my rehab days. I used to be an alcoholic—wait, I *am* an alcoholic; you don't stop being one because you stop drinking. I was the kind of man who couldn't remember 50 percent of his time on Earth because he drank it away. I'd wake up, much like Tommy, with no recollection of the night before, with rips in my clothes, lost wallet, smelling like booze and sweat and barf. And I called that living for more than twenty-five years.

Tommy is passed out in the chair, his arms bruised and skin broken open again, the shackles having ripped into his flesh from fighting. Not as bad as if we didn't have Amelia, but still not pretty. Takes him a week to heal up. He'll wear a white arm brace and roll the sleeves of his white shirts down to sign autographs. His fans never know what his arms look like; they can't see him like this, or like he is on those nights when Tommy is lost.

His head lolls back and the sunshine hits like forgiveness.

Unstrapping him, I think, *good for him*—he gets all that money and all that fame and all that love and all that grace because no one knows he's a monster. I admitted to myself and others that I was an alcoholic and I sought treatment, and just telling people that makes them judge me. I don't get treated as well as Tommy does here. Alcoholics are messed up sinners—and werewolves? Why, play a good banjo, talk about Jesus, and you'll have them in the palm of your furry hand.

⁂

"You can't do this to yourself anymore, Miss Amelia," I chide after I've put Tommy to bed, and I know what I'm doing. I know what I'm saying may make a difference.

Amelia runs her eyes over my face. We're beyond arguing this morning; she isn't playing along with my chatter. I can see a tear in her eye as if this time, this time, she believes me.

"It's not good for your heart," I say. The wind tries to catch my hat from my head.

"How do we know what's good for our hearts?" She looks over the plains of this strip-malled small town, and I know she's in more pain than I can bear to see. She needs someone. To find a new man—someone who could really love her. Pretty single girl like her, she could have her pick.

"If I don't stay," she says, looking at me with eyes I fall for every morning and every night, "we don't have a group anymore."

"You can't let him trap you," I say. "You have a life—maybe far away from here." I say this a lot, but today, I'm making it count. I'm going to nudge her away, because without her, it will all come to a head. And then we'll have to do what we need to do.

I know she's been approached by other record companies, other labels, a fiddler of her calibre. You have to hear her. Yes, she charms werewolves, but do you know what that sounds like? She can charm thousands of people at a concert, too, entire rooms freezing in place, listening.

She turns away from me, stares across the horizon at Texas trying to look busy on the highway beyond. She sighs. Her red hair falls off her shoulder.

"A life is okay to give away, isn't it? So that other people don't die?" she asks. "It's what God asks of me, right? It's the right thing to do, right?"

"It's not the right thing to do if it's killing you," I say, pouring her some coffee. "God isn't into making you kill yourself to keep someone else from killing."

35

"How do you know that?"

"Ask my ex-wife." I smile, trying not to reveal how much it all still hurts.

She nods, the kind of nod that tells me this time she's thinking hard about leaving.

It's me you should blame for pushing this to a showdown between a werewolf and God himself. Not her. It was her decision to leave, but I just asked her to honour that decision. That day, the morning sun played tricks with her face, making me think a person's doing better than they are. Little did we know that she'd already met someone, and that this was also tearing her apart.

❧ ❧

Tommy lives by the numbers. In the kitchen in the trailer, there is a whiteboard with the number 2 on the left side, and the number 11,324 on the right. The number on the right is the number of decisions that have been made for Christ at our concerts: lives turned around by the power of Jesus, but also literally by the music of Tinderbox—things Tommy Burdan felt he had control of. Each song he wrote, each time he played, he put everything he had into it, as if the words themselves, the tunes, could turn a heart, save a life.

The number on the left, those are the deaths. The people Tommy has killed.

"The people the monster inside of him killed," Jimmy reminds me. "Not Tommy."

It's what we say to ourselves. That there's a monster; that Tommy is not responsible. Do you know what that sounds like to me? That they can split Tommy into a monster and a good man, like two different people. I want to believe that, too. But I had a wife and a kid once, before I became their bus driver. Like another life, another Carl. And they blamed me. They didn't split me in two, and I have a hard time splitting Tommy in two—and blaming something we can't see.

I've heard it, though. Heard it growl inside the trailer, through the strains of "Wondrous Love" I heard it growl—that thing—and I want to give him the benefit of the doubt.

I once filmed it. No one knows, but I hid my camera in there, just beneath the small table, and I caught the whole thing on film. I had to watch it. I had to watch what he became so I could understand. His face stretched, his muzzle came out of his face, his lips tore back revealing teeth and fangs; his body got larger, the shackles strained, but the music, the music seemed to keep him from struggling so much. But I saw him, completely wolf. I saw it. I knew what he became. I watch that video sometimes when I want to remember what we have on our hands. What Amelia deals with.

Some days Tommy stares at those numbers, just stands there and believes, believes with all his contrite, banjo-playing heart that him staying alive and playing is penance enough for the two lives he's taken. That some mysterious number—10,000 or 12,000, or a million, will equal the loss of two.

Nothing can replace two lives. I know.

God knows it was nice seeing Amelia laugh again. I was proud of her—happy for her. When Aaron started showing up at all the concerts, a good ole boy from Omaha, with a black hat that he'd remove only when Amelia was playing, well, I knew she wasn't long for the road. And heavens, she'd been with us for ten years, and not really had much of a life. In our off-season, she'd follow Tommy home to keep him under control; his was a year-round illness, and she felt obligated.

Tommy treated Aaron with cold, unspoken contempt. When he wasn't busy, he would try to corner Amelia. I could overhear them—not his words, but his tone, pleading. Once he said, "You know what this means?" He never really loved Amelia; he needed her. I always thought of her as a drug for him, for the part that turned into an animal.

I confided to Eric while we were washing our hands after a long practice and sound check that Tommy just needed to let her go.

"He's never going to do that," he said over the sound of the water.

"Holding her captive," I grunted. "No one's gonna say that though. Because we don't want to say what needs to be said."

"Yeah, well it's her decision."

I dried my hands. "Are you sure?" I said, looking at his face in the mirror. I tossed the paper towel into the basket and left him there.

At the concert, when Aaron showed up backstage and pulled Amelia off to the side, I made sure Tommy saw it, and then pretended to hold him back. "You don't want none of that."

Eric plucked at his Dobro, glanced up at a seething Tommy. "You know, it's hard for me to say this, or for all of us to admit it, but it's time to let her go." I knew Eric. He liked to do that. It was on his mind, so it was out his mouth. He just needed someone to put it on his mind.

"I get it," Tommy said. "No one has to spell it out."

But after the concert—a double encore full of prayer and praise—backstage after the crowds had left, Tommy nearly punched Aaron.

"Bad things will happen if she leaves," Tommy told Aaron, walking into him.

"I know," was all Aaron had to say. What he meant was that he was aware. Aaron just stared at Tommy, eyes never blinking. And then he winked. Tommy leapt on top of the man, and Aaron threw him to the ground. Aaron had to be 250 pounds; he held Tommy down on the ground, and I could hear him say, even as we tried to pull him off, "You let me know if you want someone to knock the shit out of you on those nights. Maybe that's what you really need."

Tommy threw a punch, but it missed.

"I'm gonna take her," Aaron said.

We pulled him off, but not before it got worse.

"You won't be able to find her," he added.

After that, Tommy banned Aaron from their concerts, hoping that would keep him away.

Instead, it upset Amelia.

She stayed with us for one more full moon, and then disappeared the next night, completely. All her stuff removed from the bus. Only a short note, a ragged piece of paper towel, ripped off in a hurry, to tell us that she'd gone.

I'm sorry. I can't do this anymore.

I saved one. It's a different feeling when you do it out of goodness than when it's because you're a bastard. When my wife and daughter left, they were escaping me, and what I could do to them. They scared me back into myself.

Amelia just scared us.

It hit them hard. Tommy was crying, praying, begging God to bring her back; Wayne was making the necessary calls to Kate, the booking agent, to the team back in Nashville. Jimmy looked completely bewildered.

"This is the end. This is the End Times," he said.

Eric sat with him at the little kitchen table on board the bus, as if someone had died.

We were outside Evansville, Indiana. The sun was bright. Cars passed on the distant bridge, oblivious; no one here knew what could happen. We had a break before our next string of shows. At least we had that.

"She knew she was the only one who had to stay," Jimmy said. He cupped a Shasta Black Cherry soda in his hand.

I said, "Everyone doesn't have to stay."

"We're all in this," Eric said. "We all have to do the magic now."

"What's gonna happen to the group?" Jimmy asked.

Someone's gonna die, I thought.

We were on a ticking time bomb. We had twenty-eight days after she played her last "Wondrous Love" in the bus. Twenty-eight days to figure out how to contain the monster inside Tommy Burdan.

So here's the kind of meeting that five bluegrass players are forced to have around one of those pull-out tables on a tour bus.

"We can reinforce the Box," Wayne says. He talks with his hands, as if building it in front of us. "We can afford a stronger door, a chair with bigger cuffs, all metal. I bet we could get one in place."

"How're the installers supposed to catch us while we're on tour?"

"I can do it all—well, when I'm not playing bass."

Wayne is a great carpenter, but his welding is sketchy.

Drugs are no good. Getting him drunk is no good. Only Amelia had seen it full, through the window of the Tinderbox. She'd seen him change—none of us were brave enough. When he turned, the music was all that stopped him from ripping down the whole bus.

"We could play a tape and cover the window so he doesn't know that she's not out there."

"I still have my memory," Tommy says. "I know she's not going to be out there."

"Tommy, I think we need to have a conversation with just the rest of us for a bit. I don't mean no offense, but we need to talk about our commitment to this group, and what this is all gonna mean for us."

Tommy stands and rolls up his sleeves, showing the scars on his arms. They ripple across his flesh like lumpy white rivers, and he shows them to us, slowly. "No offense, but this means a lot more for me than it does for you. I'm gonna stay." He looks around at us, and no one speaks. Eric adjusts his hat. Tommy continues, leaning in, "We haven't tried electrocution, a continuous tazer."

"Tommy," Jimmy says, "who knows what that will do to you."

"We already tazed you before. It just makes you mad." Eric corrects himself: "It mad, I mean."

"You just taze me until I'm unconscious—hook it up through the metal shackles."

Wayne looks around. "I don't know how to build one of those—whatever it would take. That sounds pretty industrial."

"What if we take out your teeth?"

"And nails?" Tommy says. "We don't know if I'll just regrow them."

We all look worried. I've never heard us so desperate.

We sit there silent for a moment, so long it felt like a very sad prayer session.

"Well," Tommy sighs. "That's it. I'm calling it."

The other guys stand up; I stay seated. I want to see what happens. Call me curious, but I'm not sure that Tommy would ever take his own life. To do that meant he would end the ministry, the numbers board, the little game he played with himself about whether he'd made up for the dead.

"No," Jimmy says, grabbing Tommy's arm. "No one's ending it like this. We have twenty-eight days. We'll come up with a solution. You've been this for ten years. You've lived with this, and we've lived with this, and we've made it through."

"I'm not going to shoot you," Eric says.

"I'm not going to either," Wayne adds.

I don't say anything.

Either we had the group and we were making music that praised God, keeping that monster subdued, or Tommy was on his own and a killer, or he was dead. These are the only three choices we had, and no one here could kill Tommy in cold blood.

"The good that we are doing in the world," Jimmy says. "We—I . . . I can't believe God is just going to leave us like this."

I seriously wonder about a god that would let Tommy live. But if I can believe that black dog was the devil, then I can believe in a god that's come up with a way to contain all that werewolf.

Eric wipes his eyes. "We haveta pray harder. I don't understand why there's not a miracle for you. I don't understand it. I don't understand why someone who is doing good doesn't get cured. Or when someone dies of cancer who was doing good stuff in the world. I don't understand. Is it us? Have we not prayed enough? Am I—am I doing something wrong?"

Tommy hugs him. Jimmy hugs Tommy hugging Eric. Wayne just places a hand on Jimmy's back.

I hear Tommy say from within the bundle, "No one's doing nothing wrong."

We could have you arrested, I thought. We could ask them to put you in solitary confinement for one night. What would that do? They pray out loud for a miracle to happen. It's not like they hadn't done this before. In some ways, maybe Amelia was the answer to their prayers for so long—our little method of hiding him, or taming him.

I think about my 12-gauge under the front seat, about shooting him and saving everyone—and that he'd thank me in heaven, probably. We could report in the newsletter that he'd gone back to mission work, or that he got hit by a bus and make him a martyr. If we could keep his secret in life, we could keep a secret about how he died.

When it's a killer you become, a raging, child-killing, adult-killing monster—and the charms are all used up—there's only so much praying you can do. Surely if God could have cured him, He would have.

"I will shoot you," I say, a little frightened of my own voice.

The prayer party erupts, bluegrass players everywhere. "Carl!"

"Good God, man! Who put you in charge of that?" Jimmy says.

I stand up. "Someone has to do it if it needs to be done."

"I can see you as a killer," Eric says. "I could always see that."

I figure my soul is sullied already. "No need to dirty your souls, boys."

Tommy comes over and puts a hand on my shoulder, his eyes sincere, even gentle. I confess in that moment I'm not sure I want to kill him.

"I appreciate knowing you'll do that for me," Tommy says. "I'm so glad you said that."

The others don't look so sure. I've never been loved here, I can tell you that. But I can also tell you that the looks I get from the group chill me, as if there are monsters inside them, too.

He turns around to the others. "For the next twelve concerts we don't have a fiddle player. We need to either cancel them, do without, or find a fiddle player."

"Kate is on that, Tommy," Wayne says. "She's trying to round us up some names."

I look at Eric, and at the others, and say, "Jessica Hawley."

They repeat after me: "Jessica Hawley."

There would be no mistake like we made with Jessica Hawley, pure and simple.

Jimmy comes up to me when Tommy leaves and Eric leans outside the door to call something to him, and he whispers, "Remember Jessica Hawley, Carl. She was yours to lose."

In the long time we'd been together, only once had we needed a replacement for Amelia, when she sprained her wrist and we were forced to go in search of a temporary fix. It was hard—on the road—finding an experienced fiddler for tour dates already settled. But great musicians live everywhere; you just have to find them.

Salina, Kansas. Jessica Hawley, twenty-six years old graduate of KSU, tall as a sunflower. She performed as often as she could at the Smoky Hills River Festival, in a part-time band with her family, The Hawleys. She'd also played with The Wilderness Poppies and The Thompson Brothers when they played at the festival and in local bars.

We drove up to a huge place called "the City," a youth centre with its own basketball court, three dance halls, and a café.

Full moon was four days away.

I remember we stood in a dance hall lined with black curtains, like a bar after closing. Jessica had blonde hair curling across her shoulders. She was nervous. I couldn't blame her. This could be her Big Break. None of us would sit down because that energy was with us, like we were haunted. Her dad was there, hands in his pockets, a weathered look on his face. We introduced ourselves, shaking hands, and everyone smiled like popcorn in the microwave.

She was familiar with our songs, looking over at her daddy for confirmation. "We cover 'Walk With Me, O Saviour,' 'You've Got Another Thing To Bring,' and 'Fishing for Pearls'—but I've played your last three albums over and over. I can do it."

Tommy smiled on her, all around her—that was his magic, all right, and that day it just made things worse.

She played "Walk with Me, O Saviour" and "Fishing for Pearls," and then she played "The Son Goes Down Today"—and she was technically perfect, every note was there. Her daddy watched her, and I could sense that he was cheering for her, and that she wanted to make him proud. When she finished the songs, she was beaming.

"Play 'Wondrous Love' for us, Jessica," Tommy asked sweetly.

The six of us tensed up, but she didn't see it. "Gladly!" she said, placing the fiddle under her chin. She tapped her foot, mouthing *one, two, three, four*, and I can still see her in the trailer, standing in front of the locked, bolted, braced door, Tommy strapped down inside the room she can't see. *One, two, three, four.*

She lifted her elbow, cut across the strings, dipped, whined. I thought, *don't be good. Don't be good. I can't put you in there.* She got to that part—"And when from death I'm free, I'll sing and joyful be . . ." and she was smiling at us, hopeful. *Little girl—can I look you in the eye and tell you what you will see in a few weeks?* I looked away, acted like the music was touching my heart, but all I can see now is the moment when the door came down. How it was ripped down because this version—this version of the song was nice—but it wasn't the version that Tommy needed. Her smile, so bright; the music pouring out, eager for us to like it. It begs us for a chance. We gave it to her.

She let the last notes hang.

Eric clapped for her. We all clapped for her.

But when that door was ripped down and Tommy sprang out of it, she wasn't fast enough. I was there. I shot twice. Missed him both times.

I remember the moment we put her in front of the door. "All night?" she asked us, and I nodded. "I've been practicing—I can play for a long time, but I've never played all night."

"Little girl, you have to play like your very life is at stake," I told her. I nodded to Amelia, who would be there to speak to Tommy through the door. To the beast that would know her voice even if the sound of the fiddle had changed.

Wayne had welded the door shut, meaning that if all went well, we would need a blow torch to get Tommy out of there.

But it didn't.

There he was, hanging in mid-air—mid-leap, claws extended, his teeth working through the extra rope net we'd hung in front of the trailer door. He shredded the rope. Jessica screamed and Jimmy had the car open, so she could run into it. But Tommy leapt over the lawn and was on her in seconds—her neck, sweet Jesus— I shot. Twice. I tried to hit him, but he ran into the Nebraska night, into the brush.

"Sweet Jesus, help us!" I cried out.

Eric was by Jessica's side, her body folded on the grass. Blood on his hands. Her blonde hair covered her face. Jimmy came from the car, Amelia from the trailer. She said, "I tried to play—to help her. Oh God. Oh merciful God."

I backed away, cried, "I tried to shoot him. I tried."

"It's okay, Carl," they said.

But Jimmy could smell the whiskey on my breath. He punched me in the face. "He's drunk."

But I wasn't drunk. I'd had some whiskey to steel my nerves—just a little—because I remembered how scared I was, and how calming it felt, just a couple of shots. I was controlling myself, my nerves.

"Could you have saved her if you weren't drunk?"

That was the night I quit drinking for good, again, but it didn't matter. Once a drunk, once an alcoholic, you're never anything else to anyone who knows.

Saying "Jessica Hawley" was the same as saying "Carl was drunk."

Tommy had told us. "I can hear it. I can hear the magic in her song. We're going to be fine." But I knew something might happen anyway, and I was scared. It was our first mistake. And they hung it around my neck.

I remember Jessica smiling at us that first day like she was willing us to pick her—that this could be the moment the spotlight shined on her. This would be her great destiny.

No man is worth this much to God. Tommy was not worth Jessica Hawley. Maybe I wasn't either.

$$\mathcal{R}\mathcal{R}$$

"We save lives. Every night we save lives," Tommy always says.

He will tell you this in his defense: Tinderbox has raised more than three million for music education in Eastern European countries I can't pronounce, education that is lifting whole families out of poverty. Part of that money has also gone to microloans for building businesses in Eastern Europe. Closer to home, Tommy took over an empty factory building in the middle of downtown Faber, Tennessee, and started the Tennessee Street Foundation, dedicated to building community spaces for the homeless. Our music sales have mostly gone to ministries—not to administration, Tommy would say—but to the "hurting people on the ground, those running from disasters just licking at their heels." Yeah, his guilt has created opportunity for thousands of people.

I wonder, though, if Tinderbox could just lose Tommy and still do good in the world. I pray to God to be a better damn shot. To have more courage, better aim.

Less Mercy.

But his songs, his way of making that banjo ache—a tense, racing ache that coils around you—I've never heard anyone do that. His songs make me weep. Because I know the monsters behind them. I know the secrets behind them. They are our entire band asking for forgiveness. They sing to God himself, begging Him to take away this monster, to forgive us our secrets. Our fans had been brought through dark times on *Hiding from Your Face* alone. That album could have sustained the hearts of all our fans, but we kept speaking the words that maybe everyone else with secrets and monsters could identify with. We got thousands of letters every month—people touched, moved, comforted because the dog, that devil, was right all along. Tommy had the ache now to help others who hurt.

Right now, though, I'm torn; I'm ready to find a replacement for aching Tommy this time. I can't have another Jessica Hawley on my conscience.

I drive us through Kansas during the day, loving the Prairies, the slow roll of the hills, the clouds on the horizon, the sunshine and wide stretches where other people get bored. I'm not alone; I listen to Louis L'Amour books narrated by Willie Nelson, Johnny Cash, and Waylon Jennings. The thing about Westerns is that folks often say the characters are just gun-toting vigilantes, but it's really the opposite. All Westerns are built around people trying to settle down someplace and make a family, and some other folks—bandits, unlawful ranchers, and otherwise hostile forces—trying to stop them. Heroes in Westerns are people who solve problems to get to their family at the end. Rarely are they about a Miracle Worker, a drifter who comes in and fixes things—someone who has no stake in what happens.

Western heroes also do what they have to do—the hard jobs that no one else will tackle. Some big old rich rancher is trying to scare a town out of existence by sending in his henchmen? The other men of the town don't stand up and fight; our hero has to do that.

These stories are like pillows when I'm driving. I can rest inside of them as billboards and trucks go by, because the good guys will win and the bad guys will lose and the hero will do the hardest thing he's ever had to do to save someone.

Sometimes the bluegrass players come up and ride with me, to get a bit of a Western in as we drive. We don't talk much because Johnny, Willie, and Waylon do all the talking, and I appreciate that most days. All of us have the same thing on our minds. They all know about the shotgun under the passenger seat.

We pass through Salina. I look across the highway and nod in Jessica's direction.

It's Saturday afternoon, and we're on our way to Oakley to do a bluegrass camp for twenty-five kids between nine and fourteen years of age. They're all excited to meet Tinderbox and Tommy and Eric and Jimmy and Wayne, and to work with them perfecting their music. Without Amelia, there isn't anyone to help out the young fiddlers, to teach them songs, techniques . . . ways to control their future werewolves. Damn, I could see them growing up and having to do that one day. Who wants to have that thought in their heads? Amelia was this young once, with ambition and gumption and skill.

This time, instead of staying out in the bus, minding my own business and listening to a Western, I head in. Not that I know anything about music, but I felt I should help out since they were short. Somehow I feel like a part of them, whether they want me or not—whether I want them or not. We are all linked together in a strange way over Tommy Burdan. It's as if removing Amelia made us all responsible. We fill a vacuum.

My daughter was this young once. I don't know how old she might be now. I lost track of them. They let me lose track of them, or maybe I was always driving away from wherever they were. Her name is Janie Lee. She might be sixteen. I have no idea what she looks like now. You don't get pictures when you're branded a monster.

When we walk in the elementary school gym, the kids run up in that stop-start way that kids have, some with their instruments in hand, hoping the band members might sign them. Blonde and brown hair flying out of hair bands, laughing, so flippin' excited to meet famous musicians.

"Who are you?" a kid asks me.

I'm about to tell him exactly who I am when Wayne says, "He's taking pictures for Kate." He grins, places a hand on my back. "Would you do that? Here's my phone."

Tommy is good with kids. He has a knack for speaking to them on their level, not talking down to them. He treats them like players in his band, with respect. He teaches them some new chords, and plays a few songs with them, getting the others to play with him—thirty of them playing "On a Rhythm and a Prayer."

He also decides that they should write a new song. They write the words and music right there.

"What should our song be about?" he asks them, sitting on the edge of a stage.

"Kansas! Oakley! My house!" they shout.

"Okay, what about Oakley deserves a song?"

"Xiphactinus audax! The Palace Theatre! Buffalo Bill! There's a lotta songs about Buffalo Bill already!"

Tommy points to one boy. "Xiphactinus audax, you say?"

"It's a big fish that used to live in the Cretaceous period and swim around here, and now it's a skeleton in the Fossil Museum," the boy says.

"Does the Xiphactinus audax have a song that tells his story?"

"*Her* story!" says a young girl with a fiddle in her hand.

"Her story, then. Any song?"

"No one sings about the Xiphactinus audax!" says someone else.

"Well then we should!" Tommy roars, strumming his banjo.

The kids laugh. "The X-Fish is our national fossil now," says one.

"Our *state* fossil," someone corrects.

"So he's famous!"

"*She's* famous!"

"*She's* famous! But she doesn't have a song? How can that be?" Tommy asks. And he strums his banjo a little, and asks for some facts about Xiphactinus audax. The kids tell him, "Seventeen feet long, with massive teeth! Fangs! She jumped out of the water to eat birds! And fish that were six feet long! Deadly! Massive!"

Tommy looks over toward the guys with a weak smile.

A boy grits his teeth and bellows, "The fiercest predator in the ocean!"

"Here in Kansas?" Tommy asks, looking a little skeptical.

"We used to be a giant sea, full of sharks and big fish with teeth!" they say. The boys are very excited, but the girls are, too, as the Xiphactinus audax was the meanest, baddest girl in the Kansas Ocean.

"Okay," Tommy says. "A song for the beautiful Xiphactinus audax then!"

"Deadly! Fierce!"

"Okay, the Fierce, Deadly Xiphactinus audax—"

"Who was still beautiful!" a girl adds.

"Who was very beautiful, yes," Tommy says, strumming. "But this could be a problem, yes, being beautiful and being fierce and deadly—how will you make friends?"

"You eat them!" yells one kid. They laugh.

"She doesn't have to eat her friends," a girl says. "She chooses when she's going to bite."

Tommy looks down at his hands, twists one of the tuning struts on the banjo. "That sounds like a great idea. She's going to choose when to bite." He strums a G-chord and exhales. "Okay, repeat after me, and we'll see if we can build this song."

Oh, the beautiful but deadly (oh the beautiful but deadly)
Xiphactinus audax (Xiphactinus audax)
was swimming one day through (was swimming one day through)
the salty North Kansas Sea (the salty North Kansas Sea)

One kid corrects, "*The Western Interior Seaway*"

"She met up with a shark!" someone shouts.

"She ate the shark!" says another.

The song-writing portion of this bluegrass camp has turned into a blood-bath. Sharks and Xiphactinus audax fighting and biting, blood pouring into the ocean, clouding the water, Xiphactinus swimming as far away as she could. And just when the kids shout for her to be eaten (okay, some are rooting for her), she turns and, with the help of friends, has a last battle, teeth flashing, and they kill two sharks.

It's magnificent, I think.

"Yay!" the kids roar.

Tommy says, "Now, did you get all the chords? G, C, G, then A7, D7, then back again to G, C, G, then D7 G." It was basically "Angels Rock me to Sleep," just faster and with more blood in the water. He plays it through again, with thirty of them following him on banjo and guitar, one bass player, and three fiddle players trying to match him as best they can. They move in tandem, slowly, and then faster, adding their own grace notes and improvisations along the way.

"*And they never messed with her again. Never messed with her again!*" they sing with gusto, and in harmony when at last they have the whole song. "The Ballad of Xiphactinus Audax." She has a fight song now. "*Never messed with her again!*"

I want to live inside these two hours of normalness, laughing, playing, and forgetting. I want Tommy to live here, too. He's going to have to board the bus again, and all those what-are-we-gonna-do-now thoughts will meet him there. The kids hug everyone who came, even me. I didn't do a thing, but the littler kids hug me just the same. Something about that just hits me wrong, or right, and I swear I almost start crying because I'm standing there realizing that the last child to hug me was my daughter.

Tommy walks up to me, and something in his eyes tell me he could see what was happening. He pats me on the shoulder and gives me an I-don't-know expression as the kids chant the chorus, "*Go for the throat! Go for the throat! You better save yourself or that's all she wrote!*"

We share a laugh. If God were a person, he might have looked at me like Tommy looks at me right then—as if he knows me. I want to believe that behind those eyes doesn't live a monster, but I know differently. I can only see that thing waiting, as if in a tiny room inside Tommy's eye, shackled in a chair, and it gloats at me, daring me to think of Tommy as Tommy Burdan, good man, banjo player, instead of teeth and claws. In one eye, God himself; in the other, a monster.

We chuckle all the way to the bus, and continue down the highway.

༺ ༻

"His name is Arno Tomczak, and he's in Kearney, Nebraska. Mike Florens says he's the best thing he's heard in a decade."

"And he's not taken?" Jimmy asks.

"He's not taken, no." Eric says. "But he's a bit unorthodox. Lots of fire in him. He comes from the Canadian fiddling tradition—lots of Celtic in him."

"That's not really our style," Jimmy says.

"He's what we got if we want him."

"How will we know if he can handle Tommy?"

"We don't."

"Are we ready to offer him up like Jessica?" I ask.

Jimmy sneers. "There were other complications to that, you remember."

"We take a chance," Eric breaks in. "If we're saying Tommy lives then we're taking a chance every damn month." He glances sideways to Tommy. "No offense."

Tommy nods.

I say, "I'm not letting another stranger alone in the Tinderbox with him. If he dies, we can't say it's another wild animal attack."

"We should hear him anyway," Eric says. They're oblivious.

༺ ༻

Arno Tomczak is nothing like I expected. First, he has tattoos on his arms: pictures of a man with a green beard, and Celtic symbols, and God knows what else. He has a red beard and one side of his head is shaved, a stripe above his ear. He said his hero was Ashley MacIsaac. He wore sunglasses during the audition.

But, damn, could he play. He not only played our songs but he injected them with fire, rocking back and forth, swinging those dreadlocks as if a creature with a tail. We knew right away we could put him on fiddle solos that would bring down the house.

"Why aren't you in a bluegrass group somewhere?" Eric asks him.

He rolls his eyes a little. "I'm not exactly the kind of guy you'd find in a gospel bluegrass group."

"Do you have a faith?" Jimmy asks.

"I believe in the power of music," he answers, smiling. "That's all I have."

You can tell that they're disappointed. Their pause in judgment makes me like Arno all the more.

"Okay!" Tommy says. "Well, you play like you're blessed."

"That's my mom's fault. She raised me on the McMasters. When we lived in Cape Breton, I went to as many fiddle camps as I could. Believe me, I was blessed."

It's a new sound for us. Undeniably. Celtic rhythms could sneak in anywhere. Could they play with him? Would our fans mind?

"I don't like the way he looks," Jimmy tells us when we're alone. "Not very clean cut."

"We don't have a lot of choices," Eric says. He turns to Tommy. "'Wondrous Love'?"

Tommy looks like he might weep. That's when I think it's all gone.

"It was beautiful."

The other guys nod. "It was beautiful," they murmur.

"Was it enough?" and we look at Tommy.

"I don't know," he says. He grips our shoulders and we all stand in a circle and weep. "Dear God," Tommy whispers like someone died. Somehow we know it doesn't matter—that this is the end. There isn't enough hope left to fill the room.

We can't hold Arno out of the room any longer, and we wipe our eyes enough not to look like we've been crying. Jimmy says, "He can't wear the sunglasses, and he needs to cover the tattoos. Just to respect Jesus, you know?"

Eric laughs. *"Damn, Jimmy."*

"People are gonna talk," Jimmy says.

❧ ❧

They did talk and it was the end. But it wasn't Arno's sunglasses they were concerned with, and it wasn't the end of the band. The first concert, they introduced Arno carefully, uncertain what their audience would think of his appearance, unable to determine which side they should play—fully supportive or carefully, amusingly skeptical. They seemed to fight laughter when introducing him. They finally settled on a shtick—where Eric and Tommy would be wholly convinced that Arno was amazing, and Jimmy would play the skeptic.

Until Arno played.

His fiddle might as well have been flint and a rock; Eric and Tommy and Jimmy and Wayne were infected with fire, lit from Arno's fiddle. Every song had a different beat to it now. And when they called for something that hurt, he could crush your heart.

Our booking agent, Kate, started using Arno as part of our marketing, showing clips of our shows. "I'm lovin' the wild child," she told Eric on the phone. "And the new sound is great!"

The whole band changed. I heard something new from all of them.

Dear God, they got better. I'd never heard Tinderbox so stompin' good.

"This is a good sign!" Tommy says backstage one night, high on music and hope. He hugs Arno.

"A good sign?" Arno asks, smiling. Taken aback, maybe.

"We have to record this right away," Wayne says, slapping Arno on the back. "A live concert."

Eric says Kate had already suggested it. "She wanted to pick one of our next concerts. I told her Billings was coming up, and she likes Rimrock Auto Arena."

"Only one problem," I say. And it's my job to point this particular problem out. "That's a short night."

"That's a moon night?" Eric asks. "Damn. Well, maybe our luck is changing!"

Everyone gets excited but me. The full moon was a week away, Jessica Hawley is on my mind, and that can sober everyone up.

I push them to take Arno aside. "We can't wait. He has to know."

Tommy says, "I don't want to scare him."

"He doesn't look like he'll scare easily," I say.

"Yeah, well, he hasn't seen what's coming."

$$\mathcal{Q}\mathcal{Q}\ \mathcal{Q}\mathcal{Q}$$

The problem with a killing monster is you have to kill it. I never saw one movie where the monster gets to live. It always dies. And with Tommy, we'd all been stupid enough to believe that he wouldn't get out, wouldn't kill again.

No one wanted to spoil the new joy fevering through everything we did. No one wanted to break the spell. I could tell that Tommy was especially hopeful. He'd become fast pals with Arno.

One night, I go into the trailer and take my shotgun out from under the front seat, to get it ready. I pray to God for everything, from health issues to my sister's relationship, from war in the Middle East to poverty. But I look at this gun and I think cleaning it is a type of prayer. I catch myself saying, "You're going to shoot straight this time." I say, "You're a good gun. You have a heart in you. You don't want to kill; you want to save. But sometimes saving is killing and killing is saving."

L'Amour didn't have bad guys you still liked—they weren't both good and bad if they needed to die. Everyone was responsible for their own corruption, and L'Amour made sure you knew that they deserved it, that they were blacker on the inside than their hats were on the outside. *But Tommy is different*, I say to myself, complicating matters.

I'm about to talk myself out of this complication when I hear something above me, and I look up to the ceiling, waiting to hear it again. Music. Speak of the Devil. He sometimes spent time alone in the trailer, even when we were booked into a hotel, just to write music. I decide I would walk up the stairs quietly, not disturb him.

I take the gun.

I can hear him strumming, stopping, writing. I sneak up the stairs.

I've not heard this melody before. It was bluegrass, though. You can always tell a bluegrass song: heartbreak, gospel, missed opportunities, hometowns, a fiddle section, a chorus, tight harmonies, and voila—Bluegrass. Not that I don't enjoy Tinderbox. They're good, but bluegrass music in general started to feel repetitive after a while. Throw in some Alabama, some 38 Special, Ronnie Milsap, or Eagles, and I can take it. Variety, variety, variety. I like Alison Krauss and Union Station a lot, but maybe that's because Alison's voice is sweet as clover honey.

Tommy Burdan is a good songwriter, though. He bends over the guitar, there in the far room, just down the hall from the stairs. From here I have a perfect shot. I raise the gun. Maybe tonight is a good night just to rid us of the problem early—not risk another person.

Tommy strums and sings.

In my mind I see him as the beast that had leaped from the trailer door, claws curling, lips snarling, the rage, the moonlight touching the fur of his forehead, his muzzle.

I see him clearly through the shotgun's sights. I imagine him killing the little boy in Romania, the blood dripping from his monster lips, black rimmed, his muzzle covered in a red so red it was black in the moonlight.

My gun wavers. He continues strumming, and then stops and writes some.

I lower the gun. I have no desire to kill Tommy. I do want to kill the beast. But in this moment, I think—you have to kill him, Tommy. You can't be two different people—not when one of you is a killer. I can shoot him as a wolf, but I can't do this here, when he's singing about redemption, when he can't see my gun.

I'm going to let *him* do it. I'm going to give him the keys to the bus and he's going to drive it off a bridge somewhere, and he's going to fly through the windshield. He's going to give the world that one. If we can make up stories about Jessica, we can fabricate one around what happened with the bus.

The night sneaks around like it's conspiring with us. The wind taps the windows. Maybe it will rain. I nearly get up. Maybe it would make it all believable. *Jessica Hawley believed in you. I believed in you. How much good can one person do to make up for a bad? If I shoot you, does God forgive me for Jessica? Does he forgive you? I don't know how much good can possibly balance that out—how does forgiveness work exactly? What's the math on it?*

You would finally do something good, I think.

Is that what this is? I'm trying to even out my life with this gun.

It sits heavy in my lap.

I know God is really working miracles in this group—how many people we help and all—but can't he spare one miracle for you, Tommy? Or is that miracle me?

I go downstairs again, put my gun under the seat. I hear Tommy come down behind me.

"Oh, I didn't know anyone was here," he says.

"Just checking on things," I say.

"Hey, Arno's really working out, isn't he?"

"Have you told him? What he has to do?"

"Not yet. I don't want to force it."

I look through the front windshield of the bus at the moon. "That moon's going to force it if you don't."

So, Tommy sets it up. We sit one night in the tour bus, in the tiny living room with the fixed tables and the striped cushions. The night grows crickets, and a breeze comes through the screens—we're somewhere in Missouri. Shastas all around, any kind you want. We've just finished some of Eric's chili. We're all tense, and trying to disguise it with laughter. Tommy sits across from Arno, strumming on his banjo.

"We need to talk to you," Jimmy says to Arno.

Poor man. He looks at all of us, rubbing his hand across his face.

"I knew it. I knew you'd find out. I want to say my peace before you say anything."

"Arno—"

"No, I get to talk first," he says. "Yes, I'm gay, and yes, I have a boyfriend. And I may not be a Christian, but I'd like to at least *like* Christians, but that's been hard because this business—bluegrass—is *filled* with them. You guys may be the most Christian of the whole industry, but for the most part, bluegrass musicians are Christian, usually pretty conservative, too, and that's not been easy if I want to play at festivals. I don't mind people looking at my tats, my hair, my piercings—I don't care. All I care about is music, playing music, because Christian or not, you have to admit there's a spirit there, *in music* that *lifts* you, and I get that. I want to have it just like everyone else. I want to play with other bands, and I don't want them to make an issue about it. I've been in two bands. I won't name names—okay, The Weilands and Prairie Storm Players—and they dropped me like I bit them, and I won't go through that again. I'm not going to fight you in public, but I'm not going to just slink back into the night because you're uncomfortable or you want me to change. It's not going to happen."

You could have heard salt spill.

Eric looks at Jimmy. Jimmy looks at Tommy and back to Wayne. Then Jimmy looks at me.

Tommy says, "I think we're okay with you being—gay."

"Well—" Jimmy starts, clearing his throat for what might have been an epic speech.

Tommy interrupts. "Even Jimmy is okay with that. Because we *need* you."

"So you didn't call me in here to drop me from the group?" Arno asks.

"No," says Tommy.

"Oh, I'm sorry, guys." Arno laughs. "That's cool. I'm cool. I'm sorry. Wow. That's so good to know. I think I'm gonna tear up. I didn't know what you'd say when you found out. This is better than I thought. So much better. It's been a long haul in this business, you know. I forget sometimes. It just looked like you called me in here to tell me bad news, you know?"

We got quiet.

"You have bad news," Arno says, tentatively.

"Well, that depends on you," Tommy says.

"On me?"

"Arno, I need to tell you something you can't tell another living soul. Can you swear to secrecy?"

"Sure," Arno whispers. "I mean I figure you'll keep my secret. What's yours?"

Tommy says, "I want to tell you a story about my time in Romania." And he does. The whole story, only looking up a couple of times.

"I want to tell you about the people who have died."

Arno looks at each of us, to see if we believe.

"I want to tell you how you can keep that from happening ever again."

Tommy lays it out. About "Wondrous Love." About how many times, how long he had to play it, and what it would do for Tommy.

"This time," he says, "this time Carl is going to be in the room with us and he's going to have his gun pointed at the door, and if I get out of that room, he will shoot me. Because a monster is going to come out of that door. It won't be me. It'll be something that *will* kill you."

Tommy stops talking. "Can you do it?" he asks Arno.

I don't think Arno had breathed for about ten minutes. When he does, it comes out in a rush. "What the ever-loving *fuck* are you talking about?" he says. "Pardon me, *Jesus*. But that's about the most *fucked* up thing I've ever heard. I thought you'd freak out at me coming out, but are you playing a joke on me? Is this what you do to people who really tell a secret?"

"No joke."

"You gotta watch that mouth," Jimmy says. "For the Lord's sake and all."

"He just said he was a fucking werewolf," says Arno. "Did you hear that?"

No one moves.

"You all think he's a werewolf?"

We all say yes—our little confessional in the kitchen.

"We've seen it," Eric adds.

Arno breathes out. He looks worried, like he's on the edge of something frightening. I sympathize. "None of you are bad people," he says. He picks up his Shasta. "You have a fucked-up problem. Okay, I get it." He slurps from his drink, eyeing us. "If Jesus was a zombie and needed to eat brains, would you still do what he told you? Would he still be a good man? That's where we are. In twisted Bible-land."

Jimmy shakes his head. "That is *not* what we are saying."

Arno looks at Tommy. "You're a werewolf?"

Tommy nods.

"Okay," Arno says. "And the werewolf has killed two people?"

Tommy nods again, his eyes watering. "I don't even remember it."

"And you've told no one this?"

"Who would believe us? They have to actually see Tommy change," Jimmy says.

"The only thing anyone could do is kill Tommy," Eric says, breaking down. "Except for that one song. Amelia kept him good for the last ten years, God bless her. Was a miracle every time it happened."

Jimmy soon joined the chorus of crying—all of us desperate men now, asking for a miracle from someone we just met.

Tommy has pushed his face into the blinds, his eyes shut, crying. Arno reaches across the table and puts his hand on Tommy's arm. "Okay."

"We're concerned about you, Arno," Eric says. "We don't mean to put all of this on you. We shouldn't have put it on Amelia, but no one had a choice. Who knew it would be that one song?"

For a moment, with Arno touching Tommy's arm, and all of us looking at Arno, wondering if he would accept us or not—if he would think we were killers because we'd kept this secret—or if he would want to leave the group before the next full moon, we wait to see what he will do.

Arno finally looks at Eric. "I just have to be good," he says, his face trying to smile. "You need someone to be a little musical Jesus right now and save you guys. I don't know if I can do that, but I'll try. I'll give it a shot."

⚖ ⚖

Tommy disappears the next night. We're in Billings, Montana for a show. We did the sound checks in the afternoon, went to dinner, and, afterwards, Tommy said he was coming back to the bus. We searched the hotel, the trailer. I ran up to the top deck, opened the curtains to all the bunks; checked the bathroom, the Box, everywhere. I feared he was going after Aaron, going to beg Amelia to come back, as if she would.

I call Amelia to let her know. She's concerned. "He doesn't know where we are," she says quietly. "I'm not going to tell him."

I tell her I understand.

"I'm not trying to be heartless, Carl. But—" and she goes silent; all I can hear on the other end is her breath, and a radio in the background—country music, something bright, something happy. "Carl, I'm pregnant. I was pregnant when I left. I want a family. I don't have the strength to play," she says. "To save him."

"Pregnant?" My worst fears are realized. "I'll kill Tommy."

"It's not Tommy's. He never touched me. He never tried. He never wanted—" she stops. "If he comes here, Aaron will probably kill him or turn him in with what he knows. You can't let him come here, Carl."

"Why didn't you tell us?"

"The judgment, I guess. I just didn't want to have to explain it."

I lean against the kitchen counter, letting its angles press into my back, letting it hurt me. "But Amelia," I say. "I wouldn't have . . ."

She sighs. "Oh, Carl," and she says my name so sweetly. "You're the hardest. You're a good man, but I didn't want to disappoint you, didn't want you thinking badly about me. You would have. You would have been the hardest."

I wouldn't have. For a moment, I can't think of werewolves. I can only see Amelia's face: her red hair, her kind eyes, eyes that told me everything, that shared everything with me. A woman I missed almost as much as I missed my ex-wife, Sarah. When I didn't have Sarah, maybe it was Amelia I tried to be kind to instead, to do better than I did before. I knew there wasn't anything between us—not from her, at least. But she never knew how much I cared about her, or that I would never have condemned her. Why didn't she know that?

"I would have been happy for you." I stare at the wooden cabinets, waiting. "For both of you," I add, feeling awkward.

"Please don't let Tommy come over here, Carl. Please. I can't help him anymore."

"I won't let him. I won't let him near you," I promise. I look around the bus, and the emptiness of it chills me. "Don't worry, Amelia."

❧ ❧

Another thing missing: my shotgun, missing from under the seat.

"He's got a gun," I tell Jimmy.

The windows of the trailer seem to pulse inward, as if the oxygen were leaving us.

"Damn him," I say to Jimmy. Part of me wonders if maybe he's killed himself. I'm not ashamed of admitting that. Sure would make it easier. Let God embrace him up in Heaven, all fixed and all.

"Maybe he got himself put in prison. That might hold him. A real jail," Jimmy says.

"He should have stopped after Jessica died. We lied to cover him up. He doesn't even care," I say, pounding the kitchen counter with my fist.

"Now hold on, *crackshot*. You weren't there when he came back," Jimmy says. "He was broken. He was broken in two. We had to cancel those gigs, Carl. He wanted to turn himself in—he begged me to turn him in or shoot him."

"Well, you're the reason I wasn't there," I say, remembering the week after Jessica's death. Where was I? I was off the bus because Jimmy forced me to go into rehab. That was my punishment—as if I had killed her instead of Tommy.

"I told him no. I told him we were doing good. I took him to that whiteboard and I wrote those numbers from our files, so he could see them, and when I hung it up, I pointed to those numbers and I said, 'Here's the evidence. If

God was not blessing you, we wouldn't be changing lives. These thousands of people would be going to Hell if it weren't for you. You have to pull yourself together,' I told him. He could be a killer, only a killer, or he could do his penance here on Earth and make Jessica's death count for something—make our secrets count for something. He hates himself, Carl. He's trying to do everything he can to make up for it. What would he do without this band? He'd be dead."

"You kept this all going?"

"I have never *played* for a group that was making a bigger impact on the world, Carl. All because of him. That black dog was right—he is a better player, a better writer, a better *everything*—and because of that, we help the world. We do. He lets us be part of that. Only two people have died—only one under our watch. One. And that kid, that was before any of us."

When I came back to the band a week later, after rehab, the whiteboard was up, and Tommy was renewed, writing a new album, *Redeem Us*, that went on to be a huge seller. It bore the lyrics of his deepest regrets, written as if they were words anyone could sing; only we knew the truth.

Wayne appears at the door. "I bet he's at the Walmart Supercenter. He sometimes goes there to, you know, pray."

"The Walmart Supercenter?"

"I don't know. He says it helps him find himself, or something like that."

"He took my *gun*," I say again. Was no one listening to me?

"Who would he shoot at Walmart?"

We don't wait around to answer that question. We jump in the Bronco and head to the nearest Walmart.

"Spread out," Jimmy tells us when we get into the Billings Montana Walmart Supercenter. It's a busy place. Shoppers with carts come in with us, a man unfolding his list, his girlfriend telling him what's on it by heart. Children without parents carrying peanut butter appear at the end of a row, taking the corner fast and turning in front of the fresh flowers and into the produce.

"Where would he be?"

"Where would you go to pray in a Walmart?"

"I prefer the bait and tackle section," Jimmy admits.

"Definitely Hardware," Wayne says.

I can almost imagine this. I shake my head nonetheless.

"What? I get creative inspiration there, from all the projects that could be."

"Okay," I say. "You guys check out those sections. I'll check out the food. Maybe he's just getting some snacks."

Jimmy touches my arm, a dark expression on his face, and whispers, "Maybe he went to get some bullets."

"I have plenty of bullets."

"Well, maybe we should check there, too," Wayne says. "That's in the sports section, near the bait and tackle. You check that, Jimmy."

We spread out into Walmart. I'd been there many times. I remember after my wife and kid left me I'd find myself standing in the music section just scanning the tapes, asking myself which song would save me from all this pain. I'd bring home the Charlie Daniels Band, Alabama, Dolly. Sometimes the names would blur and I'd look up and find out I'd been there for an hour, trying to find something to soothe the ache. I'd been here in the snack aisle, too: chips, pop, frozen pizza—newly single people stay here for a while before moving to the produce section and the meats, and start cooking again.

Mostly I just see them using carts as walkers, slowly moving down the aisles, overwhelmed by all the possibilities they have to make that need disappear. Yeah, I guess, in a way, a lot of people came to Walmart to pray.

Where would Tommy be? What part of this place would pull him in and give him hope? Jimmy is checking the bullets—because, yeah, that was one way.

He would be in the music.

I get to the section and there are other people there, sifting through a vat of Blu-rays looking at every single one—three for ten dollars the sign said. Binge watching. I can see that as a form of prayer, too. I can remember what it was like listening to Alabama's "Lady Down on Love" again and again, stopping the tape and rewinding, like some damn prayer beads.

He isn't there. Shoot.

I see the sports section, but know Jimmy is there, and I see Wayne coming out of the hardware aisle and picking up a wrench set thoughtfully. Yeah, there's some prayer and inspiration happening there.

I walk into the gardening section, through the sliding doors and into the warmer, humid room full of plants you could buy to spruce up your beds, and fertilizer bags lining the shelves.

Tommy is sitting in one of them sample sets of outdoor deck furniture, the kind that looks too nice to ever buy but is in all the commercials. I call them the Happy Couples. In the commercials, they own the deck furniture, including barbecues. It's usually a BBQ sauce, a mustard or a meat that's being advertised, but they need to show you how to use it, and this is the kind of deck furniture they use.

Tommy is in the chair. I take the loveseat.

"Oh hello," he says.

"Hello, come here often?" I ask.

He smiles. "It helps me think."

"Other people's deck furniture?"

"Just the space. The space helps me think. People are walking around. They don't really look at you, or at any of the furniture."

"Been thinking about tomorrow?"

He ignores the question. I feel like a bastard, being so flippant. "Walmart Supercenters are open twenty-four hours. Have you ever been in one late-late at night?"

"No, been in a lot of Walmarts, but not in the am."

"They really get this eerie feeling," he says.

"I can imagine. It's two am and hardly anyone is here."

"You'd be surprised. There's a lot more people than you'd think at two am in a Walmart."

He looks over my shoulder at an older couple picking out a ceramic pot, something for an indoor plant, and they touch them all, saying, it seemed, blue or green or brown?

"There are miracles all the way through the Bible, you know? Sarah has a baby when she's in her nineties."

"That's a curse, I think," I say.

"She wanted one. Some people think she got younger."

"They're stories, though."

"Well, they're stories to some people, and to others they're real lives. They're real to me."

"But they make people want a miracle."

He nods. "Yeah, I want one."

"You don't think Amelia was a little miracle every month?"

"She was. She was a little miracle."

"Kept you sane."

His eyes start to water.

"Do you think Arno can do it?"

"I don't know. He's practicing hard," he says.

I lean back on the deck furniture cushions.

"I want God to do this one."

"I do, too."

He looks away. "I want to *push* him."

"Pardon me?" I ask, not sure I heard him correctly.

"You still want to shoot me?"

How can I answer that? I say nothing.

He looks at me like he understands. I don't even know if I understand. I just know that I know him better now than I did before, and don't think that Tommy has to pay for the wolf.

"Sometimes I come here because the plants make me feel like I'm coming to the Garden of Gethsemane, except everything has a price on it, and there's no one staying up with me while I pray, and there's soft rock playing—and I don't know why, but that combination makes me—" he stops, chokes back some emotion "—*beg*."

He looks up, and I think, he's searching my eyes for an answer. I know my eyes aren't going to say anything, but I'm lost as you, I think. Or a silver bullet. That's what I have for him, maybe all that I have

I can hear Jimmy and Wayne entering through the sliding door. They're talking about lures, and then they get quiet.

"I'm not ready to leave just yet," Tommy says to all of us when we stand around him. "I'm good here. Oh," he adds. "I almost forgot." He pulls my shotgun out from the floor on the other side of the chair. "I had it cleaned."

"You didn't have to do that," I say, knowing that I had cleaned it the night I snuck in on him writing that song, but I couldn't tell him that.

"You had a gun in Walmart in the gardening section?" Wayne says.

"Montana is an open carry state," Tommy says.

"But that's not something you see every day in Walmart. People could be frightened of you."

We all take a moment to look at each other.

"Okay," I say. "We'll leave you here. You've got the other rent-a-car."

"I do."

We turn to go, and I looked around at all the plants and the people walking the labyrinth of aisles and things around us, slowly, pondering, and I hear the bell of the register ding and ding and ding.

I turn back to him. "Do you want us to stay? You know, while you pray?"

I think I catch him off guard. He chuckles, waves us off. "Thanks, but no. No, I'm okay. You don't have to. I'll be home soon." He breathes in. "I gotta face the music tomorrow."

Wayne and Jimmy and I take our leave. On our way back, I notice how every person seemed to wake as I passed, turning from their wanting, their scanning, to watch us walk by. It's the gun, I realize. It makes them see me. Makes us visible. They look us over, three men and a gun. I imagine that Tommy got the same stares. It makes me feel dangerous.

Like a killer.

And I don't like it.

✌ ✌

It's a short night for us. We don't usually book concerts for the full moon nights, but our booking agent doesn't know why, and sometimes she'll just plant one on that day and we have to work with it. We've done it before. We just time it.

Tonight's full moon was set to rise at 9:10 pm. We had to be off the stage by 8:30, in the lobby signing autographs, and then out the door by 9. That wouldn't be easy, except by moving the concert up to 6:30. And since it was a Sunday, we could do that, giving the audience the rest of Father's Day to spend with each other.

We typically had no opening act on nights like this. I would find myself wanting to watch the concert from the wings, and at intermission I'd go get the bus, park it in the back, have it ready for Tommy and Arno, leaving Wayne and Jimmy to play and jam with people after the concert was over.

It's June 20, and it's an important night for the city of Billings. The mayor, a tall, lanky man with a moustache and wearing a western shirt takes the microphone. The crowd of about twelve thousand cheers. "We got some fine music for you tonight. Tinderbox!" More cheering, lasting for what seems like forever. I thought the guys would go on stage at that point. Usually they had a slightly longer introduction, but I'm glad it was short—this is no ordinary night.

The mayor waits till the cheering dies. "Now, it's also another special night. Six years ago this afternoon, we were hit with an EF2 tornado that ripped the roof right off this arena. One hundred and thirty-five mile per hour winds, that twister just sat over this arena for fifteen minutes. It destroyed where you all are sitting now. It ripped apart the Billings Dance Academy, Fas-Break Auto Glass was a skeleton of walls, tore up the laundromat and a hair salon. It toppled trees. It damaged homes and businesses. We declared a state of emergency because the damage was so severe. But you know what?"

"WHAT?" the crowd calls out like they're one person. They'd done this before.

"Not one life was lost. Not one injury."

Cheers erupt from the audience again—I thought they'd never end. The mayor says, "We give praise to God for that day!" The noise rises like a wave, all over the arena. "He saved us from disaster! We lost things! But things can be replaced! Look around you! These things got replaced! You are sitting in the things that got replaced!"

Wild yells and whistles for minutes. I look at my watch.

"There were nearly four thousand people here the night before for an Outlaws football game. If it had happened the day before, people would have been killed. But the building was empty, by the grace of God, the building was empty!"

The crowd was with him, almost speaking in chorus to the things he said now, like a great call-and-response song.

"We lost things! We did not lose people! And we did not lose our faith! Tonight, to celebrate that miracle, to celebrate *all* miracles, we bring you the three-time Grammy Award-winning bluegrass band Tinderbox!" And the band members run on stage and grab their instruments—all but Tommy, who taps me on the arm, leans in, and says, "What you need is in the extra banjo case."

And then he runs on stage, and the lights have him, and he picks up his banjo and grabs the microphone. "Who wants a miracle?"

I walk over, kneel down and open the banjo case. Inside is my gun, and a card with my name on it taped to the top of the inside of the case:

It's up to you. I don't want you to miss this time. I know you had mercy last time. I know that's what really happened. I know. This time, you can't miss.

I look behind me to the group singing, "Tonight, You're Gonna Save Someone."

It's then that I know something is very, very wrong.

Tommy Burdan throws himself into this concert, probably thinking it would be his very last. Wayne and Eric and Jimmy played and harmonized, *gonna save someone, gonna save someone.* You can tell they believe it, too.

Arno had assured us that he had it, though. He'd been practicing for weeks. "I can do this," he said.

Unfortunately for him, he had, to Jimmy's shock, shaved the other half of his head, leaving only a mohawk.

Which he'd dyed red yesterday. As red as a rooster.

"Boy, what kind of fresh hell are you trying to get us into?" Jimmy said. "We run a respectable Christian bluegrass band."

Arno only smiled, "Aw, now, Jimmy, I give you a story. A little Celtic bad boy heathen in your midst. Who knows if they're thinking you'll convert me, or I'll convert them. It's charity or it's *danger*," he laughed. "Besides, you won't care tomorrow."

Jimmy stopped and nodded, repeating, "I won't care tomorrow."

I look at Arno now, dancing, the crowd going wild. He didn't cover his arms; he's wearing a jean jacket with the sleeves cut off, and his tattoos were dancing, too—Pan, Neptune, all those gods all over the stage, his music like fire, bow vibrating faster and faster, *someone's gonna get saved tonight, someone's gonna get saved tonight.*

The crowd moves like an ocean of hands.

I close the banjo case.

Tonight, everything may depend on the battle between a shotgun and a fiddler.

჻ ჻

"What are you doing?" I ask Tommy when he comes off stage.

"I'm gonna get me a miracle tonight," he says.

"What do you mean? What are you going to do? Why did you bring the gun here?"

Tommy looks glassy eyed, like he'd seen the Risen Saviour on stage. "It's all gonna be good tonight. You won't need it really. I brought it just in case. You'll be fine. Enjoy the concert."

"I need you to tell me what you're planning on doing? Tell me we're going to the bus at nine."

"Whatever you need to hear," he says. Damn him.

I grab him by the shoulders. He pulls out of my hands, says, "It all comes down to tonight. Everything gets fixed either way."

"If you're thinking—"

He pats my shoulder. "I got this. Can you feel it, Carl? Did you *ever* feel it so strong? Twelve thousand people with such gratitude—the air is thick with thankfulness, with joy, with miracle—it's intoxicating." He widens his eyes, knowing that word would hit me. "Yes, intoxicating. You can get *drunk* on that kind of prayer and belief. But it's not a bad drunk; it's a good drunk. Hope is a belief that lifts you, Carl. And I'm being lifted tonight. The boys are all being lifted. Arno is *amazing*! The beat. Did you see when Eric brought out the bodhran? Miracles are happening out there. It's not going to be the end of something. It's gonna be the beginning. You won't need the gun. You won't need it, but tonight you're going to witness the power of God."

He's drunk all right.

He walks away, and I go to Jimmy. "He's planning something, Jimmy. He's going to do something stupid. He thinks God is going to save him."

Jimmy beams at me. "I feel it, too."

God, no.

"If you were a spiritual man, Carl, you'd feel it, too. A little hope can build like a wave, and we've got waves out there. Maybe he's right. Maybe Arno's gonna save us tonight, and we'll be back to normal. I don't want to be frightened. I'm tired of being uncertain. It's exhausting."

"But I think he's planning on turning right here on stage."

"Naah," he assures me. "That would be stupid. We'll be off stage by eight thirty, no doubt. I'll walk off the stage. I'll bring him with me. Stop worrying. Sometimes I think you just need to believe more in *us*." He slaps me on the arm. "We're stronger than you think."

He isn't listening; he's drunk, too.

"He put my gun on stage, Jimmy."

He just laughs.

Wayne and Eric and Arno are snacking on salami and cheese and fruit, laughing, drinking water. They're feeling so good.

I'm feeling worried.

Jimmy catches me before they go back on stage. "I'll talk to him. I'll make sure," he says. "I'll close it all down if he tries. If I have to break all my strings, okay?"

They're back on stage before you know it for the second half, and the crowd pulses like a field of sound. Arno pulls his bow back, scraping across the fiddle, one note, fluttered—a minor key. He scrapes it across again, and the crowd erupts, because Amelia had always done this song slow, but the ache, the ache that Arno put into it—and then *bam*, Eric hits the side of his guitar for a beat, and suddenly it's a faster, more desperate version of "Valley of Darkness" than anyone in the crowd had heard before.

Going down, going down, going through, going through.

I leave and get the bus, bringing it 'round to the back.

Tommy had said he was going to *push God for a miracle*.

When the crowd is like that you can believe anything. Could I believe that God would contain him? Does Tommy want me to shoot him on stage? I sit in the bus, wondering if I could do that. Could I shoot him on stage?

I could shoot a werewolf on stage. I imagine that; I imagine him turning into the beast. I think of my video, the one I made in secret, where Tommy's face stretched into a muzzle with teeth, where his eyes lost all humanity. I knew seeing those eyes—he would kill us all. I could shoot that.

I get out of the bus.

Eight ten.

I walk back in and they're playing "Walk with Me, O Saviour," the music flowing over everyone like water. Tommy has the mandolin out, playing it like a love song. I look over at the spare banjo case and my heart thumps.

I know the set. "Walk With Me, O Savior"; "River Jordan"; and then the "Fiery Furnace Bluegrass Stomp," which is typically their closer, with an encore of "Going to Heaven with a Chariot in Overdrive."

But something happens in "River Jordan."

Tommy appears to get lost.

He has the microphone during the instrumental part, not strumming on his banjo, and he starts talking to the crowd: "Lord God, we're with you tonight, deep in the waters of the River Jordan." His hand goes up, and thousands of hands rise with him. "But we can't get across. We're waiting on a miracle." The rest of them keep playing, just repeating the song. "We're waiting to see your face, feel your hand help us cross. We believe tonight in miracles. We believe that you're with us. And you can help us cross this deep, deep, powerful river."

Eight thirty.

I stare at him, but he has his eyes closed. I stare at Jimmy; Jimmy and the rest of them are so into what's happening they might as well be alone on stage.

We have two more songs after this, gang. There's no time for an altar call. No time to bring people forward to confess their—

"Lord, help us cross, help us cross this river, the water—it's taking over, it's coming up over our shoulders. If you've felt like the whole world is running over your shoulders, if the problems of this life are about to pull you under, walk through this river with me, walk up here to the edge of the stage because we're gonna pray."

And they start coming down from their seats. Hundreds of people—hundreds and hundreds of them. They leave their seats to the music, and they flow down like streams.

Eight forty. They're still coming, and Tommy is still speaking to them. Hundreds of people with their hands up, their faces tilted to catch the light as if it is the warmth of Jesus.

"Ask him for his hand; ask him to lead you through the River Jordan, because if he'll just give you his fingertips, you can make it. You need that hand. Ask for it tonight; ask for the real hand of God tonight. You are not asking for ways to feel good; you are not asking for some warm feeling; you are asking for that hand."

He's completely off script. Eight fifty.

"We don't want nice thoughts, Lord. We don't want wish fulfillment. You saved your people in the fiery furnace. You saved Daniel in the Lion's Den. You saved David against Goliath. You gave Sarah and Hannah children when they'd lost all hope. You did things so long ago. You were more than a whisper in church from a friend, more than a sermon, God, you were real, and we're asking for real."

Now the boys are looking at me. Jimmy nods. Eric looks like he isn't agreeing with the theology.

But the people, oh God, the people, they swarm around the stage. Still pouring down from the top deck, still coming through the entrances at every side. Their hands up and their hopes high, they want something real from God.

Nine pm. Ten minutes! I go to the banjo case. Don't make me do this . . .

Tommy is so far out on stage their hands are almost all the way around him.

"You have real people with real problems asking for real support, Lord. I know it's difficult to answer every need, but we're asking for a miracle. We're asking for you to save us."

Nine oh-four. I have the gun out. I have it pointed at Tommy. All I can see in my mind is the video—his body becoming a monster—and it was about to happen here, in Billings, Montana.

Arno sees me first. Sees that I'm pointing the gun straight at Tommy, and he steps in the way, seamlessly changing the song to "Wondrous Love."

Tommy's hand is in the air. "I'm gonna push you, God. We're gonna push you tonight. We don't mean to be disrespectful. We don't mean to ask for too much, but it's always wait, it's always be patient, and we're drowning. We're going to ask you for a miracle."

He's threatening everyone with his change unless God himself stops it.

Jimmy's eyes go as big as silver dollars when he hears the song, and then he turns and sees the gun pointed at Tommy. He looks at his watch and stops playing, walking over to Eric, who also stops. Wayne, thinking there's a Dobro solo going on, jumps into the empty soundscape with his whining.

Tommy falls to his knees, the microphone still in hand, his back arched, his face begging to God.

"If you don't give us a miracle tonight, we will all die."

"Wondrous Love" comes out of Arno's fiddle as sweet and soul-searching as I've ever heard it.

God, Tommy lurches. His arms crack. I can hear it.

Arno, still playing, starts *singing* the song.

"What wondrous love is this? Oh my soul, oh my soul."

Oh, get outta my way, Arno.

People, now surrounding the stage, their hands lifted to Heaven, sing, *what wondrous love is this that caused the Lord of Bliss to bear the dreadful curse for my soul.*

They've picked it up—all twelve thousand.

I can't see what's happening to Tommy. If he turns here in front of these thousands of people, he'll kill more than two. I move toward the group, walking with my gun, still protected in the shadows. I weave to get a shot, thinking of Jessica Hawley, thinking of Amelia, thinking of Sarah and Cleo. Thinking in a flash that this is my whiteboard—that if I make this shot, I could balance out everything I'd done; and that if I make this shot, I could never take it back. You're asking me, God, to kill the star of our group, the man giving hope to millions in front of the world.

When I was sinking down, sinking down, sinking down, oh, my soul, the crowd sings as they surround Tommy, on his knees, his face turned to the floor.

Tommy's face stretches; his muzzle, his claws, his teeth—and suddenly I have a shot.

I fire, a crack so loud no one could miss it. The bullet shoots out at the moment the boys join in harmony with the song. And that's when the miracle happens—the one I see in front of me.

The bullet stops in mid-air.

Later, the boys would say they never heard the shot. But I could see it, this little silver bullet hang there, spinning and spinning.

Tommy is on the ground, as if he's been shot. The song continues to rise, the whole arena singing. He does not look changed; he looks human. I run on stage. I had to see. I run past the spinning bullet, into the lights with my gun pointed to the ceiling. I run through the group at Tommy's side. Could he have forced God into a miracle?

As soon as I'm on stage, the crowd gasps, and their singing starts to falter, to stutter, just Tinderbox keeping the song going now. People must have wondered who I am and why I have a gun. I turn Tommy over. He has a face. A human face. Not the face I thought I saw a moment ago when I fired. I look back at the bullet and it's still there, spinning. I can tell. It's the only thing catching the light in the darkness of the wings.

Tommy looks up at me and suddenly scuttles away.

I put down the gun, put my hands up and in front of me, fingers wide, even in this crouched position. "It's okay, Tommy. It's okay. You got your miracle."

He looks from me to Jimmy and he jumps, dodging away from Jimmy.

Eric tries to help him stand and he falls backwards away from him. "No!" he cries.

The room is silent now.

Wayne says, quietly so we can just hear it, "Look at you. It's past nine ten. You're the same. You forced a miracle. A frickin' perfect miracle."

I stand and walk toward Tommy, and Jimmy and Eric are there, kneeling around him, whispering, "It's okay."

He looks at Jimmy, whispers, "You're all werewolves. All of you. All of you. You've all changed. I look at you—" He puts his hands in front of his face and he cries, and we try to pull him to his feet but he resists. "Tommy, Tommy, it's Jimmy."

It's Eric.

It's Carl.

"No," he yells. He gets up, breaking through our arms, and runs from us to the edge of the stage, as if he might leap into the crowd. There people are waiting, their hands outstretched, their expressions wondering what was happening. God loves you, Tommy. *God sees your pain, Tommy Burdan. We can help you through your River Jordan.*

He stops, recoils, yelling with his hands out over the crowd, as if he were blessing them. "Oh God! Oh God. The entire room! The entire room! Everyone, everywhere! You're *all* werewolves!"

And you can hear the bullet drop to the floor.

⮩ Old Lions

If his mother were around, she'd be the heavy here, the one to tell him he can't take the gun and shoot the old lions. But it's me leaning against his bedroom door, eyeing the .22 on the bed—hardly the instrument to take down African lions, but enough to kill the two roaming the hill country of West Texas.

"Where did you hear it?"

"Tom told me."

"He doesn't know shit." I want to punch his friend, not my sixteen-year-old.

"Well, I'm going to see for myself." He finds the cartridges in his top dresser drawer.

"You planning on shooting one?"

"If he gets too close, yeah." My son sits on the bed and cartridges roll down the slope his weight creates.

I find myself leaning in. "You want to prove you can take a lion."

He concentrates while loading. "Maybe I'll put him out of his misery."

My son looks up, sporting a face soon to be on the cover of the local newspaper: Boy Kills Lion. No "old" in that headline. Not ragged or tattered or bag of bones or flapping floor rug. No such thing as an *old* lion for a story.

The lions came when I was seven. A Mexican circus ambled through with wild animals in a big yellow tent. No one knew if it had been negligence or compassion on the part of the circus, but two of the male lions "escaped" into a vacant canyon. The circus owners conducted a very short search, as good as any performance under the tent, and then they gave up. They let the tent drop to the dust, but a few of us boys stayed at the lip of the canyon, watching for signs of anything untamed. Our fathers asked to rope off the whole canyon. "Nothing you'll want to see down there, sons. Leave them be." But we heard roars at night through windows our fathers hadn't shut.

By morning, we'd slipped into the crevices to explore our new Serengeti, seeking glimpses of pulsing flanks among the rocks, chasing after any distant, echoed roar. They leaped on heifers wandering into the canyon; we'd seen the buzzards skulking, loitering sideways around the carcasses. They drank from a thin stream of water tangled in white stones; we'd found their footprints, side by side in the mud.

And then, one morning, we found them. Two man-eating killers dozing against each other in the blue shade of a boulder, their manes caked in rust-coloured dust. One of them lifted his head and licked the other's ear. The other stretched his white neck back, his head lolling gently on a familiar stomach, and let himself be washed. For twenty minutes we sat there against the chalky canyon walls and watched.

Then one of us said, *We could take them, easy.* We beat the boy up, there against the rocks. I remember some blood from his lip on the ground under my hand.

❧ ❧

Today, my son swaggers past my hands, a half-smile on his lip, a grass burr for me in his gaze.

I tell him, "You can't give some people the truth. They do stupid things with it. Just like you can't give some people whiskey—even if there's nothing wrong with whiskey itself."

"Guess you would know about that," he says, swinging open the screen door.

❧ ❧

I stand on the porch watching a pink sky. A hundred yards ahead the earth cracks open an entrance into which my son descended, a gash that deepens until the canyon walls are twenty feet high. The sky has drained of colour when I hear the shot. The second shot makes me sit down on the porch. I can't go back in. I'll wait here until he gets back, and I won't yell at him. He'll be upset. He'll be upset because he missed a lion, or because he shot and killed it. I have to comfort him either way. And if he drags something home, or comes to fetch me to help him cart it back, I will not remind him about the other lion, now alone. I'll squat down and look closely at the lion in repose. I'll note its large paws, its worthy struggle, its mighty head at rest.

"That's a *fine* lion, son," I rehearse.

The Moon Over Tokyo Through
~eeeee~ Fall Leaves

Yumi's husband was the eleventh person she texted the night his plum wine won gold at the Tasters Guild International. She typed, "Gold. Marconi's." This was nine pm. He wouldn't show up. Marconi's bar was crowded, with small lamps at every table illuminating faces from below. On the karaoke stage, pink, white, and yellow lights coloured the singers. She'd come with her husband's coworkers, both her own age, but she felt guilty of the garishness. She could see it all through her husband's eyes, and this was why he wouldn't come. She remembered where she and Masato used to sit, and how he sang, "I see trees of green, red roses too," how he closed his eyes, put his hand out over the crowd. Now, he'd close his eyes if she told him how much fun she still had here.

On stage, Taro sang "Wake Me up Before you Go-Go," and the two women cheered every time he found the melody. He got into it, charging the edge of the stage, his flat, blocky face exploding with emotion. He loosened his tie. He cocked his hips. The women laughed and clapped. Yumi knew what her husband's excuse was—that he didn't come because he was strengthening the evocation in the wine. But the wine was fine. It did win an award. Maybe he wouldn't want to see them like this. She stood up suddenly, in the middle of Taro's song, and cheered.

Though it was their celebration, they weren't allowed to drink Masato's wine. Time-Wines weren't served in public places, more so to protect the customers from theft and date rape, and the establishment from lawsuits. But every staff member who knew about the Kuri no Yumi label celebrated their win tonight with "normal" drinks on the house, the kind, of course, that could leave you wasted and riding home in a cab—so Yumi wondered what the difference was anyway. That night, she ripped out a steely version of "Don't Stand So Close to Me," pointing the microphone out the neon-lit front window on every open beat in the song.

Yumi got home around midnight, knowing he wasn't there, either. She flipped on an angled, long-neck black lamp, casting a warm brown glow on the wall. She dialled his cell, wanted to wake him up, but he didn't answer. She sat on the sofa under the lamp, slipped off her shoes. They thumped on the floor and the silence afterwards bothered her. It bothered her everywhere. "Miss you," she said brightly into the phone. It wasn't the first thing she'd thought of, but it would keep the peace.

Their house had lost colour over the last few years, as Masato's tastes had changed. He had the living room painted brown, put up framed, bleached bamboo rugs on the walls. She thought they looked more like framed Frosted Mini-Wheats. On the walls, traditional Japanese paintings—a goose landing over reeds, a snow scene—had replaced the smoky pastels of jazz scenes they'd had there for years. She found him adding pieces to the house, slowly replacing "her juvenile tastes." The only piece left of hers, the only one he'd kept, stood on a table beneath one of the Mini-Wheat rugs. It was a red ceramic bull painted with purple and green flowers, something he'd picked up for her in a shop in Mexico, when she had her head turned looking at a wall of wild, wooden masks. He'd returned later to pay for it. It was home when they arrived. Ten years later, staring at its loud redness, he said, "It goes with nothing we have."

"It goes with me," she said. It stayed underneath a track light like a performer.

She wanted to drink his wine.

She took out a lotus glass, smaller than a traditional sake glass, designed for perfect full evocation. She opened the wine cabinet in the dining room. The bottles were clear, the plum wine a golden colour with four or five green plums nestled at the bottom. These were the wines he'd made for her: Borrowing the Chair at the Jazz Café, which recreated their first moment together; and Return to Grandfather's Home with Yumi, a wine with a specifically long evocation, nearly seven minutes of transport. He didn't particularly like the second wine anymore, not since he'd come to San Francisco, since he'd discovered his grandfather's shame after the war.

Letters from his grandfather in Japan to the American educational authorities in Japan found their way into the hands of a collector of Japanese

Occupation ephemera, and now lay bound by twine in a safe. Masato had paid more than he could afford for his grandfather's shame.

She remembered the mistake she'd made when she told him that this collaboration wasn't that significant. "So he rewrote history in some children's textbooks. It happened," she said. "You wouldn't have known about it if you hadn't read about it in a book. It's history."

"Yumi." He looked at her gravely. "That is the whole point."

After that he never spoke about his grandfather again, and he certainly was never willing to return to his house, not even in a wine. He wanted to destroy the whole batch. She wouldn't let him because in that wine, Masato told her he loved her. And she hadn't heard that in person in a long time. When she drank them, he was there beside her, for seven minutes at least—he said the damn words. "And the damn words," she said, mocking him, "are the whole point."

Tonight, she opened *Moon Over Tokyo* because she wanted to see.

Taro had pointed out that the judges had missed the flicker.

"It's a full-on smudge," Kichi said. "He's not finished with the evocation."

"The judges said nothing about the soldiers! They totally missed the details."

Yumi didn't care about the American soldiers; what she cared about was the flicker, the image of someone coming over the Togetsukyo Bridge. Probably a woman. He obsessed over that last detail. Only Taro got him to enter the *umeshu*, the plum wine *The Moon Over Tokyo Through Fall Leaves*, because they needed something in the competition. He could work on further evocation for himself. The wine was already good. It had a seven-minute transport, fully realized evocation, sound, visuals, smells—what more could one character add? He relented.

She poured the *umeshu* into a lotus glass. She looked at the painting on the dining room wall of two figures balanced on separate clouds, the woman reaching down. But you couldn't see the figures in this light, just her own reflection, that of a young woman in the house of an old man. She drank the wine.

The judges remarked on many things about *Moon Over Tokyo*—not the least of which was the body, the bouquet; those subtle notes of hickory, the smell of sweet liqueur—but they bowed down and worshiped the entire transport, from the first moment to the last.

Yes, yes, the transport was amazing. Around her now was her husband's best work. Tokyo, 1947: dusk in Rikugien Park, north of the city; the pond reflecting the harvest moon, the drooping pines, their branches in the water.

She could walk down to the edge of the lake, hear *yama-gare* sing *tzu . . . tzu . . . tzu*, flitting their chestnut bellies and black caps among the branches of the matsu pines—for a full seven minutes. Peace.

Masato Nakashita was skilled at giving peace, yes, at least to most people. She turned her eyes to the bridge that arched over a lily pond, the moonlight dappling the wooden planks, the trees, the ground beneath. Who was Masato trying to re-create?

The figure came from behind the taster, so you might not notice it if you didn't turn. It came across Togetsukyo Bridge, blurry, un-sustained, a flicker on the perfect image of dusk in the park. She could glimpse the figure only for a moment, a smudge—perhaps a woman. The figure moved quickly, sped unnaturally from the edge of the bridge to where every taster would stand in the evocation, as if it were a sketch of something not yet finished. You are a problem, she said to the figure. To the judges, perhaps, it meant nothing; but to her, it was something her husband cared about. It was frightening how fast the image came at her, how it seemed to smear everything else around it.

Yumi tried to make the present as important to Masato as the past. But then time had always been between them. At a mere thirty-five, she was twenty-five years younger than Masato. He would turn sixty this year, a birthday he dreaded.

"Sixty is an unfortunate label. Age is only good for wine."

She felt obliged to say he didn't look sixty, but then felt like she might be seen as covering, and by covering, admitting that he indeed looked sixty. So she said, "We don't have to remember the day."

"Good," he said quickly. He seemed shocked at himself for saying it. "There were other days," he told her, "more important things to do than watch a man grow old."

He'd only begun to look old recently. Ten years ago, they both looked young, and no one could really tell that he was that much older. You could say that Masato's eyes and hair started giving him away a few years ago, but she knew that there was no aging like the aging of attitude.

Overnight, he didn't want to sing karaoke at the bar, go out to parties with her. He left her watching television by herself. He started scolding her for her behaviour—she laughed too much, too loudly. She was in her thirties and should act more like a lady. He didn't approve of her short skirts, her white schoolgirl tops. He didn't want her moving with the fashions. His tone of voice at the mirror in the morning sounded more like her father than her husband.

"Do you have to spend all night out?" he asked.

The irony was that he now spent his nights at the winery, though she had tried to curb her own social schedule. Lately, she'd become used to letting her arm extend to the edge of the mattress, her fingers curling around the edge, spreading her body out to cover the whole bed.

She tried to get him to talk about the wine, especially this wine, *Moon Over Tokyo*.

"I'm not sure what will survive the fermentation. We will see."

"I'm just interested. I'm not trying to steal a secret."

He'd look at her as if she were a child. "I don't have any secrets."

But he was very busy. Orders for Time-Wines, or Piku Wines, as they were first called, had exploded. Wines that evoked specific thoughts, specific vignettes, were marketable, he said with a smile. "As long as one can find the right moment, something universal and healing."

ꙮ ꙮ

Yumi had a list drawn up of the kinds of scenes she wished recreated. She wanted the day of their wedding, but he said it was not commercially viable.

True, *The First Time We Made Love at My Apartment in Yokoshima* wouldn't be a wine she'd be willing to share with the staff at the winery. But maybe the *Absence of Tourists During the Rain at Inokashira Koen*, when he made her run through the fallen cherry blossoms to the lake, when she fell and skidded and he pulled her by her feet to him; or *Drinking Chocolate Shake, New York City Under the Saffron Gates in Central Park*, where the fabric of the art installation came loose and swung for a day, and people let their bodies become works of art as the saffron draped them in the wind and just their shapes remained. How he thought they were like people fighting to be seen. Couldn't he fit these in between these more difficult, historical evocations? Why not shoot for 2005 instead of 1947? Who remembered that anyway?

Tonight, she felt like creating a wine that evoked a crumbling feeling, and the ticking clock, and the traffic sounds outside, and maybe a long list of expletives in her voice. Drink that.

But Yumi was not skilled in making wines. She was a travel agent. So there'd be none of that shit. She'd have to wait until he was finished with the wine to understand whom it was he was trying to make.

Weeks later, Yumi still had the image on her mind, that flickering woman on the bridge. She found herself mulling it over even as she sold vacations to Guadalajara to couples that couldn't afford anything but love. Masato seemed happier. He did come home two or three times a week.

He said, "The wine is coming along. I'm very proud of it. I think." He stopped at the stereo and played Ornette Coleman on low volume, a good sign. "I think it's important." He looked at her.

"It must be important," she repeated from the empty couch where she curled into the pillows.

But important was obviously not what he meant. He padded to her in his soft house slippers, from light to light. He sat down across from her. The lamp softened whatever features of his face she thought had hardened, made his blue polo shirt vibrant. She waited for him to go on because it looked like his thinking face—his fingers around his mouth, his eyes squinted.

She prodded him. "You've worked on it too long for it not to be important."

He didn't open his eyes. He was thinking. "I'm not sure—" he started and then stopped. Saxophone and drums in the background, low murmurs of music. She heard the clock ticking again, tried to focus on him, let him see that she was ready for whatever he wanted to share about the wine, about its importance.

She saw his eyes relax, his fingers relax around his mouth, his brow smooth. Finally, she thought, he was relaxing. Then she saw his lips purse and a bubble of air puffed out. He had fallen asleep in the chair.

She watched him. Having him asleep in the chair was better than having him somewhere else. She watched his eyes flutter, the same kind of fluttering you might get when you drank *umeshu-piku*. He looked around somewhere under those lids. Maybe he saw someone there as well. Her hand lay near his on the arm of the chair. She hadn't touched his yet, and touching it now would wake him, so she kept her hand close enough to feel, like a cup of coffee, his live body radiate heat. The saxophone pulsed behind them. His eyes fluttered and she knew he wouldn't notice her presence at all.

Later that week, on her day off, she made a tofu stir fry for the staff. She took it down to the winery, tried to focus on Taro and Kichi, who were thrilled to see her. She joked with them and tried to stay bright. She didn't want to reveal that at night the figure on the bridge ran at her, threw itself across her other dreams, too, even erased them.

They sat around a worktable. Other staff went off for lunch, leaving the four of them together. Masato noted aloud Yumi's ingenuity, thoughtfulness, and hospitality as she served them. She could see he was proud. She looked around for bottles in preparation. She glanced over their heads as she laughed at their stories. She talked about "new things" in her work or her house or anything that might start them discussing "new things" in the wine.

They did not talk about the wine, except to say that a new batch of *Moon Over Tokyo* had been set to ferment. Now, they waited. They had since begun another wine: *Sunlight through Cherry Blossoms*. Taro thought this would be a hugely popular wine. They took his own memories of walking with his girlfriend in Japan earlier that spring. He was very honoured to supply the base. Yumi almost forgot that Taro had a girlfriend who looked into his flat, blocky face for love. She lived in Japan. Yumi treated Taro as if he were single.

"Did you sing to her?" Kichi asked, glancing sideways for his response.

The two women laughed. Some tofu dropped from Yumi's mouth, which made the three of them laugh harder. She looked at Masato. He continued eating, reading a chart on his lap. Yumi told Taro that she looked forward to seeing his girlfriend, experiencing his beautiful memories.

"It is nothing like *Moon Over Tokyo*," he said, grinning.

Yumi glanced at Masato. "It's not as important . . ." she said.

Masato looked up. He said evenly, "You don't know what is important." He wasn't unkind; just straightforward. He corrected himself. "Very few of us know what is important. Walking along with the girlfriend through cherry blossoms makes a nice scene, a good wine. But sometimes we must strive for more." He noted each of them in his glance, cleared his throat, and looked back at his papers.

"Sometimes," Yumi began, "I think we forget what's important, though we've seen it before."

He looked up and, after thinking a moment, nodded. "Still, nothing in your collective experiences has any real weight. You have music and you have laughter and you have fun, but now you are part of something bigger, something you are creating that will be important." He breathed in, smiled, and slowly let it out. "It is never too late to learn. And to change."

Taro and Kichi nodded. "Yes, yes," they said.

Yumi smiled and seethed. She began carefully. "Please tell us how the images of Taro's time with his girlfriend are different, and less important, from the moments in *Moon Over Tokyo*. I want to know and learn about importance. I'm very interested and intrigued by what you say." She nodded purely for effect.

His eyes watched her. She trembled inside, kept humility on her face, tried to erase confrontation. Placate, placate, placate, she thought. It keeps peace. Still, the question might draw out—

"It will be most apparent when the wines are completed. I think then, young Yumi, that you will understand the weight of difference." He nodded and stood, bringing his bowl back to her. His face came close to hers as he bowed, but his eyes did not look down at the floor. They stayed locked with hers. "We must continue. Thank you, Yumi."

Kichi and Taro stood and brought her their bowls.

It was December, and Yumi convinced Taro to let her taste the wine. *Umeshu* was at the halfway point—the *toge*—a point where they could check and see how the fermentation process and the *piku* were combining, how the images were layering, if there was good evocation and transport already. It would be an unfinished wine, though, because harmonics were not sealed into the wine until the fermentation process was complete. And sometimes the wines did not come out the way you planned.

"Hmmm." Taro considered. "He doesn't like anyone outside of the staff to sample the wine before it's finished."

Yumi begged him. She started singing with him over the phone: "*Why don't they/Do what they say/Say what you mean/One thing leads to another . . .*" He laughed on his end of the phone. "Oh, Taro," she sighed. "You are very funny."

He sighed. "I'm very busy, Yumi. I don't know."

"Taro." She sensed he was moving out of the pink and yellow karaoke memories. "I want to learn about importance." She sounded as serious as Masato, almost mimicking his cadence.

She imagined his face thinking on the phone, weighing how much trouble he might get into. "You can't drink it here," he said, "but if you come, I'll have a sample ready for you."

She went to the winery, and when she saw Taro, she wondered what it was like to be his girlfriend. Did he truly sing to her? Did he take her out to parties? What did they do for fun? She would have a chance to see at least Akina, his girlfriend, in the wine.

"Will *Sunlight Through Cherry Blossoms* have you in it at all?"

He gave her a small vial that she placed in her new pink purse with anime characters running across the leather.

"We only used my memories. Nakashita-san thought that one man's memories would easily be able to pull all men into the evocation, since there was space for each man."

"Yes," Yumi said. She thought, though, how sad it must be for Akina to only see herself in the memory.

By now she was convinced that Masato was somehow having an affair with an older, more sophisticated woman, and she believed strongly that this woman would be reflected in the image of the woman on the bridge—if, truly, it were a woman on the bridge.

At home, the high afternoon sun showed through the skylight in the dining room. San Francisco traffic buzzed and hummed in the distance and a breeze came through the window. A silver bowl of apples on the kitchen island reflected her body in wide strips. She poured the contents of the vial into the lotus glass, looked straight ahead, and lifted the glass and drank.

The park at dusk. She turned immediately to Togetsukyo Bridge. Other people walked about the park now, so it was more difficult to find the figure he would have been creating. There was no rush of the body now; he'd synced it with the rest of the evocation. She watched, aware of time passing.

It was a woman. She wore a *yukata*, a cotton kimono, with maple leaves on the sleeves, which meant she was unmarried. She saw Yumi, or appeared to, as she would see any wine taster. The woman was young, beautiful, but she walked in that older way, her shoulders drawn in, her head down, her eyes flashing only to the sides, occasionally to the subject she walked toward. There was a simple beauty in this that Yumi found herself liking even more than she expected, this being the object of attention, the reason the woman came from the bridge. In the midst of all other people milling about, one direct line flowed straight to her, pulling an important event closer and closer. This was already an improvement over the peaceful scene of *Moon Over Tokyo Through Fall Leaves*; it had an event—an urgency.

The woman pulled her hands from her kimono. She began talking, but there was still no sound. Yumi tried to make out the words. The expression on the woman's face was flirtatious, demure. She wanted you to follow her. And the images did. When the woman turned her back and started to return to the bridge, Yumi found herself walking along beside her. Again the woman was talking. Her bright red mouth moved, her eyes darted and connected with Yumi's as if with a needle's precision. Then the woman blurred, smeared across the park's landscape, and smudged away. There was a strange pull then—a yank from the middle of Yumi's stomach—and then Yumi was back, alone and frustrated, in her kitchen.

She threw the lotus glass into the sink where it broke. She felt like one of the people who first tried the *piku* for memory loss, because every memory of herself and Masato came back to betray her. She sobbed standing, holding herself up by placing her hands flat on the kitchen island. She sniffled and opened her eyes. At least she was not maddened from the memories. She hoped that the feelings would just disappear.

They did not. She found them creeping up on her as she created perfect travel arrangements for happy couples at work. She kept the feelings low in her belly, feeling them seep upwards in her chest at times when couples would look at each other or talk in that coded way couples have—those unfinished sentences, those looks—and when they reached out and took each others' hands, a subtle, unconscious gesture, Yumi turned to her computer to find a better deal for them.

She could not confront Masato about this, though her instincts told her that he loved the woman on the bridge. She was old-fashioned, she was demure, she was quiet, she was painted up like a geisha. Masato was in love with history, with the past. And there was really nothing Yumi could do about that.

I am a modern woman, she told herself. At one time, he loved me because I was modern. At one time, he loved the new things, the modern. Somehow, living with her in the house, he had changed his tastes for more than just art.

Over the next six months, she thought about what she might do. Options. She could become the woman he wanted. She could leave him and find someone younger. She didn't think he would be changing anymore—he'd settled into his final personality.

She continued having lunches with friends, talking at breezy cafés about books and movies and going to her friends' baby showers and wedding showers and walking in the parks by herself at dinner.

It was in a small park that summer when she saw something happen that made her decide to confront Masato. There was a black dog running through the park with a red leash flying behind it like a scarf. His tongue was out, his legs raced across the grass. She laughed when she saw him, and she laughed more when she saw the young couple running after the dog, calling, "Shiloh, Shiloh, Shiloh, come back." The man and woman were both young, in their twenties, and they ran as hard as they could, the man ahead of the woman, both racing for Shiloh. They called out directions to each other: Go that way, head her off by the bush; I'll take this path and meet her around the lake; she's headed toward the ice cream vendor! Yumi watched as they tried to catch her. The dog appeared joyful; the couple did not seem worried. They laughed. Shiloh tangled herself up in children, playing with them and knocking them down, and licking their faces until the couple found her again. At that moment, Yumi burst into tears, not knowing quite why at first. She moved under a tree and hid her face with her arm.

She drove to the winery that afternoon. Her husband had been working feverishly on a new set of wines. She did not see him on the floor of the winery, so she walked past Taro and Kichi to his office. They called out, "He doesn't want to be disturbed."

I am his wife, she thought. I disturb him all the time.

She walked into his office, a small room with a shoji screen hiding a small sink and a desk with no pictures on it. His coat was draped over the chair, but he was not there.

Taro was behind her. "Yumi, he wanted to be alone in the *piku-ma*." The room of memory, where the *piku* was stamped—where it was copied for every bottle of plum wine.

She turned and looked at Taro; his eyes had aged. She could tell. The edge of his voice had gotten older.

She said, "He's not alone, Taro. We can be honest about that."

"What?" Taro said as she pushed him to the side and walked to the *piku-ma*.

The *piku-ma* had warnings on the sides of the doors referencing the delicate process, the possible contamination. She did not knock; she tried the handle and went in.

Masato stood with his back to the door. He leaned down over a microscope. The room was blue, like sky all the way around. He looked up suddenly. "Yumi?"

She closed the door behind her.

He sighed as if destiny had been decided for him—or a decision made at least. Five bottles of wine sat on a white table in the centre of the room. To the left, a black, elastic cap hanging from wires—the brain-scanning equipment, what gathered the images, as far as she knew. On the right side of the room, other computers and imaging equipment. She didn't understand it. She just knew that this was where the woman came from. This was where she lived. This was where Masato stood now with his arms open, walking to the table. He picked up a bottle and pushed a lotus glass toward her side of the table as she approached him.

"I want you to see my masterpiece." He opened the bottle. "*Moon Over Tokyo Through Fall Leaves* has changed a bit. We have renamed this *Another Tokyo in Fall Twilight, 1947*." He grinned.

This other woman had made him younger, Yumi thought.

He poured her a glass. "Try it for me. I want you to see something special." He held the glass out to her.

She shook her head. "I didn't come to drink the wine."

He sensed her uneasiness but insisted. "Drink the wine first, and then we can talk about anything you want to talk about."

She shook her head again. "Masato."

"Yumi, it's important to me. Please, for me. Drink the wine."

But she didn't want to meet the woman who could speak now. Oh, she had already imagined all the phrases, the sweet ways that a geisha could talk to a man, what she might be saying to Masato—and now, where she might be leading him. And what was that pull in her stomach? Would there now be a physical reaction to Time-Wines? Was he creating the wino-version of a cheap thrill? Was this *piku*'s new direction? Or was this a new product for Masato to enjoy?

In his hand, the lotus glass quivered. What was he doing with such a young woman anyway? She set her purse down on the table. "I don't want your wine," she said, trying to keep her voice steady. Why was it that she felt as if she were asking her father for greater privileges? She flushed with embarrassment.

Masato lowered his hand. "I wanted to share with you something important to me, Yumi."

"I already know the evocation. I've seen her."

He looked puzzled. "Her? I don't understand. This is the first set of bottles opened with the new wine. It's very changed from *Moon Over Tokyo*, though that was obviously the base."

"I tried the wine in December, at *toge*."

He frowned. "It was unfinished. I wanted you to see it when it was finished."

"I don't want to see it at all now."

He was silent. "Did you notice the soldiers?"

"I noticed the girl, the geisha."

"Of course, that is the main selling point. But did you notice that there weren't any soldiers around? Did you watch the edges of the evocation?"

He lifted the glass again. "Try it now. See what I've created here. It's a ten-minute transport."

"Tell me who she is and why you created her."

He still seemed lost. As if he didn't know what she was talking about.

"She's a geisha," he said, lowering his arm again. He sighed, probably the clearest sign of guilt. He was no doubt remembering the images of this affair.

"Is she also a real woman, someone you know here in San Francisco?"

He set the glass on the table, took a few steps back. "I was hoping you'd understand."

"Well, I'm doing pretty good for a kid, I think."

He looked at her. Boy, did he look old now, and caught and guilty, and just a little bit angry. But she was angry, too, now; she could feel it rise up into her cheeks, into her fists.

He said, "You have missed the whole thing. How can one person see the same images as another and miss the point? We are like two people who have come to a mountain, and I am breathing in the greatness of the view while you are looking at the hardship of the trail back down. Our memories will diverge there, and I can't give you feeling, no matter how hard I try." He walked to the computer screen and opened a file.

She felt ignored, and so she repeated her inquiry. "Who is she?"

A picture came up on the screen of an old man, Masato's grandfather. "Junro Nakashita helped create a Japan that never was."

She waited for him to come back to the real issue. He distracted her with history lessons and stories. "I'm not interested in your grandfather—"

He nodded. "Nor in anything that doesn't have a movie tie-in, that doesn't sell you a purse or shoes, that doesn't have a musical soundtrack. I know. It's a weakness in you. But now you will listen for a moment, and even if you do not understand what I tell you, I will have said it and given you the picture of the mountain."

He talked for a long time about Junro and how he collaborated with Americans to rewrite Japan's history during the Occupation. He stood for a while, and then he sat for a bit and she stood for a while, and then she got tired because the shoes she'd worn were not good for standing in. She knew that eventually he would have to talk about the geisha so she sat down. He waved his hands a lot in front of him and she noticed how wrinkled the backs of his hands and wrists really were. When did that happen?

"I had a chance then," he said in what she thought was his conclusion. She was tired and upset, and it was taking everything she had to keep in her tears. "A Japan that could have been," he said. "The soldiers aren't there, Yumi; I erased them. The American presence isn't there; I erased that. For ten minutes there is no Occupation, and I can build from there. I can create a whole series of wines that lets someone experience this new-old Japan. I don't know how it would have been different. I can only think of ten minutes at a time. But one day, I will think of twenty minutes, and then an hour." He paused.

He was all caught up in himself, wide hands, wild eyes—eyes that reminded her of times he looked in her face and loved her. She didn't want a wine to say it for him again and again—she wanted those eyes and those words for her, now.

"Is she here in San Francisco? Did we move here because she's here?" She tapped her heels on the floor.

"Yumi!" he yelled at her and rushed at the table. "I am talking about something important! I'm reimagining history."

She stood up now, backed away from his face. "I'm talking about something important, too. Where are you? What do you do at night? Why are you so concerned about the past? I'm going to grow old, too, waiting for you. Why are you making women in the wine? I don't care about history. I don't care about Junro. It's in the past. Why are we here in America if you hate America so much?"

"I don't hate America. You're not listening to me. I can't explain it well. But there is something new and wonderful about being there, in that park in 1947, and being free."

She thought of the dog, the couple; how they raced after Shiloh, how they cared enough to pursue and not get distracted, to not give up; how they planned, how they ran around every obstacle to get back to her. How they wanted something and ran to get it.

He lifted the glass again. "Just for a moment. See this other world."

She took the glass from him and threw it on the floor where it shattered and spilled. "That's what I think of your other world. You can't even live in this one."

She turned her back on him, crying, crying and wanting to make it through the door before he could say that she was weak and young.

How Magnificent is the
~ Universal Donor

Jacob stumbles from the elevator on the fourth floor of Sanctuary Hospital. He's in a hurry, and feels guilty that he's been detained for three hours at a press conference helping the Deputy Minister field questions. He can still see the lights from the steady cams, purple spots erasing the hospital walls. The white hallways seem suddenly quiet. His short stride makes it look like he's running, and his beard is hiding clenched lips. He stops at the door to room 423. The sheets of the bed are neatly folded. *They moved him.*

Back in the hallway, he inhales and scans the patient screen, but doesn't find Harlin Moybridge anywhere on the list. It's probably just a mistake. He turns and looks around to find anyone who can tell him what's going on. A blonde-haired nurse in a cool blue uniform stands leaning over a desk. The desk lamp highlights her neck, and her skin looks like white fire. When he asks where they've moved Harlin Moybridge, she checks the desk, a flat screen where she moves documents back and forth with the tip of her finger.

"Oh, Mr. Moybridge," she looks up. "Your husband died this morning."

He stares in disbelief. Dead? "He was just in for tests," Jacob says. "Look. There's been a mistake. I would have been called."

She looks hurt, sad for him. She glances back to the desk. "They called you."

"They didn't." His voice is higher than normal.

"It says that you were contacted, and made arrangements to see the body."

"Where's the body? I'd like to see it."

She looks back down at the desk, flustered. "It says . . . it says you've already seen the body." Now she looks up, as surprised as he is. "You came in at ten am—two hours ago."

It didn't matter that he insisted he didn't come in. There it was in the records. Harlin always said that when it's in your medical records, it's scripture.

"How did he die?"

She scans the records, tells him, "He tested positive for BBD."

"He didn't," Jacob says evenly.

"You received the letter in the mail and came in for tests for BBD. Obviously there was reason to suspect your husband had the disease. Those initial tests are rarely wrong."

"Rare," he says, "but not impossible."

The Beijing Blood Disease, or Baby Dee as it is popularly known, is not normally fatal. Since more than 40 percent of the population has it at any one time, it is rampant, but transfusions seem to keep those infected in check. But Harlin Moybridge has the strongest immune system he's ever seen.

"I never been inoculated, never had flu shots, never been sick. I'm fine, and they *hate* that," Harlin once told him. He smiled, arched his back and spread his shoulders. "I'm on a black list somewhere because I don't take their damn shots." No antibiotics, no synthesized medicines ever entered his body. His father made sure that none of his kids got shots. He was a homeopathic doctor, but his children were fine examples of health. He faked the shot records himself, enough to get his kids through schooling.

"They don't like people who say they don't need doctors," Harlin said. "It's a scam, you know. To make you need 'em. They want you to need 'em. It's about control. But everybody's smart enough to take care of themselves." It's that rebellious streak that Jacob loves. And wasn't Harlin proved right? At fifty-six, he was in perfect health, robust, full of life. He could have given any man twenty years younger a run for his money.

"I *don't* have Baby Dee," Harlin said when he opened the letter. "They just want me in the hospital."

Like a subpoena, a summons from the World Health Organization is pretty much unbeatable. Jacob read the letter. It indicated Harlin was a "health risk to society." Baby Dee is contagious. He was to report to the hospital for more tests and possible treatment. "They *loved* my blood. They *envied* it. Dadgum 'em, they'd never *seen* finer blood than mine. The bastards!" When he was angry, his Texas drawl really showed.

Everyone has to give a blood sample, just a tiny needle's worth, at the front of every supermarket, a quick, nearly painless touch. This ensures that on a continuous basis, every person who needs food is screened. Harlin balled up the letter and threw it across the room. "From now on, *you* buy the groceries."

"It's a mistake," Jacob told him. "It must be. We'll go down to the hospital, and we'll retake the test and we'll show them that they got yours mixed up with someone else's."

Harlin argued against it, wouldn't be reasoned with.

"Look, if we just go and prove to them that your blood is fine, this will be over."

Harlin growled at him.

Jacob smiled "Let them be stinking envious. You have to clear your name."

The nurse invites Jacob behind the desk and lets him read the report for himself.

Harlin died on the transfusion table. His body is awaiting incineration. They have to burn it—an out of control BBD could infect so much of the population that it would be impossible to contain the spread. No, Jacob isn't allowed to view the body. "Again," she adds. Yes, he will have to be screened as well. Could he stop by the main floor and give a blood sample? He cringes at the lack of compassion.

Looking at the document, Jacob is sure he will sue the hospital for negligence. There on the document is his phone number.

"I never came in to see the body," he tells her again. "I was never called."

She nods.

He walks away from the nurse. She calls after him that there is a chapel and a counsellor on the second floor. But he's not going there. Harlin wouldn't be in the chapel.

The elevator doors shut and he's alone. He looks at his blurred reflection in the walls of the elevator. He's angry at the hospital. What man, playing Jacob, came and saw the body? Who would do that? He's angry at the nurse. He's mad at Harlin. How could a man with an "unbeatable" immune system go and die during tests? And finally, as the elevator sinks farther and farther down, he thinks, *I should have stayed*. Then, thankfully, he finds a way to blame it on the Deputy Minister, and lastly, China, and this gets him prepared for the doors to open.

He wipes his eyes with his sleeve. But he needn't. An aerosol antibacterial mists the air. The spray is wet only for a second, but he feels it on his face, and when it evaporates it leaves his skin dry and the doors open to the basement, the morgue.

"You can pull off anything if you're confident enough," Harlin told him before his first interview for the communications position with the government.

"Yeah, they call that false confidence," Jacob said.

"Unjustified confidence," Harlin smiled. "Who knows? You may be a whiz at it. Just act like it till it comes natural." Harlin liked that he was transparent. "You're an honest man," he said. "You got no guile. But sometimes, buddy, you have to learn to fake it."

Press conferences are great testing grounds for faking it. And Jacob ended up in more than his fair share as the communications analyst for the Deputy Minister. But even when he learned to hide nearly everything in front of a camera, still Harlin would tell him, passing his hand warmly across Jacob's face, "You can't fool me. This face is a map. And I got the legend memorized."

⟡ ⟡

On his way to the morgue, he passes three pathology labs and an autopsy room. He walks through the retracting door into the morgue. It is bland, sterile; he expects to smell formaldehyde, but there is no strong odour. A shiver runs through him. *Harlin should be here.*

Silver panels line one wall. He imagines they have bodies tucked away behind them. There are tables with bodies on them in four rows, each draped with thin muslin. Should be plastic, he thinks. One table has the muslin, but no body. He looks around first, and then begins to uncover the faces of the different bodies.

They don't shock him. He's determined to find Harlin, to see that white-haired, clean-shaven face, smiling even in death, underneath the muslin. He does it quickly: a flip off, a flip back on. The faces are peaceful. Nothing in their skin gives it away that they are dead. They're pale, yes, but not blue-lipped. Some women, mostly men. They all have their clothes on. This is not at all what he expected. But he checks each one in turn until he has looked at them all. Harlin is not here.

He looks up. He walks over to the computer controls on the wall. The silver panels are represented by a green LCD number display. On the main screen is a list of names, none of which are *Moybridge*.

These are all the dead bodies in the room, and all the bodies in the slots. *Where the hell is Harlin?*

In the back, he discovers a change room. Lockers. Showers. It makes sense. If the nurses burn their clothes because of disease risk, he can see why showers for pathologists might be available. He just didn't expect them in the morgue.

He expected Harlin.

But if Harlin isn't in the morgue, where is he?

From the corner of his eye, Jacob sees something stirring.

A body on a table moves, stretches. One of the dead bodies. He sees a hand come from underneath the muslin cloth, pulling it slowly down its face, and then its body. It exhales and then breathes in deeply.

Jacob slips into the locker room. His breath is shallow and his heart races. He hears the squeak of the table where the body was as the person steps down. Jacob remembers the faces of the dead—still and peaceful. He hears them moving and feels trapped. He looks around the change room for hiding places. Lockers are too small, showers too open. And what about a weapon?

He hears another squeak. "I thought Jardin was on today," says a voice.

"Jardin's sick. I'm filling in," says another.

They're conversational, casual.

"He's just a third year."

"Sad, isn't it?"

Jacob takes off his shirt and lays it on a bench. Maybe he can pretend to be someone, anyone, dressing after a shower. Maybe. He has his back to the footsteps as they enter the locker room. They're talking, hardly noticing him. They pass by.

"I don't want to work today," one says.

"Are you third year?" There's a pause. "Oh. Well, I can understand."

Jacob acts as if he's just putting his shirt back on. He looks at his shoes, trying not to think about *them*.

Two of them stop talking. "Hello?" one says.

Jacob turns slowly. He remembers them from the tables, how they looked when they were dead. One is shorter, blond hair and stocky build; the other is taller and lean.

"John Lake," Jacob says, not extending his hand. "From St. Mary's. In Omaha."

They introduce themselves, smiling. They seem to buy it. These dead people. He looks at their faces. He would not be able to tell they are dead. He starts to think maybe they were just asleep. But this is the morgue.

"I'm here on a visit," he adds.

"Oh," they nod. "How are things in Omaha?"

What would they want to hear? He waits. It's always good to wait in an interview to hear a follow up question. People clarify themselves. They do it all the time in press conferences.

These two don't. They shuffle awkwardly. The tall one looks at Jacob's hands as he finishes buttoning the shirt, watching his fingers work the buttons. Will they notice his hair's not wet?

"About the same," he says. "You know how it is."

The short one smiles weakly. "You kind of think it's better somewhere else."

"Especially somewhere more rural," the other one says. He turns and strips off his shirt. "Less people to worry about."

Jacob doesn't say anything back. He's hoping they find him aloof. Maybe they'll shut up. He tucks in his shirt and turns to the door.

"Did you leave your jacket in Omaha?" says the tall one. "You can borrow one here. I'm sure no one will mind."

They both approach him helpfully. They filter through a rack of red coats against the wall. "Jardin's not here," the tall one says, holding out one to size him up. "But you could probably use any that's your size." They are friendly. He doesn't want to touch them; he wants to run, but nods politely and takes Jardin's coat. It is a bit large; Jacob is a small-framed guy. "This is great. Thanks." His shoulders are swallowed in the coat.

"Hmmm. Try this one. It was Eamer's." The short one gives him another coat and he slips it on. It fits. They both smile. "He's gone now. It's good to get some use out of it." The shorter man brushes the coat down.

"Thank you." Jacob feels the need to explain himself. "I left mine."

The short one smiles. "Well, I hope you enjoy your visit."

Jacob wants to leave. He thinks he can smell death on them. But they are smiling; they seem sincere.

A door opens behind him at the far end of the morgue. An older man walks in, already taking off his coat. "We need to wake up the others," he says. "Dr. Esterhazy's found a new donor. Impeccable blood, no impurity."

"No BBD?" the tall one asks.

"No anything. Pure. Almost unheard of."

Jacob feels a lump in his throat. They have to be talking about Harlin.

And donors can't be dead.

The shorter one turns to him. "Good day to visit, eh?" The two are beaming with pride as if they are offering Harlin as a miracle to be performed in an hour, something to break out the cameras for. Jacob can't help but grin and his eyes start to water. If Harlin's still alive, it *is* a miracle.

The two turn to the older man as he comes into the locker room. "Dr. Lake from Omaha," the tall one says.

Jacob must look ridiculous, about to cry. Scared to death of this man approaching. Of these two *men* that have come from a room full of dead bodies.

"Mercy?" the older man asks. He has thick black hair and bushy eyebrows. You can see the veins in his hands, and they look younger than his face.

"Mercy, yes. It's been a day," Jacob says.

"Mercy *Hospital* in Omaha," the older man says.

"*St. Mary's*," the shorter one replies for Jacob. "He's up for a visit."

"St. Mary's?" the older man asks, looking as if he's trying to remember any hospital by that name.

"A small clinic," Jacob says, "big name. We aim to grow into it."

The doctor smiles, extends his hand. "Philip Gontard." Jacob shakes it. It's cold. The doctor seems surprised, holds Jacob's grip, a curious look on his face that fades as quickly as it appeared. "Enjoy Sanctuary. There's a lot to see. I'd suggest room seven ten in an hour." He looks at the other two men, suddenly in a hurry. "We need to wake everyone. Esterhazy wants everyone there."

Jacob fades back through the morgue toward the door as the men proceed to wake the others. The older doctor moves to the console next to the silver panels and presses a few buttons. Jacob doesn't want to see any more bodies come to life.

Except one.

And he already feels as if Harlin has risen, somewhere.

The seventh floor. If you are infected with Baby Dee, you come here. The walls are white. All the doctors wear redcoats, as does Jacob. They are all specialists in blood identification: hematologists, hematopathologists, phlebotomists. The names of their specialties make him queasy. He hated needles as a child. His parents were like most—they believed in booster shots, flu shots, and in taking their child to the doctor as much as they could. With healthcare being free in the country, there wasn't a reason not to. But, if he watched a needle approaching his arm, he fainted. "We got a fainter," the phlebotomists would say, chuckling to each other, as if he was supposed to be okay with people drawing his blood. There was something unnatural about it.

And yet, every time the government issued a health risk warning, his parents got "in line to get in line with the law," as his father would say.

Jacob followed rules, for the most part. But the blood, the needles, the alcohol smell—it still bothered him. Harlin, in some ways, gave him an excuse to run from the whole thing. As if they were playing a game with the medical establishment. "Let's see if they can catch us," Harlin said.

There was a time without Redcoats. Before Baby Dee. Hospitals were scarier then. There was a sense of the unknown, of the unpredictable. Then, after Baby Dee, the WHO appointed all these specialists to treat BBD before it could become a global crisis. Smart-thinking, dedicated Redcoats were credited with averting disaster. "In the war for your life, Redcoats are the front line," went the commercials. Jacob watched tv specials on their procedures—it looked like a common transfusion to him. But the transfusions—the frequency of them—were "the reason the world stays safe" the nations' Presidents assured their citizens. The Redcoats found new treatments for several more blood diseases, and cured Leukemia. But BBD was a constant threat that the doctors could only contain. These doctors worked as a team, cooperating with hospitals all over the world. They earned the respect of the world, and most people revered them.

Jacob was indifferent. He just wanted to avoid doctors and hospitals. But Harlin was skeptical—and adamant. "It's a show," he said. "Where'd all these specialists come from? Phlebotomists were the low man on the totem pole. Why'd they all of a sudden rise up the ladder? The medical profession is fulla secrets, Jake."

Well, now Harlin knows some of them. And so does Jacob.

On the seventh floor, he sweats nearly through his red coat. He pictures every other doctor he meets lying under the muslin cloth on a shiny silver table. Dead. Or asleep. Who are they? *What* are they?

He feels like a guided missile going through the hallway, reading the numbers on doors, smiling at people. He's gone past confidence and has moved into determination. Harlin is alive. Or at least, he will be for the next hour.

Jacob encounters more and more Redcoats. The hallways are flooded with them, plus a few white coats, floating in among the nurses and general staff. They look vibrant in the over-whitened space. He can't take his eyes off them. They even look back at him as he passes.

"Dr. Lake?" says a voice to his right. It's the older doctor, Dr. Gontard, who now walks beside Jacob, matching his pace. "Could you assist me here?"

The man's heavy eyebrows overshadow the slits his eyes have become. The grin on his face isn't pleasant. He grips Jacob's arm, and Jacob feels small pinpricks as Dr. Gontard pulls him into a dark room with a central set of lights illuminating a patient on an angled platform. The patient, a man who appears to be his late twenties, looks unconscious; the light creates a rapturous expression on his upturned face.

"Dr. *Lake*." He says the name as if he's savouring it, amused by it. "I need to conduct a transfusion and we need a hand." He indicates another doctor in the shadows wearing a red coat, operating a tower of blinking lights and some cords, none of which are connected to the patient.

Dr. Gontard walks over to the patient and climbs up onto his body until he is straddling the man. "This man has BBD. If we don't transfuse him, he'll eventually succumb to the neurological side effects: tremors, loss of muscle tissue, the general wasting away of a healthy individual. *As you undoubtedly know*," he turns and looks at Jacob, continuing wryly, "transfusion is all that works right now, and this will eliminate 99 percent of the disease. We've never been able to totally cure an individual. All we can do is keep them as healthy as possible, despite the ongoing infection."

The man on the board isn't strapped down except at the waist, to prevent him from sliding.

Dr. Gontard places his hands beside the man's neck, far enough away for Jacob to notice as the nails on both middle fingers elongate into needles, the tips sharpening into fine points.

"This patient will eventually die of BBD if we don't do something, but hospitals can't handle the number of complete body blood transfusions, which is why they have relied on us for the past twenty years."

He inserts both needles into the man's neck and cups the chin in his palms. His fingers puncture first the skin then the veins. He leans his own head back and sighs. "If only we could keep all the blood for ourselves instead of just the nutrients. But I suppose our job is to purify as much as we can, and then return it."

Jacob steps back. The other doctor, the one by the blinking tower monitoring the situation, is behind him.

"What does this have to do with me?" Jacob asks. He has to stop himself from backing farther away. Dr. Gontard's fingers are fat sausages, red and flush with blood as the patient's blood transfers through the doctor's body. What *are* these people? He gulps. "I know all this," he says.

"Do you?"

Jacob reaches into himself to extract as much confidence as he can. "I've performed these transfusions for fifteen years."

"Have you?" says Dr. Gontard. His head turns so that he is peering over his shoulder, eyes completely blocked by his oppressive eyebrows.

"Well, I think you have this completely under control. As a guest, I do appreciate you showing me your technique; however, you didn't need my assistance. I'm not sure your positioning is best for accomplishing a transfusion. In Omaha, we do our transfusions from the side of the patient so as not to restrict blood flow. Thank you for your time, Dr. Gontard. Perhaps we'll . . . we'll meet again."

Jacob turns to go, and looks directly at the Redcoat standing between him and the door. The man hesitates but eventually steps aside, and Jacob leaves the room.

In the hall again, he feels sick. Faint. The hallways are filled with Redcoats. He wants a bathroom more than anything else. But instead, he scans the numbers above the doors, counting backwards. He weaves in among the medical personnel, hoping he won't fall. If they've hurt Harlin already, Jacob doesn't know what he'll do. What he *can* do to people like this. If they even *are* people.

He feels a rush of relief as he spots room 710 and pushes through the door.

The room is small, empty of people. There's a little desk that glows from the LCD imbedded in its surface, blinking lights and a tower, and rolling silver tray tables set against the wall. The room is a circle, in the centre of which, beneath a light, is a body on a table.

It's Harlin, flat on his back. A sheet covers him from the waist down. He looks like he's sleeping.

Jacob hurries to Harlin's side to see if he's breathing. He looks so alive. His cheeks are flush, his hair is combed, his lips half parted as if he has just lain down. For a moment, it's as if Jacob has only turned over in bed to see Harlin sleeping. He has done that so many times, just to watch the man breathe. He often thinks of that breath as keeping rhythm with the night, a way of knowing that everything is secure. Jacob is such a light sleeper; if the breath stops, or if Harlin turns his head, Jacob wakes. Is he afraid of losing the man? Or is he just . . . afraid?

"Harlin," he says.

But Harlin doesn't answer.

Jacob feels a pulse in his neck and, most importantly, finds no needle holes. No one has gotten to Harlin yet, but there are two lines marked on his neck. His chest moves up and down, slowly but steadily. "I got the body of a thirty-year-old," Harlin often said. "From hard work and good livin'. I'm gonna live to be a hundred and twenty."

"You're gonna live," Jacob says to him now, pats him on the chest.

He moves to the computer in the desk. He saw how the nurse pulled up files; he searches for *Moybridge* and finds Harlin's records. He needs an ace in the hole. If the Redcoats are afraid of Harlin—if he doesn't have such perfect blood—they won't want him so badly. And they will let him go.

The file opens, and Jacob creates a disease. He adds a note at the end of Harlin's records, as if a doctor added it.

It's not so different than a press release, really, just subtler.

Medical records are scripture. He just hopes that Harlin will forgive him for messing up the scripture as it pertains to him. Muddying up his reputation, his perfection.

Finished, it's time to get Harlin and himself out of there.

Quickly, he reaches the gurney and begins to unlock the wheels. He is busy covering Harlin to his neck with the sheet when suddenly lights come on all around him.

Jacob finds himself standing in the middle of a surgical theatre. Above him, surrounding him, are windows, and at those windows are Redcoats. Fifty, seventy-five, a hundred. All peering down at him, watching him, as if he is a drop of blood on a slide.

"Ladies and gentlemen, may I introduce you to Dr. John Lake from St. Mary's Hospital in Omaha, Nebraska," a familiar voice booms through the speakers. The Redcoats clap. As the clapping dies, Dr. Gontard continues. "We are indeed privileged that Dr. Lake is with us. Today, he is going to tell us a bit about a new donor that we discovered among the pool of applicants that have come to the hospital. And, I believe," and Dr. Gontard smiles, "he is going to show us a new transfusion technique. Is that correct, Dr. Lake?"

Though initially frightened, Jacob suddenly feels at home. This is a press conference. Instead of being the communications man behind the scenes, whispering the strategies, the lines, every second, he is now the minister himself.

"Thank you, Dr. Gontard," he says broadly, "and to the staff of Sanctuary Hospital for your generosity, and for the honour of demonstrating to you the Omaha method of transfusion, popular at our clinic, but also a technique that is becoming popular in other hospitals."

He stalls, looks around the room. "I wish we had this kind of staff at St. Mary's."

The crowd murmurs their pride and approval. It's a cheap shot, but it gives him time to think. "I would like to tell you about this donor; first I'm going to need his records."

Dr. Gontard taps the window twice and small screens appear at intervals around the glass. A projected holographic display, shoulder height, appears in front of Jacob. The report is two pages, which include his additions at the bottom.

Dr. Gontard begins. "With your permission, Dr. Lake, I'll give an overview of the patient."

Jacob nods, even as sweat runs down his back. He sees the door behind him, and knows that most of the Redcoats are close by, too close; he might have only minutes to escape, if that. He can't be too obvious.

"As you can see," Dr. Gontard begins dramatically, "the patient, Harlin Moybridge, is in peak physical condition. Even at fifty-six years, he is as healthy as a man half his age."

Oh how Jacob wishes Harlin could hear this. It would stroke his ego.

"Harlin Moybridge has never had any man-made chemicals invade his body. He made a point to list on the patient application that he has only eaten organic foods all of his life, drank purified water, that he'd never taken antibiotics, and only employed homeopathic remedies. He is chemical-free, and therefore chemically unaltered. His blood cells possess the ability to regenerate at an astonishing rate. He could be a universal donor, and the answer to our own dilemma, even as we are the answer to theirs."

What did he mean? Jacob suddenly remembers the doctors talking in the morgue. "*Jardin's sick*"; another doctor was "*gone.*"

Someone calls out, "What is SVD?"

"Excuse me?" Dr. Gontard asks. There is general curiosity.

"At the end of the record: *evidence of SVD. Patient not safe to transfuse.*"

"But the top of the form has him approved."

Curiosity becomes confusion as they each check the records.

"I don't know SVD. And who is the doctor listed? Esterhazy." Dr. Gontard looks up. "Dr. Esterhazy. What do you mean by SVD?"

"I didn't put that there!"

"It's on the records."

"But, I don't even know what SVD is."

There is now rumbling among the Redcoats. Jacob knows he has only seconds to convince people. They are so much like reporters hearing something they can't believe, something they fear. You can calm that fear. Or not. He watches the slow chaos forming, wants to wait till it hits a peak. But Jacob hears a murmur from behind him. Harlin moves his head and grunts.

"May I address the doctors?" Jacob asks.

They quiet down. Jacob continues. "It is what I feared I might find at Sanctuary. Something only recently discovered in other hospitals. SVD, or Shanghai Ventricular Disease, has started appearing in our patients in the heartland of America. It is not confirmed yet, so WHO doesn't want rumours spread.

"First discovered one week ago, SVD is responsible for three deaths at our hospital, two of those doctors. Harlin Moybridge, it appears, carries this disease."

He keeps his face as straight and convincing as possible. "Which means that anyone who transfuses him will contract SVD."

The silence tells him they are waiting for one last word.

"This man is no longer of use to us." He moves to the head of the gurney and begins pulling it backwards. "Gentlemen, for your own safety, please keep back. I've already been exposed and will take this man to isolation. Thank you."

He moves quickly toward the door.

"Jake?" says Harlin. "Jake. That you?"

He tries to place a hand over Harlin's mouth.

"Jake," he's slurring. "Got me strapped down, buddy."

"Dr. Lake?" says Dr. Gontard. "Please stop."

The door behind him opens and two Redcoats stand just outside it, blocking his exit.

The gig is up. But the spotlight is still on. What would he say to a minister caught in a lie? No comment, no comment, no comment. He doubts that will work here.

"It's not Dr. Lake, is it?" Dr. Gontard says. "Convenient that you come on the day we find a universal donor. That the universal donor has a mysterious disease no one else has heard of, and that you are able to, equally conveniently, provide us with a definition, and a history of the disease. No, I think not. He called you Jake."

"He said Dr. Lake, but he's sedated and is slurring," Jacob says.

"Jake, where am I? Who's talkin'?" Harlin asks.

"It's okay, Mr. Moybridge." Jacob turns to him. "We'll have you fixed up and back in your room soon. Don't worry."

He places a hand on Harlin's arm. *Not great timing, Harlin.*

"Ah!" Dr. Gontard says, smiling, as if he holds all the cards now. His voice has a lilt. "You're listed as next of kin. *Jake Moybridge, husband.* Well, that makes sense."

No comment. No Comment. No comment. These are the rules of politics and media.

"My name is Dr. Lake and I have come from St. Mary's in Omaha, Nebraska."

"Mr. Moybridge . . . Jake, there's no need to play any roles now. It's valiant, trying to save the life of your husband. We're doctors. We hold to the same values. We want to save lives. Your husband is a universal donor." He pauses, looking around at the Redcoats.

"Dr. Gontard, we can argue over my identity all you want, but this patient is a health risk to this hospital and I must insist that this be our priority."

Dr. Gontard smiles. "By all means." He waves to the men in the doorway. They step to either side of the gurney.

"No!" Jacob says instinctively. He pulls one of the doctors away, hitting him across the face with the back of his arm.

"See?" Dr. Gontard says through the speakers. "The actions of a husband, not a doctor." He waves again and the two Redcoats back away to the door.

"Mr. Moybridge, you are standing at the edge of the greatest opportunity you will probably ever have to make a difference in this world. Your husband has impeccable blood—a kind of blood that will save our lives, even as we save yours. We are filters. We take out disease and give you back better blood. But there are so many of you, so many people with BBD, that we filter too much. We finally succumb to it ourselves. And who is here to save us? No one. We are discovering our own limits."

He turns to his right and begins to walk the length of the circular room, as if he's in a lecture hall and Jacob is his only student.

"But Harlin Moybridge has a chance to change that. His blood—with its purity and exceptionally rapid regenerative quality—will give us the ability to transfuse without consequence. We'll save more lives, and be under less risk ourselves. Thousands of people, Jake, will benefit from Harlin's blood."

"You want to do a transfusion of his blood?" Jacob asks.

The doctor stops walking. "Jake, we need *all* of Harlin's blood. We can't give any back. It's not a transfusion so much as a *donation* that we need—a donation for humankind. Harlin's blood, combined with our skills, may allow us to duplicate his blood type and strength for all doctors."

"Did you ask Harlin?"

Silence.

"No." Jacob steps more into the light. "You listed him as dead. You didn't consult his husband. Where are the patient's rights, Dr. Gontard? You didn't want to bother with someone saying no. How many people have you done this to already?"

Dr. Gontard snaps, "Don't look at us with disgust, Mr. Moybridge. Surely you can empathize. We were just like you once—a minority no one cared about. We were forced to feed in the dark, forced to put who we were into a back alley. We cleaned up your poor, your diseased, your refuse from your streets. And now we hold respectable positions. We save lives. We don't often take a life on purpose anymore—but we *could*. We could still feed off of you, you know. But we don't, because society gave us a chance. And we rose to the occasion. The world needs us. And we need your husband. And when you are that badly needed, what is one sacrifice for millions?"

"Then sacrifice *yourselves* if it's that important to you," Jacob says.

Dr. Gontard places his hands against the glass. His fingers elongate, becoming needles again. "Who is looking out for us, Mr. Moybridge? Can you honestly say that you would sacrifice the lives of other people to save your husband? Can you make that choice?"

Jacob drops his head, feels like his feet are taking root, but it's just because he's pressing them into the floor. "First of all," he says, "you and I have nothing in common. Gays as a group do not kill people, nor feed off anyone. You were a minority that had a skill, and you volunteered that skill. Your choice. You benefited from that skill and from your choice. Second, Harlin Moybridge has a choice to become or not become your saviour. You have to obey the same law that gave you benefit and power. You can't say you're saving lives when you decide who gets to be saved. Hospitals are obligated to heal *everyone*. It's part of the Hippocratic Oath to 'Do no harm'—even if harming might save millions."

"One interpretation of a law," says Dr. Gontard. "You want to ask Harlin Moybridge? Let's ask him." Dr. Gontard calls out, "Harlin Moybridge!"

Jacob's voice rises. "He's half *asleep*. He's *sedated*. You can't ask him to give up his life for whatever reason if he can't understand the question."

"Harlin Moybridge, would you like to save the world?"

"Harlin, don't listen to him," Jacob tells Harlin. His fear, his real fear is that Harlin would *love* to save the world. It is the kind of question he has been waiting for his entire life. He loves swooping in with a heroic, helpful hand. Sacrifice is something he would do if given the shot. To be the Messiah . . . what if he says yes?

"What's he saying? Saving people?" Harlin asks.

Jacob looks up at Dr. Gontard, walks towards him. "You can't believe that his answer is binding in any court of law. He's drugged!"

"Harlin, you have perfect blood," says the doctor.

Harlin smiles, slurs his words. "I know. I got a helluva pedigree."

"Harlin, we need you to help us."

"What? What do you need? Just ask. Jake, tell him he can have what he wants."

Jacob turns to the crowd of Redcoats, pleads with them. "How is this right? *You can't be doing this.* I'll expose you to every news media outlet. I know everyone in the media, everyone." He realizes he's just threatened people with needles on the ends of their fingers and tries to calm down. "You're still taking innocent lives."

"Harlin," Dr. Gontard continues, "we need your blood."

"You want my blood, don't ya? It's good, damn good blood." Harlin is smiling. Eating up the attention.

"We need that damn good blood, Harlin. We need you to donate your blood for sick people everywhere. Your blood will save millions of people, Harlin. Do you want to save millions of people?"

Harlin grins, looks at Jacob. "Millions of people?"

"Yes, millions of people. But we need all that blood. You have to give us your life, Harlin, for the lives of millions."

Jacob grabs hold of Harlin's bare shoulders. "Harlin, they want to *kill* you."

"Harlin," the doctor says. "We want you to *volunteer*."

Jacob starts to cry. He can't help it. He's powerless. Harlin reaches out and touches Jacob's face, traces his right eye. He cups his chin in the palm of his hand and stares into Jacob's eyes.

Then he turns his head to address Dr. Gontard. "All these sick people you're talking 'bout . . ." He looks around at the Redcoats standing above. He sounds almost awake, but slightly drunk.

The Redcoats silently wait to hear what he will say. Jacob waits, scared that if Harlin gives his permission, that Jacob will have no power to do anything about it.

Harlin frowns. "Why should I give up my blood for them? People don't take care of themselves today." He throws an arm into the air. "Lazy *assholes*. Let 'em get their own selves better. Sheesh! How many times you gonna drain one of us to save one of them? Get your own damn blood! I made mine myself, took good care of it, stayed healthy—and now I gotta die to save millions? You're full of *shit*, that's what you are. And I mean that, from the bottom of my bloody, damn-good bloody heart. You bastards!"

He lolls his head back. "Sheesh. What do they think I am now—a bloody blood bank?"

Jacob smiles, barely able to suppress it, and looks up at the doctors. "Satisfied?"

The doctors murmur. Someone speaks up. "Mr. Moybridge is right. Perhaps we *should* ask Harlin Moybridge when he comes out of the sedative. I think if he understood the question—"

Jacob laughs a little to himself. They don't know Harlin. And he realizes that, for a moment, *he* didn't know Harlin. He looks at his husband, who is rubbing his eyes, complaining about the strong light in the room. Jacob loves him for being a damn curmudgeon at the right moments.

Jacob glances at the Redcoats standing at the windows above, at the way the doctors are looking at them, at how their fingers elongate, sharpen into needles.

Jacob reaches for Harlin's hand and holds onto its warmth. Harlin squeezes, using the leverage to sit up, then stand.

Redcoats pour into the room through the door, surrounding them. A red river. "There's only a hundred of 'em," Harlin says. "We can take 'em, buddy!"

Bondsmen

What if Tom were sitting at the end of a green-lawned casino table, martini to the left of him, girls to the right of him, across from a fat man in a red fez with a cat on his arm? What if he smiles, turns and *stirs the martini*, and everyone gasps because they know him better than he knows himself?

And what if that simple stirring sets off a small panic, no bigger than a small plastic exploding device, enhanced by the waiting at the table, the crowd that has gathered, and the fans that are spinning overhead in a slow-moving rhythm on a cream-coloured, high-vaulted ceiling, where Tom could make an escape using a small gyrocopter if he had one in his pocket, but he doesn't.

And maybe the crowd cannot possibly know, but they do, that this man isn't the man he claimed to be when he entered just an hour ago, sauntered over to the table in his impeccable tuxedo, stunningly exotic woman on his arm (who never spoke, but purred), manoeuvred casually into a seat and challenged the fat man to twenty-one, and ordered a drink, which was the same as announcing his name to the world, down to the very directions by which it would be made.

And perhaps now, as the crowd anticipates this familiar stranger doing something that will win their belief back, Tom slips off the seat to an effortless stand, holds up his drink, and, with all the style expected of him, accuses the house management of stirring his drink, threatening the man if he ever gets the drink wrong again, but never actually getting red or spitting in his face.

And what if he enters the bathroom, with its heavy blues and dim lamps and sectioned mirror, goes up to the sink, washes his face, looks into the mirror and sees six men—not actual living, breathing men, not as if they were there to actually help him, but just images in the mirror—and they know him and he knows them, and they are Sean, George, Roger, Timothy, Pierce, and Daniel, each in his own mirror, and Tom begins to talk to them and the whole thing sounds something like this:

"You blew that one," Sean snaps.

"I came in with the confidence, assurance . . ." Tom begins.

". . . but if you can't handle the card game," Roger continues.

"It was the drink. I couldn't get the drink."

"Shaken, not stirred," Timothy reminds him.

"Oh, that part was easy, but I stir my drinks afterwards."

"But you can't," George says.

"But I did. What do I do?"

"You stop your hand," Pierce reminds him. "You move it under the table, out of sight."

"Well, perhaps not—he might think you were going for a gun. A fat man did that to me once . . ." Roger just confuses Tom.

"Then you punch him, or chase him," Daniel says.

Sean interrupts: "A card game is not an action sequence. Tom, you tell yourself that you cannot stir the drink, no matter how much you want to. It's not in you."

"Then why is it there? Why is that characteristic there if it isn't in me?"

"It doesn't matter," Pierce says flatly. "It isn't there now, and even if it is, you'll be aware next time. You'll suppress it. We're good at that."

"But what if someday I go off and order a daiquiri? I've always liked daiquiris."

"You can't." Sean is emphatic.

"The banana ones especially."

"It's against your character," Sean continues. "You must preserve your sense of character over anything else. You must be consistent. No matter if the world spins off in its own tawdry rhythm, you, of all men, must remain the same. And you wouldn't order a daiquiri, banana, strawberry, or any other. Martini—"

And they say it together: "—shaken, not stirred."

"You were right before." Tom wipes his face with the blue towel. "The card game is intimidating."

Roger grins. "I was always very good at the card games."

Tom looks around sheepishly. "Then why don't you fill in for me on this one? I'm feeling overmatched."

"Never," Sean shouts, "*never* let yourself say that."

"But it's true. The fat man is intimidating."

He's got Sean fuming now. "It doesn't matter. You are a *legend*. Legends don't run into bathrooms and complain about life being a little hard—"

"Who've you got for an escort?" Roger asks.

"Norwegian chess player, Rook. She's very stunning."

Roger adjusts his tie. "I'm sure she's a good match."

"Perhaps a good mate. You'll have to check."

"One game only." Roger reaches out of the mirror and takes Tom's outstretched hand.

And when he emerges from the bathroom, Roger strides over to the table to finish the game.

So *what* if somehow that enduring crook of a smile, the one with the hook at the end and the teeth just emerging, isn't crooked at the same angle that it was when he was there before, at the card table, next to the purring chess player named Rook. Because when he orders the drink again there's a sigh of relief, perhaps (though not everywhere) as he takes it, pitches the olive to his right, and sets the glass again on the table. It tells everyone that the momentary excursion to the bathroom was enough to snap the man they know back into something they can believe. It tells the fat man with the fez and the cat at the end of the table that he shouldn't have doubted because everyone has an off day.

So when the agent wins and slips Rook a hand on her hip and a whispered rendezvous in her ear, what if he goes back into the bathroom, strides up to the mirror and says this:

"Well, I've put you in a position to castle, Tom."

"Thank you." Tom, uncertain, retreats further into the mirror, afraid of the hand that might pull him out again.

"He does everything for you, doesn't he?" Sean says. "You have to blaze your own trail. Soon, boy. What will you make of yourself, our self?"

Roger dismisses the question with a hand, looks at Tom. "You'll have to move fast—the fat man you were playing cards with has rigged Austria to explode at nine. I've arranged for you to be at the symphony when it does."

"The symphony?" Tom says.

Roger reaches into the mirror, and despite the intrepid avoidance techniques and skilled hand-to-hand combat training, Tom is easily snagged and pulled back into the bathroom.

He shakes his arms and legs out. "What do I do at the symphony?"

Roger talks to him as if he is a child, and normally he doesn't mind because he could use the training; tonight, however, Roger seems arrogant. "Mozart has written a very special part into his fortieth symphony—a duet between violins and cellos. When the cellos reach the *allegro fortissimo* and the violins have been riding on top so long that they must hit the eight-second *allegro grande* with the staccato high b flats, the entire symphony hall will shower down like confetti in a parade."

"So how do I—"

"You should know this part. Think." Timothy sighs and begins to walk away. "I'd say it was hopeless. No more of those little Vienna sausages."

"And you mustn't forget the world leaders," Roger says as Timothy fumes in the back of his mirror, thanking God he only saved the world twice and did it perfectly.

"What *about* the world leaders?"

"They'll be at the symphony. They're at a conference now debating important issues like export quotas." Roger pulls on a black glove. "But later they'll be hamburger."

"What if I don't want to save the world tonight? Has anyone ever just once felt that way?"

"It doesn't matter what you want. It's what you are," Sean growls, assuring him that if he is to learn, it will be tonight, before the symphony explodes. They disappear then, leaving a worried Tom alone in the bathroom.

He exits, grabs the arm of Rook and whispers through gritted teeth, "We have to go to the symphony. They're about to rock Europe."

But what if what actually happens is that he reaches the world leader's conference first, in order to stop the catastrophe early, having the most noble of intentions—even if he didn't have the slightest idea what or how to do it—and, spying a certain table, he suddenly has other ideas in mind, ideas that include the taking of nametags on that table—one for himself and one for his escort, waltzing into a room crowded with several world leaders, and spending a good portion of the night saying something like this:

"I am *too* Xi Jinping! I am *too* the President of the People's Republic of China."

And so, that is where we are. It is where things have led us. Beyond the table, inside the room, where several international delegates will sit discussing not quotas really, but graver issues that they will never really find agreement on. And probably, over the course of the next few days—if they weren't all perishing together tonight at the symphony—they would find it harder and harder to discuss anything other than the weather, the food, and the lack of good toilet facilities to accommodate the expectations of every culture.

So, maybe everything begins here, in the burgundy-carpeted hotel conference room, with two hundred representatives in colourful hats and cultural attire crowding around a man they seem to know, are sure they recognize, and are trying to convince themselves that he is. It is not that they are quizzing him in conversational Chinese, or noting the fact that the mole on his chin is gone, but, knowing exactly who he is—his reputation having preceded him, no doubt, with an obvious show of bravado and a hefty supply of superlatives—they are adamant in their cross examination.

"You are not the one who operates submersible cars?"

"Gyrocopters, exploding briefcases?"

"An agile fighter?"

"Carrying a large black gun?"

"Protector of world peace . . ."

"Guardian of the free market . . ."

"Defender of all human life?"

And with perfect English he answers them, while gesticulating in several other languages at once. "No, no, no. I'm the President of the People's Republic of China. It just wouldn't be me."

"But your face is so familiar," notes the Burmese Prime Minister. "You've saved my life before from a man who was mad with power."

"I'm mad with power! I'm trying to tell you that I am Xi Jinping, President of the People's Repub—"

"Yes, yes, you've said that. But the way you move in a tuxedo, you can only be the man we've come to know as—"

"Shaken and not stirred!" someone in a yellow turban yells out.

"No. I will prove it to you. Do you see my escort?"

Everyone nods.

"She is not really the world chess champion, Rook. She's actually the assistant to the assistant of the Press Secretary for Tuvalu." Rook, looking at her nametag, confesses this is true. "Would your man dare to be seen with less than an heiress, a mysterious escort, a deadly but fascinating arm drapery?"

And they begin to see that maybe they are wrong. Slowly, the leaders of the world begin to react as if he were truly the man he claimed to be. As long as he speaks in ultimatums and makes impossible demands on neighbouring countries, he is terribly convincing.

And, at least twice during the evening, he sighs a deep, troubling sigh.

Still, the mirrors get in his way.

The room is mirrored every other panel, and as he walks the room, his reflection pairs with a passing Sean, a droll George, a pleading Roger, a furious Timothy, a wry Pierce, an impatient Daniel, each reaching their arms out to be taken into the scene, to restore their fine name to its former glory. Tired of their protests and disgruntled faces, he smashes the mirrors as he passes. When asked about his peculiar behaviour, he comments, "I'm the President of the People's Republic of China; I can do as I please," and passes over to the next image and gives it a good whack with a chair. Of course, this causes several rumours that the Chinese regime is unstable and about to fall, or that Communist China is ruled by a crazy man. It also causes quite a row with the hotel busboys, who follow Xi Jinping with a broom, dustpan, and trashcan.

But it is really much later when Tom, or Xi as the nametag reads, is involved in a card game with the leaders of Burma, Chad, Iraq, and the Czech Republic—and pulling out ahead it should be noted—that Roger, Timothy, George, Daniel, and Pierce, spearheaded by a bold Sean, leap into the room via the shiny, reflective, wine-glass tray sitting on the heavily sculpted buffet (given as a token of gratitude from the Republic of Guatemala) that Xi for a moment touches, and all hell breaks loose.

Suddenly, there are seven of them and every mouth drops. Xi Jinping is taken to the floor with a full Nelson.

"It's all right." Timothy stretches out his hands, warding off the unbelief.

"Perfectly under control. We have the impostor," Roger adds.

"The impostor of what?" the French Prime Minister says, standing.

"This man is not who you think he is." Daniel struggles with Xi on the floor. Sean explains, "He is not Xi Jinping. He is instead—"

"Aren't you that detective fellow?" someone calls out to one of the men.

"Yes!" Pierce shouts in rapture.

The Brazilian delegate smiles, knowing that is who he is, knowing that the face is finally pegged—not Chinese, not quite at least, but something else, something more familiar, daring, dashing.

"I am—" Xi struggles to his feet. Sean knees him in the abdomen. "I am—" Pierce chops him with the edge of his hand. "I am too—"

"No," George says, "He's someone else. Think. Who is the man who saves the world from mad, power-hungry moguls?"

"The man." Timothy crosses his arms in a way that should show them—gun in one hand, leering smile on the other side of his face. "This representative of British Imperialism, who always comes out on top in fights with villains from foreign governments?"

"The man who comes out on top with all the ladies?" Roger adds.

"The man whose cars turn into boats," Pierce says, "whose watches turn into lasers, whose pens turn into machine guns, whose shoes turn into submersible breathing equipment, whose name terrifies the treacherous, conjures up the most relentless pursuit of one-upmanship in the history of—"

"I *know* him." A man stands at the back of the room. He is distinguished, greying, thin with powerful strides as he comes up to the three men standing in black tuxedos with peerless smiles, to the men on the floor struggling to find who will be what they really are. "I know him."

"Then you also know that the situation is serious." Timothy shakes his hand.

"Always," the man answers.

"And that millions may die," Pierce says.

"Such is often the scenario."

"And that this man needs to know who he is, who he represents," George says.

"Exactly. I should say he needs heavy debriefing." The man brings Xi to his feet.

ℒ ℒ

So, now they are all sitting in a room together, the seven who look so alike, the distinguished man who is willing to help, the men who represent the world as they knew it, and Rook, who is devouring pastries.

"Everyone dies at nine o'clock." Sean is sure this is highly irregular, and that they are going completely against standard, so he shuts the curtains in the room that look out onto a beautiful view of Symphony Hall.

"But I can do things as Xi Jinping that I can't do as the other fellow." Tom pulls out a chart. "In five years, I estimate, with the proclamations I hand down through this government, I can improve trade with foreign countries, thereby increasing the cash flow coming into China—while still maintaining a communist nation."

"Why that's ridiculous," Roger snorts. "You can't do that. I never did."

"You can't have a capitalistic society and a communist society together."

"You're wrong, Sean. I can be the only business in town. I can make my country export things that other countries depend on. I can be a benevolent Communist dictator."

"You can be a blithering idiot," Timothy says.

"I was meant to be Xi Jinping," Xi says.

"Perhaps you're right," the distinguished man says.

"But he can't. Who will save the world's leaders?"

"Oh really, come on," says the distinguished man. "You know and I know that second-in-commands are always a better judge of world economics. The destruction of the world leaders might be a good thing. We can't really know."

He turns to the crowd. "We've never really known, have we? Someone always rushes in at the last moment and saves everyone, now doesn't he? I see by your looks, your smiles, that you agree. At least one of these men, every time, has come by and whisked trouble away from you. And so, the countries you represent have always run along their merry courses because democracy, or monarchy, or communism was safe once again. No one's allowed a dramatic regime change, permitted you to explore the effect of outside interference, of disaster, of the effect of sympathy upon your nation. No one's ever mixed up the pot before."

"What do you want to do?" Timothy asks him.

Sean says to the man, "You want them all to go to the symphony, listen to twenty minutes of Mozart's greatest work, and scatter their intestines and brains all over Vienna. I see what you mean."

"That's not it at all," the distinguished man chides, his fingers on his chin. "The elimination of the world leaders would cause a mass rethinking of government as we know it. It could have the greatest possibilities for new ideas to emerge, and come the closest to world peace."

Sean puts his hand down flat and loud on the table. "You're talking about sacrificing the lives of men who have earned their way to the top of their country's ladder, taken on a load of responsibility. This is not the way you repay hard work."

"I'm thinking of something else entirely," the distinguished man says. "Something spurred on by the thinking and rethinking of one man. This man, this man I will call—Xi Jinping."

And of course, as anyone might have guessed by now, Xi is a hero. But the night is still young. And as Xi stands, and the distinguished man shakes his hand, the smile that so wanted to flood across his face many times before, between costume changes and explosions and nights of white satin, suddenly finds its way to Xi's face. He feels comfortable—not so wanted, not so needed, but definitely noted. And the distinguished man makes a suggestion that forever alters everything. Literally everything. He strides over to the punch bowl filled with punch and dumps it onto the carpet, wipes the bowl out with a towel, and walks around the room passing the bowl to people, so they can throw their nametags within its shiny reflective roundness.

"We should have done this long ago," say the Haitian delegates.

"It doesn't matter now," the distinguished man says. "If we can have a new Xi, we can have a new anything."

One by one, inevitably, the men and women, now incognito, begin drawing out countries and names from the punch bowl. The British Prime Minister draws Senegal; the President of the Czech Republic becomes President of the Philippines; the Prime Minister of Greenland becomes the President of India.

"Now, look at what you have. Look at who you are!" The distinguished man sets the punch bowl down on the table where all the pastries used to be. "Imagine what could happen when the former Irish President goes 'home' to Peru."

"They won't know what the bloody heck he's saying," laughs the old British Prime Minister.

"He will have to lead a country with different needs, different problems. You have an economic crisis on your hands, Mr. Peru. You have an environmental and economic war to figure out. Refreshing, isn't it?"

"I suppose trees are easier to work with than people," he says.

"It will put everything into perspective, I imagine, Mr. Peru."

"And you think they'll go for this?" asks the new Senegalese Prime Minister.

"I think they'll embrace it. Most countries are tired of their regimes and the ways to do things. They want a fresh start. They want new blood. A new perspective, one who is not persuaded one way or the other."

"Like having your bartender as your president," says the United States President, now the leader of Iceland.

"Exactly!" says the distinguished man. "These men—" and he points behind him "—they never brought *change*. They always reset the world—with its problems intact—back to the way it started. If you want to move the world forward, you need to embrace the change, wield the creativity, share the knowledge and be willing to break a few things."

The phone rings and the busboy answers. It is the symphony and they wonder if there is a problem, and if anyone will be joining them for a nice rendition of Mozart. The busboy hands the phone to the distinguished man, who politely tells them that they will not be attending, and they can very well send Mozart out to sea for all they care. They are tired of Mozart being the hallmark of culture.

"But he's also the patron saint of Vienna," someone says.

"Maybe we'll put all of those in a punch bowl as well," says the distinguished man.

And, while the distinguished man opens the curtains, the President of the People's Republic of China asks the six men, who all looked and behaved alike, to be his marketing team, to work very hard marketing a gyrocopter for China. When they agree, he feels very satisfied, and yet, as the Symphony Hall explodes in the picture window, and everyone realizes that, yes, this is the dawning of a new age, he cannot sigh with relief, and his banana daiquiri sits all night on the table, untouched.

Et Tu Bruté

Brutus, our multi-million dollar signing gorilla, slumps behind glass, pining away for my ex-boyfriend, Pete. He hasn't eaten for days. He shoves all the food we give him to the observation window—offering it back to us in exchange for Pete.

Pete's not coming back, and I've gotten used to it.

Brutus draws a policeman's badge, Pete's symbol, in the dirt of the Outdoor Facility. I want to tell him that Pete broke up with *me*. I never pushed him away.

Primatologists record everything Brutus does to show us he misses Pete. When he draws a badge on the glass with his feces, they say, "Look how he loved him."

"Shelly, maybe Pete could drop by," Dr. Jim suggests. "Just for an afternoon. You could take the afternoon off if you wanted."

I feel invisible. We all want to know of Brutus' grief, as if we're bored by the human version. How blessed to have a team of caring observers!

"If you don't want to write the letter, I can," Dr. Jim says.

Well, it's unanimous then. Everyone wants Pete.

Honestly, Brutus is making us write you, I write. *He won't eat. Pete, I'm not asking for me. Just for him.*

This irks me on a deep level. Like I'm begging.

I'm not begging you. One afternoon, then it's over. Visit a gorilla—save some primatologists. If I were going to ask you back into my life, I'd be more creative than saying the gorilla made me do it.

I picture Pete's mouth in a smile under his bushy cop moustache.

He used to wrestle with Brutus. Yes, wrestle. Brutus was gentle with him; he knew it was play, and would sometimes kiss Pete softly on the forehead after he'd worn him out. We're pretty sure Brutus is gay. Jezebel, the female gorilla shipped over from the Primate Institute, is pretty sure he's gay, too. She went back very disappointed.

It'll make your gorilla happy, and everyone here needs a happy gorilla.

I picture Brutus giving me a thumbs-up, his leathery eyebrows conspiratorial.

I wish I'd had enough dignity to walk out on you first. You called me a "lab rat!" You were embarrassed to be with me in public. I can't believe I tried to be "worthy" of your affection, I write. But I crumple up the sheet and try again.

Hello, Pete. I'm writing on behalf of Brutus, who is holding a hunger strike in our lab. He's demanding you. Dr. Jim has asked me to write you—see if you'd drop by. It would be good to see you. I erase the last part, suddenly afraid of scaring him off. Again.

I look away to see Brutus flipping through a picture album, stopping at Pete's pictures. He sighs heavily. Should I tell him Pete wouldn't stay? No. I can't even tell myself.

Pete won't fall for this, I know.

Maybe I'll let Brutus smear some feces on the card for emphasis, for love.

he stalked into the room, w...
emanding th...y she foun...
emaine... Hern all
all kinds
no breez...

look on his face
only water
when she qu...
So, in a dense
or what they t...
ground of the
? She c...
pathol...
stroll

I. C...
hat

urther
ntain
boo
a
troll

hea...
t he...
how
lif...
sc...
u...
on
her

operation bu...
Love, had
and pooped it
This would always
squirrels again she w... short herself.
"LOVE," she said with contempt, "makes
us all." She drank from the cup — he...
Unbeknownst to her, Kevin had
raffle
lesson to her

Why the Poets Were Banned from the City

He drives with his foot hard on the gas all the way to our café. I've imagined him a hundred times as he was before we met him, before he broke down in front of us, or pulled the gun, or shot it, because I want to understand who he was before he left us—and maybe what he discovered with us, if anything at all. So I have him driving his car out of the Republic, passing the checkpoints, keeping the gun hidden well enough to pass a scan. I don't know how he did that. I imagine he has to fake it really well, his emotional state, and act like a tourist; say that no, he's not planning a long stay. Yes, it's just for research for an ad campaign. No, he doesn't know anyone here. Just coffee, conversation, a pleasant time. Has he brought the necessary emotional inhibitors? He shows them a handful of blue pills. He's ready, he says. They let him through. Probably the info hasn't hit his profile on their scanners yet. It's too fresh.

He's coming away from the suicide of his only daughter, Samantha. Sam. He calls her Sam when he talks to us. So I need to call her Sam now. She was good at illustration and ad design, top in her fifth grade class. She played a tin whistle in her school orchestra. In the picture that he shows us, she has long dark hair and is smiling, but he doesn't remember the smiles so much over the last few weeks.

When the man comes into our café, it's sunny outside and the blue blinds are drawn, giving the place an underwater feel that I've always liked. The espresso machine drowns out his first words, but everyone can tell he is upset, and every poet deep down believes, as if communally psychic, that his story would be thrilling and poignant, if a bit over-dramatically narrated. We knew that even then. Out of breath, angry, the man stands with the door of the café half open, glancing around him. He's up to his neck in a dark blue business suit, looped by a red tie.

At first I thought he was emotionally unstable. I wanted to see his questions to the poets, his accusations, as the result of a man pushed to the edge of rational behaviour, not someone who thought about this a lot—a crank, a policrat. He was someone who had been through a rough morning. Maybe it was he that found her drowned in the bathtub. Maybe he knocked on the door several times because he needed in. It was morning, and suicides usually happen at night, so he had no reason to believe that anything was different. Except that she didn't answer, and this part I'm assuming, though Charlie has written that he killed her, but I don't think that's the case. At least, that wasn't in my first draft. Later, when I'd read his version, I thought that he presented the whole story as that of a man on the edge for other reasons—his job, his wife, something missing in his life. And he accidentally drowns his daughter.

But, while that's thrilling, I don't think of him as a murderer, at least not a practiced one. So I graded Charlie's story pretty low when workshop time arrived. Mainly because I hadn't really come to terms with who the character was—I mean the man—but what his character was like. We all agreed on *distraught*. We all agreed that he was dangerous, walking into a café like that, pulling out a black snub-nosed revolver.

But we don't agree on backstory, motive, or anything else. And I wasn't satisfied with even my version of the story, so I went back to him driving to the café.

He picks out our café even though we're not the first he will pass. He passes Haloed Grounds first, and then a rapper bar on the corner, and then us, Lethe Bank. He makes a clear choice. Does the number of cars make a difference? Do the names make a difference? While most of us have written ad copy for the city, we don't think much about advertising *here*. Mostly we cater to regulars, so why would we think too much about name recognition, or what those names might mean to Republicans coming out to see us? We don't. We concentrate on our games, our stories and poems and essays we write for each other and ourselves, the secret workshops we hold inside the city, memorization groups we've started. We have a lot on our minds.

And he does, too, that day, but I didn't know what it had to do with us.

This is the kind of thing they said we were responsible for, which is why no one comes when I press the secret buttons under the bar. Which is why the Republic Police do not show up in time, why we are always told that we have to handle it ourselves. This is the way it goes when imaginative literature, poetry, anything with a scrap of decency is banned from inside the city. We cause emotions without product directive, emotions without prescription. People read our writing and feel something, and they don't know what to do with that emotion. In the city, all those pretty pieces of writing you see—most of them done by us when we absolutely have to earn money—have a directive: buy this tooth cream, explore this underground chasm, invest in this high-rolling casino. So if we make you feel sad or happy, you can find resolution in a purchase. But literature, on the other hand, doesn't let you off the hook that easy, and that's why there was a time when we were blamed for a lot of murders and mayhem that went on. Music caused *this*; fiction caused *that*. This man saw this movie and committed this crime. People thought about things the government didn't want people thinking about. Now, ad campaigns are so personalized to cater to your every taste that they've become specific in their manipulation—which, apparently, is our skill. So, while we can't write what we want, we write what will sell.

The man accuses a table full of poets and writers of killing his daughter, Sam. To prove it, he produces a scrap of paper taken from her hand that had on it the following phrase: *Because I could not stop for death, he kindly stopped for me.* And he asks who wrote it, and we could recite the whole thing by heart, but Starla tells him it is Emily Dickinson.

I can see him, back at his house, busting down the door of the bathroom when he knocks and doesn't get an answer. The wood splinters at the lock, so it would be sharp to fall against when he finally does go through. I see her like a Waterhouse painting of Ophelia underwater, only fully dressed in her school colours, a black and tan uniform perhaps, or blue and tan, with her white face under the water and her black hair rising like a silk cushion around her head. She must have had a lot of courage and strength not to come back up to the surface of a bathtub. It would have taken only a nod, you know, to bob her head back up out of the water. She had to hold herself under. And I don't think of her eyes as being open when I imagine the scene, not like Scott does. She's not horrific or startling; she's quiet and buried, like Snow White under glass.

He wants to see Emily Dickinson. And I know the group shouldn't have laughed, but it's the irony of everything that comes back and kicks you in the ass. Would he have been this angry if he knew that Dickinson was dead, that she wasn't a living villain, out to hurt his daughter or other young girls in the Republic? Would he have sought her in the OutSkirts, among us, if he'd remembered that, oh, she died in 1886? No, she won't be out there. And this galls us, that the poetry that is the most moving, that causes the strongest emotions, isn't even ours. And the other poets have no idea that the man is looking to kill someone, only that their poetry is hardly as effective and that this man is ignorant of literature. The kind of irony we chat about daily in the café. Some of us slip real poetic lines into advertisements all the time. For wine, Keats: "Oh for a draught of vintage!" And then they show the bottle and the man dying of thirst. Eliot for selling pickups to men: "And there will be a time to wonder, Do I dare? And, Do I dare?" Blake for oven mitts: "What hand dare seize the fire?" We sneak them in where we can. But these are in-jokes, for us, because it doesn't matter.

And now, after a long time, maybe years, of no "literature-connected incident," this man comes in doing exactly what people supposedly did when reading literature, though this rarely happens to us and we are exposed to the deadly emotion-producing stuff all the time. The media call us immune—we see through fiction and poetry and we can handle the emotions because we bend them, and are, therefore, ourselves unstable. So there are thousands of us who have the power to manipulate people— we've drunk enough of the poison to be immune—and we have to pay for any unstable words of Dickinson that cause a young girl to drown herself. Powerful and responsible, but exiled and needed at the same time. For the people of the Republic then, literature moved them, really moved them, and that's the biggest potential audience for a bestseller—only there aren't any; just full length action-oriented infomercials and novel-length ads, But this man, this Dylan Hailey, was affected by a death. Not a poem. The girl was affected by her own life going in some bizarre way. This explanation is unacceptable to Mr. Hailey. Because when you see your daughter underwater in that blue way, her hand holding onto something, she is telling you that the piece of paper is key. And you will go anywhere to find the answer to that key, and you will not believe anyone connected to that key is innocent. And you will point your gun at a mystery writer, an environmental essayist, and two poets looking for the answer to that key, and maybe the key to Emily Dickinson's apartment.

I think Starla's chapbook, *The Bend of Light Through Water*, an excellent collection of poems she wrote following Mr. Hailey's visit, returns to the central problem I've been trying to understand. Light is distorted in water— not only the light that enters it, as if seen from below, but also light as seen from above. When he looked down at her face through the water, he didn't see truth. I don't think Hailey ever saw the truth, even at the end. I think he came close, but he had no references, no way of understanding context. Is context what I want to say? It's close. Maybe narrative is better. Or practice, as Barry said in his essay. Hailey did not have practice with contextualizing his experience.

He sits down at the table, still holding the gun, and asks for a glass of water. I bring it to him, setting it down as he leans back to let me move in front of him. I think about being a hero—I write adventure fiction and ads for *Boy's Life*—but it's one thing to think about being the hero and another thing to actually be one. Those punches are easy to write—"he fit a right cross under his chin"—but have you tried one? So I don't. I bring him his water—I offer to fix him a coffee, and what am I thinking? He doesn't need the caffeine. He asks me to sit, so there are six of us at the table; Joan, the mystery writer who eventually filled in some of the blanks, stays at the table in the back, moving to the blue couch under Van Gogh's *Starry Night* only when he asks her to.

Joan interrogates him. She's good at that, having written a slew of mystery novels and some good mystery storylines for pharmaceutical companies. "Tell us about your daughter," she says. He hesitates, asks for Emily.

Joan takes the biggest risk. "She's dead," she says.

And he looks at her, moves the gun in her direction.

"All the people she loved died. She died of grief." She says this in a matter of fact way, so that he will know the truth and not want to hurt anyone. In the way that Charlie tells this moment, he grossly overplays the man's grief. But, even if it's badly written, the man does break down. Big sobs. He covers his mouth, as if he is trying to hold them back, but they keep bursting through his fingers, out of his eyes. He still holds the gun, but it wavers at all of us in a casual way—an afterthought of malice, though still dangerous. Charlie makes this the reason the man fired the gun in the end. He says the turning point was right here, when he makes the connection between himself and Emily Dickinson—and I think it's important—but I see the connection as also being between his daughter, Sam, and Emily. Because what the others don't write down, not even Barry, was what Joan said after that. She says, "Emily wrote about dying a lot when she was trying to understand the death of her friends." That's what I think has to be the moment when we started helping him contextualize and grieve. And maybe I'm oversimplifying it, but I'm trying to find where the narrative line is inside his head. What leads to what leads to the gun going off?

I think if Emily had been alive, she would have died that day. He needs to do some action—just like he's been taught by all those commercials. He has an emotion. He has to take some action. And this is what makes it difficult for everyone at that table, I think. Everyone knows that he is going to have to do something—at least fire the gun. That's one of the first rules of mystery writing: if you have a gun in a story, it must go off.

Instead of getting angry with Joan—she's kind of a mother figure here, and older than Mr. Hailey—he starts talking about Sam, telling us what she was like as a baby, how she had to be held all the time, how he had to get permission to wear her in a pouch to work. She secured him a toy account with China. Barry tells him that she was that image of what they were looking for in a caring, paternal ad campaign. He said that the Chinese even suggested that they allow this child to grow up through their commercials. They loved Sam. Her Chinese name—they gave her one that day—meant *fruit* because she looked like a fruit attached to Mr. Hailey. When Charlie writes this scene, he has Mr. Hailey say that he always looked at the campaign as the fruit of his fatherhood. But this is essentially wrong. It's because, I think, he couldn't make those metaphorical leaps that he lost it.

Starla tries to ask about the weeks leading up to this morning, tries to get him to think of what his daughter was doing, what she was thinking. There was no diary that he knew of. But she'd had a best friend end a relationship with her. She had come home crying, shut herself in her room, but that was more than a week ago, and she had been pleasant the last few days—not happy, but friendly and calm. Starla tells him that this is sometimes what people who are planning suicide do—they become resolved, happy, because they've figured out what they will do. How they will leave the pain. And I almost think that he could have walked out of the café a calmer, happier person himself—and maybe he did in the car—but he remembers the poetry, and even if Emily was going through a hard time, why did she take his daughter with her?

He stands up and points the gun at Starla—not Joan, but Starla, the woman I see nearly every day. She teaches a private workshop in a basement apartment for three women. Their work is getting popular out here, and we print it like mad because we're happy when any fiction or poetry, or any real writing gets out of the city. She has red hair, curly, down to her shoulders, and we have been seeing each other for a few years. So like Sam meant something to Dylan Hailey, Starla meant something to me. And I knew that the gun would have to go off sometime. This is where I played hero and maybe changed things.

I am faster than I think with the coffee mug, but I'm sloppy and Starla could have been killed. It hits him in the head. The gun does not go off, but the man falls over in his chair. I get down on top of him and, originally, I was just going to hold him down so he wouldn't hurt anyone. He looks at me pitifully, as if he wants to be punched, to be shot, and won't I do it for him. Charlie and Barry both have me wrestling on the floor with him, and I think they wrote that because they were doing an homage to my adventure fiction, but I really hate that part in their narratives. They claim I punched him. And I don't remember. I do remember thinking, *I don't want this power you think we have. This power to hurt you with emotions.* So I thought I didn't touch him. I didn't hurt him. But maybe I did. I took away some dignity, some different resolution he might have been coming to. He wrenches his arm from under mine and sticks the gun in my stomach and everything in the room stops. I can hear the acoustic radio overhead and the toilet in the bathroom that never fully stops running water. I swear I never punched him. But I almost did. After he gets the gun in my stomach we both stand up and he leads me to the door. We walk out of the shop into the daylight and he pushes me into his car and tells me to drive.

And this is the part that only I can tell. Other writers have speculated on just what happened, what was said, where things went. I wish he had taken Barry, or even Charlie or Joan (though I'm not wishing danger on these people), because they could have better explained to him what they were thinking. I knew what effect I wanted to have on him. I wanted to say things to get him to drop the gun. I raced through all the ways a writer has to make people feel things—it's what we're good at, right? Then why did I start talking about how he had to contextualize things?

I try to tell him how to tell a story to himself. I don't know what else to do. The car races down the street as I drive, and he keeps telling me, Faster. I say that stories can heal you, too. They don't just have an effect on making you do something, but when something bad happens to you, you can write it down and find some meaning. But he says there is no meaning in suicide. There is no Emily and so he doesn't know whom to blame, and he can't blame Sam. She was just a child. Maybe, I say, if you write something from Sam's point of view . . . ? I don't know what I'm saying. I am not so much concerned for myself. I see that he is in terrible danger. We aren't going toward the city, but away from the OutSkirts, toward the desert where there aren't any provisions or roads, and there are dunes and canyons.

"My daughter is dead and I can't figure out why she died," he starts, and I encourage him to continue, nodding, yessing. "She was so beautiful," he says. "And she would have been a great person. She wanted to be someone who designed space ships—did I tell you that? She drew pictures of spaceships, beautiful ones designed after flowers. She said that would be prettier in the sky than the metal ones. If maybe she could see a flower floating down to the ground, she wouldn't be afraid of aliens, or of space travel. Isn't that amazing? Isn't it? If a flower-shaped ship blew up in the air, the petals would be okay, because they would still be beautiful." I turn to him, and his eyes are tearing up again. "That's my daughter. My Sam said that. She wanted to make flowers in the sky."

He twists his wrist suddenly and puts the gun in his mouth, pulls the trigger while I drive over sixty miles per hour, yelling and yelling and yelling, No. The car spins out because I'm scared; the blast is so loud, much louder than you expect. The glass behind his head shatters and the car careens into a ditch because I look away from the road, from the shot.

The others have already jumped in their cars and followed. I don't remember them pulling me out of the car, but I remember standing and holding Starla, getting blood everywhere, some of it mine.

Later, when Barry writes dialogue into that scene, I explode during workshop time. I mean he's got the man still alive, barely speaking, hanging out of the car, and I know he's writing it that way to bring some sort of closure. But the man—he had no head. Part of it was on me. I was there. And how can they take that moment and try to work it differently? And later, I'll repent profusely, give him free coffees, which he turns down, but at the moment I can see *why* we were banned from the city. We're heartless, soulless.

"This was a man's *life*," I tell them and throw the manuscript across the table. The papers hit Barry. I'm half standing and I know what all of us are thinking at that moment, and it hits me like an oncoming train.

I'm the man now.

Like I caught what he caught from his daughter. I'm sitting at the same table and I am angry because I'm threatening and they don't understand my pain. Starla has risen just like me, and it reminds me of how Hailey first pointed the gun at her, and I wonder who will beat me up and hold me down and stop me from doing something stupid. But no one has to, because I can see myself and Hailey, and I know what I have to do. Starla says, "You write about it, hon. Go back and write it out, figure it out." And I knock over a chair and go to the back room, and I look in the mirror and think I see some blood that didn't come out of the shirt I'm wearing, or the apron, or my face. But I'm smarter than Lady Macbeth. I know that washing will never get it out. Instead, I take a clean white sheet of paper and I dirty it with my story, and Hailey dies again, so I can live.

You Will Draw This Life Out To Its End

Last week, Trois Frères, a gallery in Persévére, the city at the centre of culture floating above Enceladus, showed your work *The Water-Miners of Détermination*, and last night you were feted at the Orange Buddha until you were tired, so tired that you could not sketch another face on the tablecloths they'd provided for the party. You begged off the late night screening of a colleague from Uranus's film, *The Lifetimes of Clouds*, and were escorted back to your room, the highest suite in the massive Passepartout Hotel overlooking the Persévére skyline, a sight too exquisite to draw because one needed too much time to do it justice, and all you could think about were the mining cities on Ganymede and how much your body needed sleep.

Lying there, on a bed big enough for three, you knew Marie and Francois-Jacques took good care of you now that you were entering the "edges of your body's gravity," as the author Morole would say. They watched over the doddering artist during receptions, travel among moons and planets, but there was a weight they could not fully support and you knew it. You'd often said to yourself, "I am on a course, on a ship, I cannot get off of. I can't even steer it."

You could veer to projects on Uranus and Saturn and to the moons of Jupiter—you were well established and had the money to travel.

"You can paint anything you want," Marie told you one morning when you seemed the most insecure, handing you a cup of peaches and whipped cream with a dusting of orange rind. "You can find passage on any ship going anywhere."

And you had done that. But there was a responsibility in becoming widely praised. You were in sight of others, and you must keep moving for them.

Weren't artists cursed to be sharks and swim, swim, swim for their very lives? After tonight, there were shows you were expected to attend across the system, appearances you needed to make, so much marketing between painting times. Your life was not your own.

"Nonsense," Marie told you. "Besides, I don't think you could stop."

You were the artist most well-known for painting the cities of the solar system. All of them. You gave their narrative, their histories, their people, all woven into your paintings, and you connected them to Earth. You travelled and painted; you were to the art world connective tissue for a rapidly fraying human culture.

You liked it. You found floating cities like this one—fifteen around Saturn, ten around Uranus—attractive. You'd visited the Emirates, the twelve colonies, on Mars and Earth—you were always praised there and well taken care of. Ariel, Titania, Titan. You painted the cities, the people, their worlds. For most of your career, you did not have to spend much time in the mining ships that hovered closer to the surface, or the asteroid belt of restaurants and hotels and fuelling stations for travellers. You could always float above that.

Until that day you decided to draw them. Instead of painting the cities against a backdrop of planet, instead of the patrons' daughters and sons, instead of the shopping districts with their hanging gardens, you decided to draw the miners on which these floating cities depend, on which the missions within and beyond the solar system depend, and so you went there. Not without controversy from your friends, agent, and representatives. You brought your pad and your charcoal and your paints and your easel. You loved there. And then, when the work was done, you moved on from there, mining the miners for art, in a sense. And tonight, in your dreams, you go back there again, because you left something there.

But when you dream, you dream in charcoal.

This is the burnt arm of Ajax Connolly, the scar a river of tissue up his bicep, little rivulets around his deltoid. He doesn't mind them. "Battle scars," he calls them. "When you do battle with the plugs and the lingers, and the drones that jaw the strafe need fixed, you gotta fix 'em. Sometimes they needs your arm, at least parts of it."

He's proud of his arm, so you make sure to draw the scar perfectly, of course you do—you can't stop looking at him, or talking to him, so this will be an exquisite portrait. You take your time at his elbow, at the arm that disappears into the dark grey shirt with his name in crimson and his company—Helios—in yellow ochre. You notice how his shirt is unbuttoned to the middle of his chest, and how his beard merges with his chest in a darkness that compels you, and your charcoal, to create the darkness drawing you in. But you realize that you are sixty, and that your life is moving from moon to moon to moon to planet for an award, to a city for celebration, and that your life and his life are incompatible. They can't even exist in the same picture, you believe.

But we do, you think then. We do exist in the same picture. People forget that the miners and the floaters are part of the same picture, and you're going to remind them of the people they've forgotten. You are hailed as "seeker of justice," as a "recorder of the forgotten" by the people who live in clouds, and you sit through elaborate dinners as others proclaim your unending, tireless mission as ambassador for the "working men and women." But you don't feel at peace.

This is Ajax in his bed, a picture that will never be in a show—a gift to Ajax from you. He is wrapped in the silk sheets, a luxury every miner affords himself. His are deep-water blue, and they contour and fold to hold his thick legs and body as you paint. A quick study this time. For a later painting. "Do you have a dom of yours own?" he asks you. "An artist like you has a sleek dom, for sure. But you've not spoke of a love, or a dom, so I'm just asking to know you better."

But he *had* known you better, earlier, and you chuckle sadly, knowing that you wouldn't be staying. You admit that you don't have a home so much as an exchange. You pay a monthly fee for a room in any hotel and the exchange allows you to move from hotel to hotel as your home. "Yours a skipper!" he laughs. "Skipping from one place to the other. That must be grand living. You don't have to be trapped." He sees that you are concentrating, maybe, that you don't laugh with him.

"Or rooted," you say.

Maybe he is sincere, but you are afraid of the sincerity, so you will later say to yourself that he was saying it to be polite—"You can always skip here, dom down with me if you like."

But you bury it and his torso in phthalocyanine blue, because it scares you to think how long this moment could last. Or what it would cost.

He makes cabbage and sausage for you, with garlic. You drink beers. The scent of bergamot stays with you for years. So does the sound of his laugh.

You sketch a hundred men in charcoal. You paint twenty men in acrylic, some of them in their jobs, suspended from molybdenum-super-alloyed steel girders above the clouded Ganymede hundreds of miles below. You are often hovering yourself, safe inside a sitejet, when you take the photographs that will later be used as the model, a bubble around you, steel separating you because you are a famous artist and you are documenting the great miners of the solar system.

"Can I have a copy when yours finished?" the young men will ask because they want to hang this in their dom—a single room with a bed and a kitchen and a beautiful view of the rigs on which they work—and this painting or charcoal that you do will be to them, and to their dom, a family crest, giving them a sense of ownership and title, a way of marking their territory with art. They are all young to you, but they are twenty and thirty and forty, and they are decently paid, mostly happy, and within a single two-hour transport of a floating city like Ruckus or Chattle or Trouble or Skirmish, to meet their needs for social activity, which is where you meet many of them. The older ones have been there for twenty years or more because it's decent pay, and "because I don't belong floatin' above it all." Most of them have not heard of you—until you do a drawing of them. And then, "You are Renault, the people's painter." They buy you drinks. They sit with you. Crowd you with camaraderie. And you spend a month there, doing portraits, paintings, all for a show—paintings that will sell for more money than the miners make in a year because you knew people liked to have pictures of others working hard on their walls to give themselves a familial connection to labour—and you shell out some of your own money to make copies for them for their doms, because it's easy, and it's friendly, and it's the least you can do.

But these days, as you succumb to your own "gravity," you don't want to be in the great cities of the Ceinture of Saturn, of Uranus, because something caught your attention on your way by. Instead you want to retire in a place that does not want retirement, a place where one cannot retire, because one is working fast enough and hard enough, and playing hard enough, that there will be no stopping for the miners—they will die and wear out young. If you do this, you will have to live faster now, draw faster, if you want to capture a new life. *Do you want a long life alone, Renault? Or a shorter one with someone?*

♧ ♧

When the morning comes and the reflectors carry the hazy sun to you in the penthouse suite of the Passepartout, you have come to the end of a life. You are writing a letter on your pad telling Marie and Francois-Jacques of your best and last project, and what they must do. When the jawline of the other of the city's spires glint in that reflected sun, you will have dressed, packed, and made reservations for transport to a Moonline, to head back to Ganymede.

What will they say? He has buried himself in his last great project! Yes, they will say that. But for you, you will be *living*, and the payment for that life will be this clever art distraction. Call it a project, not a retirement. "Look over here! I will soon show you *their* lives," you will say to them, even while you take all the time to live your own.

On the way to the transport, two women from Hérédité on a holiday will want your autograph.

It is okay to give your signature away, but you are going to keep walking. You know, as the woman who takes your suitcase leads you to the top floor of the transport, that you cannot help the miners by merely drawing them, merely making the moneyed worlds aware of the people who support them. You realize that now. You cannot change life for the miners by appealing to those who buy your paintings because for them, the painting is help enough; you decide you can only change the lives of the miners by drawing *for* the miners, giving them something. You will sink much faster in the colonies around Ganymede than you would in a floating city, you think. But you might be happier. And you are sinking fast in the floating cities anyway.

You write a letter to Ajax Connolly, hoping he is still there, asking if you can skip his direction, dom with him for a while, and paint yourself into the pictures of Ajax's life. When he asks you, as he will, if this is for a project or for more, you can tell him both. That there will be time for both; that you will paint the miners and their lives—the lives that you will spend with them this time, not leaving in a month, but staying, to give the system a true glimpse into life here. You will call this project "Together." Secretly, though, you don't know if it will change a single mind, because the only thing you truly want to show to yourself is that you and Ajax can be together.

"How long will you dom?" Ajax will ask.

139

And you will say, "As long as my gravity holds me above the planet, I would like to dom with you."

And he will say, "I'll go buy an extra cabbage then."

And that alone will make you happy.

This is what you believe will happen. You will live a quiet life. You will paint as long as you are able to, till a tremulous hand cannot be disguised as sketchy art. You will have shows only in the nearest floating city, Antigone or Aeschylus, far above Titan and around Saturn—but you will also have shows in Ruckus and Trouble and Skirmish, the bars in each, because they are not as bad as they sound. You quote Susan Sinjay Marshall in your head: "We dive down into the atmosphere to breathe again." This is what you will say you are doing when you talk to yourself. When you talk to a more and more worried Marie and Francois-Jacques, you say that this is a grand project—a long project—a *lifetime* project, because life is on such a grand scale is it not? And one cannot do justice to a life in moments, but in a collection of moments.

"It is dangerous there," Marie tells you.

"I've been before."

"The toxic levels of Jovian radiation, the mining colony, the dangerous rigs and working conditions . . ."

"All of which I know about and have experienced before."

"You are too important to stay there so long."

"It's important that I stay for the project." You cannot tell her that you are stepping away from the art world, or that you are in retirement. You must couch it this way—that it is a grand project that will take years to complete. Life takes years to complete.

You argue and you debate, and you pull against the people and the tide that would take you back out into space, until you close your eyes and commit to a show every two years, one that you will not travel with but that they may take on tour, and all but Marie is satisfied with that. Like a daughter, she pleads with you not to disappear, and you promise not to, for her, and you know that she will come eventually by the way she says, "All right." Quietly, like a whisper.

At first, the art world acquiesces to your desires, pliantly allowing you to create a masterpiece of immersion. *Becoming Miner* they rename it in magazines that you promise to stop reading. The art world has always had a hate relationship with love when love takes away an artist, destroys a band, ferrets away a soul that was perfect in his or her longing, their acute loneliness, their meditative melancholy. Love dulls the edge, they say. But you say Andrew Wyeth, Salvador Dali, the Emperor Shah, Claude Monet, Philip McCoy, Silmarillion: the Martian Brothel—all inspired by love, bettered by love, producing art for love.

You think to yourself with some excitement, as you travel by Moonline to Ganymede, "I have gotten off the ship," by which you mean the pre-programmed, autopilot course of your life as you knew it. "But I don't know where that will take me now."

❧❧

Ganymede looms ahead of you, a great round eagle's egg floating in space, splattered and speckled in greys and whites instead of browns. Be home for me, you think to yourself. But that's so much to ask of Ganymede. It isn't a friendly place. It isn't a homey place. It's difficult for the miners that stay there. We can't just choose a place to stop and expect it to be everything. That's why you've picked up three bags of honey sesame-covered almonds, a case of black cherry walnut Martian gelato, and five cylinders of Inuvik Delight coffee beans, and you bring a small suitcase of whatnots—things that have the magic to create a home.

As the Moonline makes its turn, you glide over the deep crevice carved into Ganymede's surface like an old wound. Ajax and the other miners on Aethon Mining Station call it "the Mouth of Ganymede." Less than half a kilometre long, about three 300 metres across and ninety-five kilometres straight down, partly man-made partly tectonic, the crevice is the main work site of the crews at Aethon, the Miner's city floating just above the planet on magnetic lifters, using its own magnetosphere to keep the city aloft. Deep inside the crevice there is an ocean that covers the whole planet just under the icy, rocky crust.

In this slow descent, you stare at the strata left behind by the cutting and drilling and blasting, the shadow of the Moonline gliding over a billion years of history written on the crevice wall.

Ahead you see Aethon, and as you approach, you find yourself again asking the same question, this time of Ajax: *Can you give me home?* But you are certain that you can put roots down here.

These are the last years of your life, the work of a lifetime, the masterpiece *Together*.

Instead of twenty more years of life, you will have eight.

The first years of your new life with Ajax are better than all the appreciative, fawning fetes you've attended over the last forty years. Ajax holds your hand at tables in the bars of Ruckus as miners talk to you about their hopes and dreams—to take starships into the blanket of space, to take the money they earn and visit Enceladus, because they've seen photographs showing the planet looking like sky. Or they tell you about growing up on Mars, or in the Belt; a few of them talk of the green grasses across Nunavut and Russian forests, where they know their uncles and aunts live. Have you been to these places? they ask. And you tell them stories of the worlds of which they dream—and better, you draw them pictures, so many pictures. You will paint a mural inside Skirmish that will become famous—of your memories of Paris in the 2090s, with its tall hanging gardens and the rivers beneath the Eiffel Tower and the Palisades that stream like solar winds from the Arc de Triomphe. Do another, they will ask you months later, and you paint them the windswept plains of the Arctic—their long grasses, their deep steppes, the bison grazing in herds with the mammoth.

They cannot afford to go home. They cannot afford to leave, so you bring them the rest of the worlds you know: Enceladus, Ariel, Charon on the New Euphrates, anything they ask for—all from memory.

In exchange for their friendship.

You know they will not refuse you. Even in awe of your murals, you know they will ask you for a personal painting, of them and their friends, of them and their girlfriends and boyfriends, on these fragile lily pad colonies floating above Ganymede. All miners know the risks of coming here, of the voluntary temporary sterility, of the risk to their health, but the money is good, and they say they are sending it to a sister, or a mother back on Mars, or to their families who have not forgotten them and who believe the deposits to be a form of love. Or they are saving it for their dreams to leave.

You will paint them all, eventually, but every night here you absorb them—their stories, their smiles—and you absorb the heat from Ajax's palm. Isn't this worth leaving the third tier cities, to have someone hold your hand?

You take your radiation shots more regularly because you will be staying for a long time. You will notice that very few of the men are as old as you are. In the back of your mind, you hear Marie's voice: "Life is too quick there, Renault. All burned up by forty, most of them, if not mangled by the mining—you belong here with us."

Burned up lives, flickering faster but brighter. Oh, that first night you are back, Ajax, the superintendent of Aethon, cannot keep his enthusiasm inside, his joy at seeing you, and he carries you over the threshold of his apartment, lays you on the bed and kisses you. His beard is wet with crying, trying to say something about "good things never come back." You've heard that myth before from other miners—that there are no second chances, that nothing good returns. Ajax makes love to you, and even in passion, in this moment, you are an artist tracing every nuance of his body with your mind: his body, his eyes, his arms. His joy ignites the bed.

The blue bull from Mexico you put in the kitchen. "I was not always well-received," you tell Ajax. You left Paris for Mexico when you were twenty-five and you lived in a studio in the Condesa Hipódromo, and you used to walk to the Fuente de los Cántaros in Parque Mexico, that great fountain with the giant woman, just to see her pour water from the jars—such a beautiful sculpture—and you would sit and sketch people. And you were anonymous. No expectations, no crowds, and you might exchange drawings for some flautas or tacos at the mercado. You liked sitting at a set of blue arched doors, and a woman there had this cheap Guido Gambone bull knockoff on her tiled porch, and you knew that she didn't know it was a cheap copy—it made her happy. She showed it to you when she learned you were an artist, leaned over it, even stroked its smooth ceramic back, talked about its value, how it had been handed down from her grandmother to her mother to her. "That bull was about her family. It wasn't about Gambone at all," you say to Ajax as he kisses you on the ear. When you were feeling depressed about your lack of fame—everyone in the Condesas were trying to become famous—you bought this cheap little blue bull to remind you about the value of art in a life, and he travels with you.

"I think I will have a Condesa Hipódromo life again here," you tell him, which means drinking and eating and friends and days that you don't count, you just live.

But living in a place means you become curious to explore what it means to live there.

Eleven times over that first year, against the worries of your patrons who hear that you are becoming reckless, you take trips down to the surface of Ganymede. How can you not? The lives of the miners are not just lived above the planet. The long oval elevators descend on needles of metal tethers, like raindrops travelling the length of grass to the ground. There are hundreds of them. You paint them. You travel in them with Ajax and his crew, several hours of slow descent. When you hear a rumbling, Ajax tells you that they will soon have an upgrade, but until then the tether's surface behind the elevator is corroding; there are rough patches, but "nothing dangerous." However, there have been times when they stop working and you have to call in to the Command Centre for assistance.

It is on the third time you're there with them that you see a miner crushed between the giant pincers and the drill, his body snapped in three places by the force. His arm and face are enveloped in the metal, his helmet light illuminating his surprise; the drill has broken away from the hoist, and his arm emerges from between strips of metal in the great pincer-suit.

You paint the memorial service held for an hour in a bar in Ruckus, where he is remembered. The service is recorded for his parents. He was twenty-three. His ashes are placed in a golden, fluttering mechanical bird and dropped into the thin atmosphere of Ganymede, where the metal, after a few weeks, will corrode from radiation and spread his ashes onto the surface. The sun tips the bird's wings in gold as it flutters from their hands.

Only a month later, you paint the miner's strike. Their union has asked for better equipment, upgrades that were promised years ago (after the last strike ended): upgrades to drinking water safety, better radiation shielding, upgrades to the elevators.

"I'm just going to watch," you tell Ajax. You sit atop a table with your easel and paint the negotiations—the growing tensions, the strikers, the frustrations, the human-ness. In an especially explosive moment the moderator looks at you. "Did you get all that, Renault?" he laughs. Ajax is the moderator, and he's in every sketch and painting. It breaks your heart to paint him so wearied by negotiation. His head lowered, his grief, his fury. His impassioned speeches and his cool head.

Over your shoulder, though, Ajax nods, kisses the back of your neck. "Oh. I want to help that man," he says with seriousness.

"So will others," you say.

"I wish I knew him."

"If you knew him like I knew him, you would love him."

He chuckles behind you. "Did you come here to escape the art world only to paint the miner's strike?" he asks. "Do not give up the quiet life you came for. Did you come here to escape it all and fall in love, or be a part of all this weary life?"

"Yes," you say.

His face softens; you give him peace.

"I came here to have a life with you. And this is your life."

Someone sends images of the paintings (not without your permission) to those who recite the news. The paintings get incredible coverage—the *strike* gets amazing, helpful coverage—because of your paintings. You receive frantic messages from Eustachi and Helios that you are not a miner; that you cannot comment on the strike.

"And what would Picasso say to that?" you write back. "Was *Guernica* meddling or documenting? Was it a meditation on war?" You call this body of work *Meditation on a Strike*.

You sketch the meetings, ink their fiery rhetoric into the canvas. The raw sketches find their way through the ether to Mars and Earth and Saturn. These become your fastest selling compositions, and the more you do, the more you sell. Eustachi becomes rich off the miners' strike, even though they are accused of taking sides ("we cannot control Renault," they say in their defense) and the art world becomes activated for the cause, the media now a gallery for your work for weeks.

Helios, to answer a growing tide of resentment across the system, sends a massive system cruiser and docks it to the colony. You are there, painting quickly, sketching the white arrow of the ship as it stretches over you, and the lawyers they bring—for both sides. The media accompany them, and the negotiations are calm and rational. You paint this as well.

The union is partially successful in their demands, receiving promises from Helios and immediate upgrades to their equipment via the shipment on the system cruiser.

You are hailed as a revolutionary by both the miners and the art world. But it is not all positive.

"Young painters might be asking if there is a place for art in politics, if you are sullying your reputation," a renowned art magazine says to you in an interview being recorded for later broadcast. "What do you say to them about the nature of true art and its neutral place outside the quagmire of human rivalry?"

You laugh for such a long time the interviewer has to cut the interview off.

✧ ✧

Some negotiated improvements never come, now that the strike is over. Helios looks good to have acquiesced and given you new equipment. They tell Ajax via messages that they are working as hard as they can on upgrades to shielding, to pipes, all of which are massive undertakings costing millions.

Ajax presses his hands on the window in your room. In the reflected light of Ganymede, he appears a faded blue. He's angry, and when he looks up it seems as if he might fly through the window. You will never paint this scene.

✧ ✧

Marie comes as you knew she would. You love her because you can't really tell how appalled she must be by your living conditions—not on her face, not as she greets your friends, smiling, and Ajax, hugging him. She says, "I know we've never met, but . . ." and you know she is hugging him because he cares for you. He says, "I know," finishing her thought.

You offer her water, and she gives a momentary grimace because she's told you the water is full of contaminants. Instead she pulls out a bottle of wine from her suitcase.

Of course, after a jambalaya dinner and wine, she wants to see what you have, for the show that you *did* commit to before you came. She doesn't say it like that. You just know. It's the little price you pay for freedom.

You guide her to the bedroom, your work hanging in every available space, some of it stacked against the wall. This is what's not being broadcast, the work that went beyond the strike. She is amazed by your new work.

"It's more *visceral*," she says. Several times she gasps. You know you have done well when you hear that sound.

She holds up a set from the surface of Ganymede, and she notices what she's never seen before in your work. "That's *you*," she says.

"I am not separate any longer," you tell her.

You immediately see her fear. "You're not a trained miner."

"No, I'm not. But I can't stay up here and record their lives down there."

She knows better than to argue with you. You are stubborn, set in this course. Besides, it gives you a rebellious arc, even further from the patron's wishes.

"Is it safe for you?"

You look across the table at Ajax and think of the three birds you saw fly over the Mouth, their gold surfaces mottled by exposure, carrying the ashes of three different miners set free from Ruckus or Skirmish. "Is it safe for them?"

She takes forty paintings and drawings with her on the Moonline out, kissing you on the cheek, whispering, "Stay out of your paintings, yes? Be safer."

ℒℒ

A short time later, you hear that the corporation will be upgrading the water lines throughout the grid. New air filters are sent, of a higher quality this time, and a team from Helios has brought a great cargo ship with upgrades for the tethers.

And for Aethon, the promised changes do finally happen, with a raised eyebrow from Ajax. Unfortunate and controversial as that is, they would not have happened if you had not been affected. To Ajax you say, "Let's see what we can do with this old face."

He is angry that it took a painter to convey what he has been telling them for years, when men have been dying—only now will they listen.

You put your hand on his arm. "Let's see how much they will help you to help me. Let the celebrity work for you—let them care about you because of me. That is the way it happens for everyone in the rest of the worlds." It was true. A mother loves you because of him; your boss likes you because you are associated with a school you both went to; everyone is helped by the favour of another face. Why not let your face get all of them favour?

One would be well within rights to say *no, if you can't do it for the right reasons, don't do it,* but why not exploit the wrong reasons if they lead to the right actions?

Finally, you are helping the miners in a way that could improve their lives.

"Let's get as much as we can," you tell Ajax. "It will not cost us much." You chuckle.

He looks at you, and then away. "It could cost us our lives."

ℒℒ

This is Ajax's mechanical hand, the blue one, with translucent blue skin, so that you can see the gears, the pulleys and ropes, the cables, the tethers of his hand beneath.

You were down on your knees, screaming for a medic when it happened.

On the dais beneath the elevators, the broken cable whipped at your face,

147

and Ajax reached across to catch it, or at least to protect your face, and the tether severed his hand.

You held his arm, tried to staunch the blood, using the now-ragged sleeve of his groundsuit, until someone brought a kit, a tourniquet, a stasis cap. You can never unsee his face—his helmet holds his scream in, his mouth stretched wide, eyes clenched shut.

You sit with him in the mining corp's plastic infirmary, like nesting fish tanks around you, and you can see other injured men and women, their friends talking to them, sitting with them, though you cannot hear what they are saying. Ajax says, "I've been thinking about New Australia on Titan. They have forests there. I miss trees. I grew up with trees until I was nine. Maybe that's why I like very big things all around me, watching me," he says, nodding towards Jupiter outside the windows. "It would be nice to go back there again one day."

You sit uncomfortably in the cactus green chair and imagine the loved ones of the other injured men and women are saying similar things. *I want to go far away from here. I can't wait to travel to the casinos. To the pools of Europa.*

You are angry at those who own you both.

"Where do you want to go in the end?" he asks you, and you forgive him because he's under the influence of many drugs for the pain.

What can this old face do for you? You will see.

When they build a new hand for Ajax, they have to cut into his arm, and you ask to have the blood saved. Because this new work will have blood in it. You have them draw a pint of yours as well.

You paint a portrait of the two of you, holding hands, looking at the viewer. In it, you hold his blue artificial hand over your own hand. *We Break For You.* The painting you did of the scene caused more controversy at the show on Antigone, and Marie tells you that if you are going to use your own blood, the Helios Mining Corp says it wants to bring you home.

When she comes the second time, she sits on the edge of her chair, nothing of her quite touching the world around her. Except you—she holds your hand and pleads for you to return with her. "Eustachi has said they fear for their favourite artist, and I do, too. I don't care about the art, love," she says, wincing at what must be a betrayal to even voice, "but I don't want you hurt." She looks up at Ajax. "Would you let us take him to Antigone for a medical check-up, please?"

You fear going with her, some uncontrollable fear that if you step with her into a Moonline transport, you will never see Ajax again. Even you cannot escape their gravity, not with all your celebrity. They want to pull you back into their control, and they use Marie to do it.

You do not think she is aware of this. You love her like a father. You pat her hand. "Would you like more wine?" you say.

"Will you go with me?"

"I am not going to stop my work here until it is finished," you say, pouring her a glass.

"It will never be finished!"

"Oh, yes. It will one day be finished."

"When? When will it be finished, tell me so that I can tell Eustachi and Helios. Tell me when my nightmare of losing you will go away. It is not like you to be so selfish. So many want you, want to see you. I want to see you."

She takes the glass and you let her explode like this all over your living room, because she needs to say all of this or she will not feel as if you know the pain you are causing her.

"I know what this is. I know what you are doing," she says, glancing at Ajax. "You are trying to run away from us."

"No, Marie."

"I can find a nice place for you and Ajax to live—some place that doesn't kill you slowly. The radiation here is ten times what you would have if you were living on Antigone, on Daphnis—anywhere else. Both of you could have a lovely apartment, a house." She listed things as if she were hoping to get a reaction from you, a light in your eyes, as if she might stumble on whatever it was you wanted.

"I will tell you what I want," you say. "I want to live here with Ajax, within the mining community that is our home. I cannot take the mines with me, can I? I cannot take the other miners with me, no? It would be absurd, yes?"

"Yes, that would be absurd. The miners have to mine here."

"They choose to mine here, yes. And I choose to stay here with them."

She slaps the bed, shakes her head. "No, it is unacceptable for you to be here," she says, tearing up. "Because I cannot be with you here."

You know this is the crux, the tiny key to all of this. That in moving away from the art world, from the demands and pressures of performing, you moved away from her—you took yourself from her.

"I did not want to break your heart," you say. She is quiet. "But I needed to do this, all of this, here. I am happy, my dear," you tell her, but she stands and you can feel her cooling down suddenly, and it frightens you.

She steps away from both of you, now hovering near the door. "Eustachi Group and Helios are refitting the shielding here. They told me you would not come home. They told me to tell you that they are wrapping the mining company in protective shielding. They are doing this for you, to preserve you. They do not want you to die, Renault."

You stand and she hugs you. She says, "I do not want you to die."

"I am going to die," you say, and it comes out much worse than you thought it would, as if you are willing it, some incantation of death. Even Ajax looks horrified.

She cries and heaves into your shoulder, grips you, her little hands turning into claws, holding your skin through your shirts.

"I am going to die," you repeat for all. "But my work will travel even more than I did."

She does not answer. She cries. Ajax stands and waits, and you hold Marie until she stops crying.

She pulls back. "Think about coming home with me sometime, please."

You cannot stop thinking of Marie. You know she will come back, and that she will bring others with her. You are sure of this.

You leap into your work, painting and drawing.

The new shielding comes, and for two years they install it, starting with your wing of the mining colony. This is how you know they have come. You see them out your window, hanging above the moon, dangling in their Helios suits.

A supply of those suits also comes with them.

"See what my face can do," you say to Ajax. He hugs you from behind. "New suits for your men. New shielding."

"What is it about your face?" he asks.

"The problem with my face is that I have promise."

"And no one else's face here does? Do they only value you?"

"When I no longer have promise, they will tire of me."

You do not know how to make them value the miners more than what you are doing. "It's insulting, I know. But we will take what we can get."

"And what happens when you die? Will their concern disappear?"

You look at him, and you don't know how to be more immortal than you are. "It looks as though I shouldn't die then."

He comes to you, puts his arms around you and kisses you. "If Marie is right and you are being killed here, and you want to keep doing good for us, perhaps go for a check-up. You might live longer, do more work."

He doesn't understand what he's saying, you think. Instead you bask in the warmth of his breath.

A celebration occurs on Ruckus for you and for the new supplies. The miners know it is you, and they are not upset. They do not know these things have happened to keep you safe, but believe you have negotiated with the mining companies, used your influence. Let them believe it.

You paint the miners celebrating, and send just the image to Helios. *Worth Every Penny*, you call it. *See their smiles and their mugs raised?* you write in your letter to the mining companies. *It is for you and what you do for them.* You soon see the picture used in their marketing and recruitment. You bet the image is netting them a tidy little sum. They paid for it, you think, looking at the floating colony with the new radiation shielding. They paid a lot for it.

Will they see the value in the miners now?

The galleries are upset with you. You sent the image directly to the mining companies, bypassing them. It's not in your contract to be so dilettante with your work. You explain to them that you were giving them something they could use, and there were still plenty of paintings and drawings for Eustachi to market. One made no difference. They mention the contract you signed for their exclusivity.

You ask for their forgiveness on this one painting, telling them that you will pay the commission they would have received. On videophone, they look mildly assuaged. They have always looked mildly assuaged.

"Who cares for your work like we do?" they ask.

"No one. You have always been there for me."

"How can we care for your work if it does not pass through us first? We do not want your patrons to abuse your work. Or commercialize it," they say with disdain.

You imagine that one image has travelled all over the system by now. *Worth Every Penny* is the one everyone will see.

You're thinking about Uranus, and how the clouds speak to each other. You've finally seen the film *The Lifetimes of Clouds*, with Ajax and others in the bar last night. It's about scientists trying to decipher the language of the clouds around Uranus—their multi-stratified conversations, the passing of light from cloud to cloud to cloud. How does language and meaning pass from a body to another body? How can we convey meaning without words? You've spent a lifetime trying to learn that elusive language.

You've tried painting their lives as they live them—in danger, toil, and harsh conditions; you have painted their injuries and pain. You have humanized them. But this has cost the mining company money and public relations. Now to make the mining company happy, and to thank them for their gifts, you have painted miners as happy and content. This also gets you in trouble, but maybe it will help them. Still, if anything is done to help them, it is done because you are there with them and the miners receive residual benefits—leftover sunshine, spillage of the bounty.

How can you make the miners themselves into what is cared for? After four years, you have done your best.

It is in the mirror that you notice how thin you are. Ajax notices, too, and sometimes whispers in the cobalt violet night. "Are you well?" he asks. You say, "Yes, love," every time, and he covers you with his arm as if to protect you from the lie hovering above.

Marie comes.

You're wearing your best, bulky burgundy silk robes to hide the fact that you have lost weight. You've opened the screens to get full view of Ganymede, and Jupiter, vague and mystical in the distance. You've opened a wine. You know why she is here.

When she enters, there are two others representatives with her. They are tall, sallow men, wearing expensive little hats and dark robes.

She nearly trips running over to you, trying to run ahead of these hounds she has set upon you. "Oh, sweet Renault, do not hate me. These men are doctors. Real doctors. I know you will not go with me to Mars, so I brought them here for you. Please, it is the least you can do. Humour me."

The doctors first must tell you how honoured they are to meet you, what you have done for all of Sol—knitting together the system in paintings, keeping the face of humanity present, making sure that no one is forgotten. They ask for your autograph, first for themselves, for which you use your special pen, and then, yes, just one here on a form. *It is just a form saying that you give your permission to being examined.*

But you don't trust it and won't sign it.

Marie crosses her arms. "You must sign it, my friend, please. It is the only way that Eustachi and Helios will be assured that you will finish your project." She taps her foot because she's nervous. She suspects, you think, that you have tricks up your robe.

You act affronted. "I did not sign a contract with them guaranteeing the completion of a project, only that they had exclusive rights to work I produced."

She pulls out a contract as if it were sitting on the very top of the bag. She points to a phrase: "will own the complete project *Together*."

"When it is finished it will be complete," you say.

"If you were to die, the work would not be complete," she says.

"If I die, the work is completed automatically."

"That is not how the contract reads. You promised to complete the project. So you must complete it. Then you are no longer under contract."

"So I am their employee until I finish? And if I don't?"

"The doctors are here to make sure that you can finish, and if they find you are not in good health, they will recommend that you be sent to Mars for treatment, or at least to Antigone. Please, please, it is for me."

She seems overly proud of her use of lawyers to define the word "complete."

"It is commonly known among artists that death is a completion."

"It is not commonly known in contracts. Death is default."

"Default? Well, I don't think that any contract, in that case, is sound. Everyone will die leaving their lives 'incomplete' and their body of work unfinished."

"It would be much easier if you allowed the doctors to examine you."

You back away. "Eustachi owns my body of work. They do not own my body. No contract I signed gives them that authority."

She pleads with you now. All pretense of being in charge is dropped; all tête-à-tête is gone. "Renault, this is the compromise I am making with you. I can see the spots on your arms, and you are thinner. Let them check you."

But you are not listening to her; you are re-reading your contract, scanning for important phrases—important life-altering phrases. *Care for the life of your work in perpetuity.* Eustachi owns all of your work, yes, but must take care of whatever they do not sell to private collections, or lend to museums, forever. Forever.

You look at Marie, and you do your best impression of a man finally giving in to reason. "Let them look." You give yourself over to their scans, their murmured ponderings, their analysis, but your mind is thinking about that clause in the contract. You draw a plan. A careful plan. All while she is talking to the doctors.

The doctors, of course, do not find anything they didn't expect. They find high levels of radiation; high levels of lead in your body. What other miners deal with on a regular basis all cause a mild panic when it is you. "I will not receive any treatment unless everyone on this colony receives the same treatment," you say.

Marie says, "You must come with me to receive treatment. It requires equipment they do not have here. I cannot take every miner from this facility to Mars. I am only authorized to bring you."

"Tell Eustachi and Helios they should build the machines here for this infirmary."

"That will take a year."

"Then I will take the treatment in a year."

She sees your game. You will not budge. She stares you down, but you are doing this for something so much bigger than yourself.

"I am trying to save your life," she whispers. "You are not making it easy."

"Until they see every miner here as they do me, I won't be saved." She begins to cry. You speak softly, almost like a prayer. "I have become a part of this place, and you can't take me out of here without killing me. You must save the place, the whole place. You must be my advocate to the art world, to Helios. You must tell them I am no longer an artist alone. I have become a colony."

The doctors take various equipment from their floating bags, administer shots and rays, some a brilliant green, others emitting a deep cerulean blue. They admit that they can only do so much if you do not go for treatment.

"As long as I am here, I make a difference. Marie, help me make that difference. Be my accomplice. Be my partner-liaison to the others. Make them listen. They have already done so much and I thank them, but the day I die, they will forget about the needs of the miners."

She puts her fingers on your face, holds your cheeks and your ears and wants you to look her in the eyes. *Bring Ajax and come live with me on Persévére.* She dines with you that evening. *Come be a part of the life we once had together.* She witnesses the turning of the Ganymede day from the balcony of the bar on Ruckus. She holds your hand as Ajax drapes his arms around you both. *Remember when we used to set the planets on fire?* she says. When she was first assigned to you twenty years ago, and she couldn't speak because she believed she would only prove herself stupid in front of the Great Renault, and how you passed gas at the table. *And you knew I was just another old fart*, you say.

She rests her head on her hands, and with half-lidded eyes gives a small bumblebee laugh, almost talking to her hands as much as to you. "You tell the story of humankind in the cosmos. You were born when we moved away from Mars, and the rest of your life has been movement, moving around the planets even as we did, telling our story."

You say, "And now I am not telling a moving story. I'm telling a different one. Now it is making a life. Just as the rest of these wanderers did. We settle. Every artist eventually roots and tells the story of a people and a place."

She hasn't heard you. "I do not know how you create art out of so much chaos. You make us look beautiful and meaningful."

You look at Ajax. He looks below the balcony, beyond the sheer shielding to the moon below. How much like the stars all the craters look.

She whispers into her hands as if they are a cup for her words. *Beautiful and meaningful.*

⁊⁊ ⁊⁊

Over the next several months, you work on a new project with the help of three other talented artists who work on Aethon. They operate out of a parlour on the Pavilion side, nestled among other shops where miners spend their pay, and they, too, are always busy creating art. On their wall hangs a painting that you painted, of the three of them leaning over the miners, interpreting their dreams for them. Many times the four of you have talked to each other, sometimes sharing art and designs, learning from each other. Many times small versions of your work have ended up on the arms of miners, and that's why you are there to visit the Swordsman, the Quilter, and the Harpoon.

Today, you open up the large black portfolio case and lay plans across their table for a project for which you need their help. They take a break from their own art, their customers rest, and you show them *The History of our Sol on the Arms That Built It.*

They stand around your designs for a multi-panel work—a collaboration with them. The Quilter puts her hand to her mouth. The Swordsman inhales deeply. The Harpoon calls out instinctively.

You say, "Any miner who wants to participate should be encouraged. But I will not enlist anyone. It's all voluntary. I don't want to be accused of using miners as things. Inevitably that will happen, but we will remind them that the miners chose to complete the project with me—and we put their names on the artwork as well. Once we know how many will want to be part of this, that will tell us the scope of the project—how many months, how many arms. But there won't be a painting that correlates with this. It can only be seen if the men and women stand, or even sit, together, which makes it unique. Which makes it *valuable*."

You are designing the entire history of human endeavour through the solar system on the arms of the miners, each containing a piece of the whole—an expanse of progress from Earth through Mars and the Belt, through Saturn and Jupiter; through the cities they created, the moons they mined; through Uranus, Pluto, the base on Charon, reaching to Enkidu, the wild planet that hovers on the very edge of Sol.

The Swordsman strokes his long black beard and asks, "And what about miners who already have a tattoo on their arm?"

"We could incorporate their design into the work, altering it to fit with the overall painting, if they want. I think that will add your own art, and their own personality, into the work. It is about them." You take a step back. "In every way this should be about them as much as it is about the painting. They are integral, and not just a canvas."

The customers are now around the table, looking. "So my Chinese dragon can be a part of this?"

You nod. "Yes, that would be perfect. Everything will add to the design. It will be a multi-layered work, but it will take time, at no cost to you."

"But no one will buy this work. They can't possibly buy hundreds of miners. Why not do something that will sell?"

You smile, as this is the core of your plan. "They won't buy it, no, but Eustachi Group are sworn to protect all my work. The miners will be carrying my work with them, on them. They will then have to protect the miners for as long as they live."

"And we can travel?"

"Oh yes, I have a feeling that anyone who signs up will be doing a lot of travel—at the cost of Eustachi. The Ceintures, the Starred Balconies, you will see the system by the time this show is done, you can be assured of this!"

The man smiles. "My girlfriend will be keen on this. My mate, too.

You turn to the Swordsman. "We should document how we do it, film it, for authentication purposes."

"You should be part of each segment of the process, from design to application," the Quilter says.

"And with that I will need your help."

The horrible thought weighs over the table like a stone about to drop, that to give the miners value it must be inscribed. There is a moment where no one speaks, the truth of that sinking in.

"I'd be beefin' honoured," says the Harpoon, reaching across the table and holding your hand. "Let's ink it."

You expect there will be thirty men and women who sign up, but there are hundreds. The artists never balk, and once you have a secure number, you design *The History of our Sol* for their arms. With the help of the artists, you create a painting that is 200 feet long, made up of the arms of the miners on average six inches across. Sometimes you sign your signature into each arm with a needle and ink, as part of the design, showing the movement from Earth to Mars and to the very boundaries, the cities, the mining colonies, the workers themselves, aching and lifting, pushing metal into place for others to live well.

❧ ❧

"Auguste," Ajax asks when he hears of this, "what will they do about their jobs if they leave to go on these art tours?"

"The touring schedule doesn't have to be long. They offered to use vacation time. The important part is that they will be looked after for the rest of their lives."

"You know this?"

"It's in the contract."

"The way you're interpreting the contract."

"They will have my work on their arms—there'll be no denying that."

"No, there's no denying that. But what if they lose something big? They aren't you. They can't risk without punishment. The work here will suffer. Helios will not be happy."

"But I am securing their future."

"I know. But you are trading their present for it."

"It's their choice."

"Do they know the choice?"

You don't answer because you don't know if they do. Only now are you realizing what you may have done.

Ajax can see he's disturbed you. He stands up. "You came for a quiet life, but look at you. You are touching everyone with fame, and it is unpredictable. You are making people angry with your art. Is this what you want? Is it worth it?"

You think he means, *Are we worth it?*

"It's easy to be an artist passing through, but it's false and it's lonely." Ajax reaches around you. "It's hard being an artist in a place, grounded. Monet at Giverny; Renoir at Cagnes-Sur-Mer; Benton in Kansas City—especially Benton. It is hard not to tell the story of the people around you, for good or bad. Art can't stay above a place where the artist has chosen to live. It just can't. It has to root, too. I am living with you, together. That means everything we experience is part of my art."

You let him enfold you for a while, and then you quietly reach out and sneak one of the rapidly diminishing honey sesame almonds.

❧ ❧

Seven months later, you ask Eustachi Group for five Moonlines to come and pick up your latest show. Eustachi tells you that the museum on Archimedes on Mars has already asked for it, and you can certainly guarantee several shows on Earth, Antigone, the Ceinture. You ask for Eustachi and the museum to take special care of the work, that this work is fragile.

You will not be coming, no, to see that the work is properly installed. "The people I am sending with the work will help you install it." You warn them, "It will be controversial."

"Good. I'm sure that will be a bonus to them. Controversies pack people in." He is so excited. Instead of your piecemeal work, a collection that takes five Moonlines to transport is an event.

The Moonlines arrive and 169 miners board them, carrying luggage for their extended vacations, their tour through Sol, with their boyfriends, their girlfriends, their friends, smiling and waving at you, hugging you for giving them this opportunity to see the worlds. Standing with them are the Swordsman, the Quilter, and the Harpoon, promising to speak on your behalf wherever they go. You stand with Ajax at the platform, and he doesn't have to whisper the warnings into your ear, not right now, that this will cause more trouble.

"It's not a strike," you tell him later.

"They aren't working," he says.

They go to Saturn, where they will all board a system cruiser to Mars. You wish you could go with them—just to see the faces of the gallery officials when they ask where the paintings are. To see Eustachi, hoping to be there to personally care for the paintings, and not seeing them at first. Asking, *Where are the paintings?* And hearing the Swordsman tell them that they will reveal the paintings when they get to the gallery. How they must be feeling when 169 miners come into the gallery, line up, and take off their shirts, revealing one long history, that of the system from arm to arm to arm. What did they say? Did Ernest Eustachi bat an eye at your cleverness? You can imagine him—he loves your work—recovering quickly from the initial shock as the miners ready the line, as he sees what you and the Swordsman, the Quilter, and the Harpoon have done. He will examine them for your signature, your style, but he knows it. He will see the universe beyond their arms because the three artists are that good, and he will see the ships, and the people and the moons and the bases, and the building of the mines, and the building of the colonies.

And then, the miners will speak.

"I remember coming to the colony when I was eighteen," one of them will say.

Another one will begin her story. "I've hauled salt water from the great crevice we call the Mouth for three years now. Ice pebbles under my feet crunch like gravel whenever we inspect the drones."

And then another person: "Mars sent a crew of sixty-one pioneers to Saturn in 2062."

Occasionally, they will stop and say, *This is the History of Our Sol on the Arms that Built It.* But they won't just recite these lines; they will also talk with people, tell their stories, interact, because they are as much the painting as the tattoo—as much the history as the *History*.

The gallery officials—there will be close to forty or fifty of them—might think it brilliant, but they will also recognize the cost. They will recognize your work, and more importantly, they will understand what you are saying, and what the miners are saying about their part in the building of the worlds as we know them. It will be filmed.

You will hear about it from Eustachi when they realize they have to cover the safety of those paintings, those miners, for the life of the miner.

"You cannot ask us to insure people as if they are works of art. We cannot take care of them for the rest of their lives just because you decided to paint on them."

"You already agreed," you will tell them. "In the contract, you insured these works. Now you have to protect them wherever they go."

"Renault, I think the mining colony has damaged your mind."

You laugh it off now, but he will do something about that. They cannot pay for the tour of the solar system for close to 200 people for a year, and they have no means to support 200 people for the rest of their lives.

Helios representatives can barely speak to you without yelling through their videophones. Their employees are not working, are not harvesting the water and air to deliver to Callisto or Saturn because they are being used to make a statement? You have gone too far, they tell you, and they mean it. They intend to make Eustachi pay for the lost earnings since they have kidnapped 169 miners. How could you be so careless with their property?

"They're not your property," you say.

"No, it appears they are the property of Eustachi now. Congratulations— you've just shifted assets. Eustachi has stolen our property. We intend to press intersystem charges on both you and your management company for loss of income and assets."

"We didn't conscript them. They volunteered."

"Then they just changed jobs. Hope you can give them years' worth of work. In effect, you've just destroyed their livelihood. They can't afford to be activists, Mr. Renault. You can."

"You are mistaken, sir," you tell him. "The miners are doing more good for Helios on this small goodwill tour than they are doing here in this mine."

"Says who?"

"Says the people who see this show. Read the reviews, talk to the people before you take action, or you'll find that your profit margins may suddenly go down when they were going up."

"You are living on Helios property. I want you off the colony or you will be taken off by force. Do you understand?"

"Mr. Salazar, I guarantee you, you will benefit more from this than anyone else. You should wait a few weeks."

"By force!" he says and ends the transmission.

He doesn't understand what you have done. By giving them value, you've increased the value of Helios. Eustachi Group will not be liable for the men forever, but they will insure them as they have insured you. This is all you wanted. For someone to see these men and women as the world sees you—to ascribe the same value to them. An equity of vision.

"But you did trick them," Ajax says, with a hint of anger. You are staring out at the ever-changing atmosphere of Jupiter, a swirl of color—Jupiter was like oil paints, all mixing, blending into one another.

"I have good intentions," you say quietly to the moon.

"You should have talked to me about this project. Those are my men."

"They own themselves," you say, adding, "don't you think?"

He runs the dishes under the micro-atomizer, which hums.

"Auguste, this was irresponsible of you. You can't take people and make them your message—"

"I didn't. I asked. They volunteered. I'm trying to do something for them. I'm trying to—"

"I am too. I'm employing them for ten or twenty years. I'm responsible for keeping production up here at Aethon. Those men committed to me, and I committed to Helios. They are under my command. You can't just do what you want here without permission."

"Without *your* permission," you say.

He slams down his hand on the counter. "Dammit, yes. My permission. I earned this position and god knows I have to answer for the decisions that are made here. I have to ask permission. It's the way things work when you're not a celebrity. You can't just write fame on people and expect it to change everything. Fame is a crazy thing. I don't know how you live with it, and it worked well for us, yes, before, but now . . . I'm afraid. I'm afraid it's going to do mess everything up."

You are listening, but you are not looking at him. You are thinking about the moons of Uranus. It's not that you want to go there. It's just that all the moons are named after Shakespeare characters, all the moons of Uranus but two. Twenty-seven characters all mixed up from stories running into each other again and again, just passing by. *Hello. Oh hello, Caliban, Desdemona says, have you seen Ophelia?* You once saw a play on Philostratus by Hobii Andropolis, Uranean playwright, born and raised, very nice fellow that used to put olives on his fingertips—but the play had all the moons of Uranus in it like they were in a Shakespeare play, and Andropolis had them revolving around the stage just as they do in space and asked them to only speak lines they would give from their respective plays and it was quite profound. Puck meeting Cupid, Portia meeting Rosalind, Prospero talking to Lear. Every night the play was different. But it matched the 'movement of the spheres.' You look at the faded giant of Jupiter in the distance. You feel like a revolving Prospero, always running into people and revolving away, passing things by, and you'd like to stay longer, but you never could. Until now. And now you may have messed it up.

"I'm sorry," you say.

"No one was listening to us before you came," Ajax says, coming up behind you, calmer now. "Now we are getting more and more heard—but I'm not sure what they're going to do about what they hear."

"Is it my fault that I can't stop being who I am?"

"Is that what you're gonna tell Helios when those men skip Aethon?"

"I gave them a gift for their retirement."

"You gave them a way out. You let them all uproot."

"I let them fly," you say matter-of-factly.

"Now we see how long they'll fly before they fall."

A few weeks later, Ajax is down under the crust for an extended haul. You are alone in the room, working on a study of Ganymede from photoscans you took from a sitejet you went up in the previous week. The starry, pocked surface still calls to you. You paint a golden eagle circling the moon, like the golden birds carrying the ashes of the men who have died. But this eagle is the god Zeus searching for his lover Ganymede.

A series of timpani sounds, and you are leaning over the video screen to answer a call. Marie sends you an urgent recorded message. Her voice sounds frantic. She cannot calm down. She is so sorry, so sorry. "The Helios ship Abraxas is already on its way to you. I've just found out Ajax is going to be arrested." As the superintendent who okayed *The History of Our Sol* using Helios workers, he is liable for the lost work, the lost pay, and they want to remove him from his position. Or they want to remind you not to be so political with your work. Either way, it scares you.

Ajax knows nothing about the ship, and when you check the colony logs, there is a ship named the Abraxas due to arrive that day. "They're a supply ship, bringing new upgrades," you're told. You almost tell the Command Centre to let them know, so they can alert Ajax. But what will you say? Will you tell them he's about to be arrested? You take your finger off the button.

You say instead, "Can you patch me through to the Abraxas?"

"I'm sorry, I can't."

"It's an emergency."

"Only authorized personnel can use the communications. I'm sorry, Mr. Renault."

You understand. This is the limit of your face.

Something grips you: you need to tell him personally.

Marie's panic, her fear, passes like lightning to you, and you don't even take off your painter's smock; you just put on a jacket. That same frenetic lightning makes you leave your dom and walk to the main shuttle platform to borrow a sitejet.

You've been outside the base before. You've been down in the crevice before. You know exactly where they'll be. And when you get close enough, the link in the suit will connect with them.

"I need to do some work on the surface," you tell the dock crewman who comes up to you to ask what you're doing. The privilege you have carries you, even when it's reckless. You tell the command centre and they ask the same question when you leave the base. "Just going out to paint the crevice."

You've flown a sitejet before, to do paintings above the surface of Ganymede, to fly around the outside of the buildings. You know what you are doing.

They ask if you want someone to go with you because, sir, you're not experienced enough to do this alone.

"Oh, I don't want to bother you. You've been so helpful in the past, but I think I'll just be taking some preliminary scans. Shouldn't be more than an hour."

Your plan is to sit at the edge of the crevice and wait for Ajax and his crew to come back up. You'll catch them first. You fly to the crevice, where the elevators run down like droplets. Many of them are, of course, ninety-five kilometres below with the team. You land the ship not too far from the other transports.

If you were a more competent pilot you would fly down the crevice to the dais below, but you are not that confident about your skills in a dark, tight crevice.

You'll sit and wait, watching the black carpet of stars above you fall until you are asleep.

⁂

When you wake, the grey shape of the Abraxas comes into view above, like a floating tool in the dark cosmic sky, as it makes its way to dock with the Aethon Mining Colony. You decide that you cannot wait any longer.

It is now a race.

You will take an elevator. They took elevators, after all. Most of them are safe. You remember that occasionally they are not.

You suit up. Your hands flutter over the straps, the helmet, turning on breathable air. You can hear Ajax's voice: *You shouldn't be doing this when you're upset. You'll make a mistake.*

"You would have wanted me to tell you before they landed," you say.

Yes, you need to warn Ajax. You also need to be with him—this

163

uncontrollable urge not to be pulled apart. *Good things don't come back*, you hear Ajax say. This time it will be Ajax that's taken from you. But now, you'll go with him. You'll stand by his side and your face, that lucky, privileged, celebrity face of yours, will buy his freedom, even if you have to use every last ounce of your influence.

You shake getting in the elevator, stomping on the metal floor, connecting to it with your magboots. *How did we get here?* You punch in Ajax's code, hoping he forgives you. You've seen him operate the controls maybe ten times but you weren't watching the details. You were almost always looking out the window at the huge crevice walls, the layers of rock and ice. You said before, how they tell the history of this planet in ledger lines, an accounting of the build-up of ice over billions of years; of rock; of impact.

It's a language, you'd said.

"It's definitely a story," Ajax had replied.

So the buttons on the console that seemed so simple are not. You may have touched some of them two or three times. Finally, something moves, the whole elevator jolts a little, and you remember Ajax saying that some of the elevators gave bumpier rides than others. Because of corrosion.

You can see Ajax saying, "They've promised us upgrades."

But the water and air business was so good. Everyone in space needs water and air. Especially this far out.

The elevator moves down slowly—too slowly. Ajax hit a button to make it speed up. You can see outside the window if the other elevators are coming up. You can't yet communicate with anyone below.

Slowly you descend. At this pace, the trip will take you four or five hours to get through the crust and arrive on the dais below.

The buttons are carefully, logically marked. You just have to be smarter than the elevator. You press what you think is the speed, but you're jolted, and realize you hit the directional buttons; up and increase look the same, you think.

The elevator crawls to a stop. You could be just a few miles into the crevice.

You hear Marie's voice in your head: *You are not a miner.*

You press the down arrow. There is rattling and scraping and resistance. It doesn't sound good. Then a big jolt frightens you. Then no movement.

"In emergencies like this," Ajax would say, "you call Command Centre and they send a sitejet."

And they will rescue you. Maybe they can take you down into the crevice—just one person. You realize now that taking one person along was not such a bad idea.

You use your communication link and call the Command Centre. "I've gotten myself stuck in an elevator," you say sheepishly.

"We'll be right there, Mr. Renault. Just hold tight." And you know they will be scrambling because it's you in danger. How embarrassing. What were you doing?

Still, you think, when they come you will convince the pilot that you need to go into the crevice.

It's a failure of your name, your face, if it can't warn the person you love that danger is coming.

You sit down and wait, and you imagine there will be a trial, and that you will testify, and that the men will testify. You practice what you might say as if speaking to a jury, and the jury is the crevice.

The window outside provides you with a good view of the crevice wall. It is a magnificent, talkative piece of art. You can follow the years down; the ice layers, the rock layers, the dark mica and the clear, reflective quartz sparkling like a diamond. It is the long history of Ganymede. You can almost hear it competing with your own narrative.

"Why did I do it?" you answer a judge that is not there. "Your honour, the case against Ajax is not that which should be tried, but the case against Helios is. They neglected their miners."

Surely any jury in the world could see that, you say to the crevice. It speaks back to you in billions of years. Your moments mean nothing to it.

As the solar system formed, it was here, gathering layers, the ice and the rock and the mica and the sand and the frozen ground all nestling together to form a layer. What does it matter, the crevice says?

You press your hands against the clear window, appealing to the jury. "We matter."

The elevator leans sideways, groans. You fall against the wall to your right, against the door you entered, which is closer to being a floor now, as it is pressed against the crevice. You don't move.

You look outside and see a shadow fly across the crevice wall, like an eagle looking for Ganymede. It's the sitejet. The pilot hovers outside the elevator with a look of horror on his face. You wave, trying to get his attention.

Your communication link clicks on. "Mr. Renault? It is you."

"Something happened to the elevator," you say.

"Mr. Renault, just sit tight," the man says. He flies around the elevator, comes back and hovers in front of the window. "I can't dock with the door. But I can take apart the panels on the top of the elevator. I'm just going to call this in, get some help. We'll cut you out if we have to. Just don't move very much if you can help it."

"I'll root myself to the floor."

And you do. You breathe in and think that it's all going to be good. Things happen for a reason. You look through the window at the crevice. *I've been waiting for six billion years for you to see me like this*, it seems to say. It's all you can see; you can't see the stars from where you're seated.

Accidents happen all the time. They don't choose who to affect based on income or importance, or race or creed or gender. They are the great leveller. They are random, though you increase your chances of having an accident when you go to a dangerous place, board an elevator of dubious condition; when you've panicked and allowed fear to take control. You have been to fifty-three memorial services in eight years and you can remember the details of each one. Most of them were young men and women; a few were supervisors and foremen. Many were knowledgeable, professional, the best at their jobs. Some of them had shoddy equipment. Some of them made mistakes. Some of them had "an unfortunate circumstance." The injured in the infirmary were broken in much the same way. This was a dangerous place. Marie was right.

You look up at the beautiful crevice and it seems to be reaching out to you, coming closer, but then you know it's not the crevice but the elevator that's moving.

You are going to fall.

"Something's happening," you say to the Command Centre.

"Mr. Renault, we are grappling the elevator with claws—"

The elevator shifts, but not up.

It falls, slowly, because the gravity is lighter here—only a tenth of Earth gravity. But you are aware that you are not in the claws of an eagle.

The drop is sheer. It never makes contact with the edge of the crevice.

You can look out the window and read the whole story now, travelling slowly by—the whole history of Ganymede. It was as if you were running down the crevice. I could survive this, you think. You're only going about nine miles an hour—that's just running.

But you are falling, and falling inside something that weighs 2000 pounds at a tenth of Earth's gravity. You can't be sure of things like survival.

You say into the communication link, "Please tell Ajax—" But you hear static and then a pop and the link disappears.

You pull yourself in a little. The elevator is not turning but falling flat because the backside of the elevator weighs the most. So you sit on the wall and pull your arms and hands in close to watch the last movie of Ganymede on the window in front of you. You figure you have three hours.

You put your hands into your jacket and feel something wet. You look down at your hand. Is it blood? No, it is brown.

It is burnt umber.

You lean over the floor and you paint. When you look up, you see the sitejets beside you, trying to match your speed. Three of you are falling now, drifting really, like a snowflake falls, down into the crevice. You are your own floating city, rapidly descending into the deep ocean of a moon.

They say they saw you painting on the way down. They considered flying a ship under you and letting the elevator piggyback on the ship, but you were too close to the edge and they couldn't get the wings of the sitejet under you, no matter how they tried. They feared causing the elevator to turn.

You were still going too fast to make that manoeuver safely.

Another sitejet hovered over you, trying to lock on and slow your speed. They scratched the surface of the elevator and it wobbled. They pulled up.

If you hit the ocean below, it might not break the elevator; however, below every elevator was a long, connected steel dais—a platform used for haulers who took the salt water out to the loading bay.

There's a discussion about grappling hooks that you never hear, and if suddenly grabbing the elevator would knock you around, if it might hit the crevice. All you hear is the sudden slam of metal on metal, and the elevator jerks and you are thrown into the ceiling. You can see through the window as it scrapes the side of the crevice. You'll never see how much, but it leaves a mark several hundred metres wide, the swing of it, as the sitejet tries to pull the elevator up.

That scrape is your part of Ganymede's story.

And it tears open the elevator and you fall through.

When they get the ship up top and set the elevator down, gently, they notice the scrape has cut into the side of the elevator. And when they open the ship, you are gone, having dropped out of the elevator somewhere along the way.

But against the wall, they see a painting.

You loved that last hour inside the elevator. You had burnt umber and phthalocyanine blue and yellow cadmium light and titanium white in your pockets, but no brush. So, with a smile, you finger painted, just like you did when you were a child, and you smiled and you cried and you thought not in a million years has any artist been given this opportunity, to paint in freefall on the side of an elevator through a crevice on Ganymede.

Outside, Ganymede tells its own story. *Look where I began!* And the years pass by so quickly, thousands of them in a moment. *Look what I've endured!*

Inside, you told your story. Because you wanted so badly to be with Ajax, you painted him on the wall, his arms around you, and you were both looking back at you, the painter, as if they were watching you in some alternate moment. They were content, in their dom in Aethon. You lightened the blue to make Ajax's hand, tight around your arm, his other hand resting on your leg. You painted with your whole hand that middle darkness of Ajax's chest, as if you were touching him, and you could feel him.

You cried, but you kept painting, these two men who were content with the eight years they had. You didn't have to say it—even if they didn't hear what you wanted to say over the comm, they would see it here. These two men, oh they loved each other, you saw that and wished you could save them both. And you looked up to the crevice wall, the years passing by, sobbing, tears streaming down your face, and you turned back to your painting and placed the words *Still Life with Ajax*, because it will make him laugh.

You rejected *Falling in Love All Over Again* out of good taste.

For Marie you wrote *The Work is Complete*.

For the courts you wrote that you were responsible for the men and women who participated in *The History of Our Sol*.

If you were lucky, you could just stay here against this wall and the fall would not destroy the painting. Acrylic dries quickly.

The sound of metal hitting metal happened above, and then the lurch of the elevator, upending you. The scrape happened right under you.

Your helmet was broken and breached, and all the air from around you disappeared like a breath, even as you slid through the cut in the elevator and fell into the mouth of Ganymede.

You hold your breath.

You fall so much slower now, about as fast a person walks. You can't reach out to the wall to slow your speed; it's too far. The sitejets don't know they've dropped you. Above, they carry the elevator and your art to safety.

If no one came for you, if you did not run out of breathable air, you would have eight hours to fall. It is as close to flying as you may ever get. You take the paint tubes in your hands, unscrewing the caps, and squeeze out the paint, which falls up above you and stays, almost stationary, and you leave an air trail of blue, yellow, brown, and white. You squeeze them hard, getting every last ounce of colour and paint out of them. If you weren't going to die, this would be the most enjoyable, and most unusual time you've ever had painting.

There's not enough oxygen or atmosphere on Ganymede for a human to breathe, and so you suffocate, the tubes leaving your hands, finally, squeezed empty of all colour.

You don't see the sitejet, how it hovers next to you, putting a wing under your body and letting you fall there so that you don't have to make the rest of the journey down into Ganymede. Someone climbs from the sitejet onto the wing to retrieve you, pull you inside the cramped two-person sitejet. They pull your helmet off, call your name, but they can't resuscitate you. Quickly, they ascend out of the Mouth, hoping to get you to the infirmary in time, startled when they suddenly meet some of the blue, the yellow, the brown, and the white on its way down, marking the sitejet in ribbons of colour.

Together, your first big posthumous show, is in Antigone. Marie has asked Ajax for your work, but Ajax won't let it go unless he comes with it—he can't be separated from your work now. The miners also ask to bring the work you did personally for them, and in the wake of this Sol-wide tragedy, Helios participates in full, even sponsoring the show, else they might be implicated in the killing of the famed painter Renault. Of course, charges are dropped against Ajax. How can they prosecute the man whom Renault loved?

The men and women who were part of *The History of Our Sol on the Arms that Built It* are the keepers of the last great masterwork ever done by Renault, and so these miners are celebrated, envied. Their images are every- where, as if, in some way, they hold a spirit of Renault, and they will never lack for support or money. They bare their torsos and arms for the Antigone show, and tell not only how they lived as miners but also how they lived and knew Renault. People come to touch them, to touch the *History of Our Sol*, to be a part of it, too. Several of these miners eventually become artists and begin travelling through the cities, painting the people, and wherever they go, they are feted in the Orange Buddha, in Greystokes, at Atlantis Hall.

In the Grand gallery at Antigone, the paintings fill the space. Everything else is put away to make room for the definitive Renault show—your last eight years. Outside the venue, protected by a barrier, is the sitejet dubbed the *Chariot of Elijah*.

They will bring the elevator panel, not the whole elevator, grisly as it is. When they place it on a wall, it is a reflective surface inside which people can find themselves reflected as the artist had been. And those patrons of the arts, both the wealthy and the not so wealthy, find their reflection just above yours and imagine that they are you.

It brings the miners and the mining executives and the art world together, just as you hoped it would. You should have seen them meeting each other—awkward handshakes, first conversations, seeing that the subjects of the paintings were wandering around them. The barrier between art and life had been removed, as no one could tell if they weren't walking inside a Renault.

Your body was brought back to Paris for a memorial service, and sunsailed ships gathered at sunset like a flock of birds around the Arc du Triomphe, spreading across the city in remembrance of you.

You loved spectacle. You were spectacle. And everything you touched became spectacle. If you were owned by the art world, then you wanted them to take ownership of the things that mattered: people and love.

It is hardest on Ajax and Marie. Marie remembers what you said, that after you died, they would forget about the miners. As executor of your will, she fights for your wishes to make the miners the recipients of your future sales percentages, with Ajax having the largest percentage and the miner's union and their families with the rest. Inside her heart, she wonders if her message to you contributed to your death. Ajax reassures her that she did the right thing, and that no one could have stopped you from doing anything you wanted to do. At what point did she think she still had control?

Ajax treats her as you would have, as his daughter, staying with her while he is there, dining with her, sharing all your stories. And there are a lot of stories. "It's difficult to see his face everywhere," he confesses. "Famous people are the most famous when they die." But he hasn't really had a chance to say goodbye.

After three weeks of staying with your show in Antigone, Ajax wants to leave, and begs the gallery for the elevator panel and the paintings that you made for him. Because they are so personal; he can see your body everywhere in Antigone, your face, and it is hard for his grief to be so public right now. He just wants to be alone with you. But the show is so successful that crowds will come for weeks to see it, from all over the system, and Eustachi knows that. It's already been booked, they say. You've lent these pieces for the duration of the show, especially the elevator panel, his last conscious work. There is a tug of war over your body of work, about who owns it—who owns you—and the Ajax that fought for miners' rights is forced to fight for his own.

Until Marie steps in as your agent, as representative of Eustachi, to let those pieces go.

"But what if he never brings them back? What if no one can ever see those pieces again?" they ask.

"There were always parts of him you never had," Marie says to them.

They place pictures of his work in a commemorative retrospective, and in a book of the show titled *Together*, and on Marie's suggestion they don't ask if they will ever see these works again. Marie helps Ajax lift the elevator panel from the wall, and helps him take the other few paintings that he owns from the gallery.

He will take the elevator panel back to Aethon and he will sit and look into it, for hours some nights, to try and say goodbye, which slowly turns into good night. Sometimes he'll look to see his reflection in your face, to try and understand what you found in him that was so good that you'd leave the rest of the solar system behind to spend it with him, together.

For a Look at New Worlds

*"Every generation has an obligation to free men's minds
for a look at new worlds . . . to look out from a higher
plateau than the last generation."*
—Ellison S. Onizuka

Benji Onizuka stood in front of his great great-grandfather's memorial. A swirl of brightly coloured paper cranes flew around the twenty-seven-foot-high copy of the Space Shuttle Challenger, the brass base, the face of Ellison S. Onizuka. As if caught in a beautiful pastel tornado of little wings, the monument had its picture taken from hundreds of different angles. If Benji wanted to reproduce this on Mars, he'd need multiple shots for the holographic display to work with.

His mother and daughter stood a ways behind him as he worked, not wanting to be in the way. A holographic sika fawn stood beside Benji's daughter, Naia, and looked around the square, as if watching the people go by. Naia, only five, spoke to it softly, saying, "Non't be scared. No one's gonna hurt you. Non't be scared."

His mother, Sharlet, watched Benji go round and round the memorial and sighed.

"I just want to get it perfect, Mom," Benji said. "I'll only get this one chance before I go."

He watched the 3D picture form in front of him on his tablet, controlling the crane-drones, making sure they didn't miss even the smallest fraction of the memorial.

She said, "Make sure you get plenty of shots of the base, too—there's a lot of information there."

"Yep, I'm all over it." He kneeled down and guided the swirl of paper cranes downward, around the base, to get pictures of Ellison S. Onizuka, mission specialist, who died in the Challenger explosion in 1985. His bronze face was smiling, and Benjirou felt as if this time, Onizuka was smiling on him.

Naia handed the deer an invisible apple; it was programmed to come to her hand and nibble on the invisible food. Other people walked by on Onizuka Street, past the shops, their shirts wildly animated and moving, sometimes too much for Sharlet Onizuka to look at. She wanted to look at things that were still, calm, peaceful.

She looked forward to visiting the Japanese gardens later today. She was sure that Benjirou would take pictures there as well. *Another something to capture and take to Mars with him.* Why he wanted to leave her, she didn't understand.

"Okay, I think I got it all," he looked up at the Challenger statue, which pointed toward the sky. "Mr. Onizuka I just want you to know—I'm going up to Mars, and I'm going to live there, but I'm taking you with me."

He looked over at his mother who'd turned away, was looking across the street at the sushi place. He said, "I just wanted you to know how much you inspired me to be an astronaut." He knew his mother wouldn't acknowledge what he was saying; she didn't want to. His wife, Audra, and Naia would join him there in a year, after he put down roots, got a place to live.

Without looking at him, his mother said, "We're not going to get a good seat if we don't hurry."

"Audra's already got them, I'm sure."

"I don't want to be late."

"I know. I just wanted to get this."

He programmed the cranes to fly above Little Tokyo now, to take thousands of pictures and download them simultaneously, so that he could bring Little Tokyo itself to Mars.

"I don't think anyone's brought Little Tokyo yet." Personal drones—even nanodrones—weren't that new, but holographic technology had taken off in the last ten years or so, and most of the Mars colonists had already been settled.

He walked toward her. "I hear they have the Taj Mahal and the Eiffel Tower and the Grand Canyon—but I really want to bring a little of me up there."

These tiny nanodrones could fly all over a place and take this single day of Little Tokyo with them. *My day with my family.* "It's a lot of work," he said aloud.

"You could always stay?" She turned, smiling, knowing it was a futile effort but asking anyway. Who knew? Maybe this time he'd stay.

"Mom," he said. "That's not gonna work."

She looked away. "I didn't wink enough, did I?"

He laughed. "It'll take more than a wink to turn government paperwork around. Let's go see what Audra's doing."

He was an astronaut and a holographic/fabrications engineer. A digital reconstructionist, as he sometimes called himself. Able to create anything, again. Useful in a new colony that needed to build, but couldn't ship the proper materials.

The three of them walked, followed by Naia's sika fawn, past streams of people shopping, talking, eating little bowls of green tea ice cream, their own animated dogs and cats following them. Some had birds that followed them. Signs on the outsides of shops read please turn off holographic projections before entering the store.

Sharlet remembered having a personal drone take pictures of her and her friends when they were teens. They'd stop and pose everywhere. Small drones followed like paparazzi, always looking for your good side.

Nothing like what you could do now—recreating monuments and cities you could walk through. If she were young, would she too want to go to Mars?

She sighed. Little Tokyo was her home.

"I want to go see the ocean wall after the service, after the gardens," she told Benjirou.

"That's all the way in Old Jefferson. We can take the LR."

"The LR is very *fast*," she said, remembering how jostled she felt the last time.

"Well, driving will be too slow. You forget how crowded it is down there. Everyone's going to be walking the ocean wall on a day like today."

⁂

Sharlet had been overjoyed when she heard that she got to take Audra and Naia to live with her for the year as they waited to join Benji on Mars. What happiness that they would be hers! But weighing on her were the years that would follow. She wouldn't see Naia grow up. The rules were pretty strict: if you went to Mars to live, you made a commitment. Naia would have a chance to leave when she was ready for college, but until then, she wouldn't be back to Earth. Would Sharlet even be alive when Naia returned? If Sharlet wanted to see them, she would have to visit on one of the Earth-Mars shuttles and stay six months inside of a shuttle, and then spend a year there on Mars. What was there anyway? There were fewer than 500 people on Mars. It was growing, expanding, but still. She couldn't imagine it. She felt claustrophobic just knowing she'd have to stay inside a bubble for a year.

"Oh, Mom, you don't go much outside of Little Tokyo now. And that's practically the size of the biodome. They have parks. You really don't think of it as being cooped up inside—the dome is so huge. You've seen pictures."

"I would miss the wind."

"They have wind."

"It wouldn't be the same."

Why did they have to move so far away? She used to think that if her children moved to New York City, they would be almost too far away from her. But now, New York seemed like it was across the street compared to where they were going to take her little grandbaby. *The terrible choices our children force us to make*, she thought to herself.

Audra waved at them across the terra cotta-bricked plaza when they arrived for the service. She wore a navy blue dress and motioned to some shaded seats. Some people sat in the sun on white chairs, but many of the older people sat in the shade. The press stood in the aisles, controlling their tiny camera drones.

Across the steps of the stage in front of everyone were racks and racks of real paper cranes—brightly coloured streamers hanging from above, commemorating the short life of Sadako Sasaki following the Hiroshima bombing, and her thousand paper cranes, her wish for peace. Naia and Benji went to the front to look at the cranes with several other people. Sharlet wished that she had folded a thousand paper cranes—she knew her wish.

"He's trying to get every moment with her he can," Audra remarked beside her.

"It's barely a year. That's nothing," Sharlet said.

"Well, considering we can't come back, it's a lifetime."

"I still don't understand why you couldn't just take a shuttle—"

"Mama Sharlet, we told you they're small. Visitors have priority. You can't build a big city on Mars if people keep leaving."

Sharlet nodded. Rightfully so. It was hard to try and build a family anymore. She spoke under her breath. "People shouldn't leave."

It was the 118th Anniversary of the bombing of Hiroshima. This service for peace commemorating that moment was also shared by the Indian, Pakistani, and Chinese people who had been through the short-lived but nuclear South Asian War of 2021. Many of them suffered disfiguring burns, and their children, like Sadako, contracted leukemia. They came because they wanted to pray for unity and peace. Little Tokyo pulled them into the ceremony as if it were always theirs. Later, on the anniversaries of New Delhi, Beijing, and Karachi, the Japanese Americans joined them in prayer as well.

As the ceremony began, Benji re-joined them, but Naia and her sika fawn still walked around the paper cranes, which gave Sharlet no end of worry. "She needs to come sit down."

They tried calling to Naia but she was mesmerized by the sudden procession of religious figures marching out of the glass doors of the Japanese American Cultural & Community Center. Buddhist monks, Muslim imams, Protestant preachers, Catholic priests, representatives from all the major religions in and around Los Angeles came to the service and stood in a line in front of the spectators. Naia and her fawn walked carefully around them, looking up at them, like Sadako herself. Some of them tried to ignore she was there; others nodded to her, as if she were inspecting the troops of prayer.

Are you ready with that prayer? she could have been saying.

Yes, miss, I am ready. My god is ready.

೪ ೪

With the world shrinking, the rising seas and oceans, and everyone crowding closer together, prayers of unity and peace were needed every day, not just once a year. Still, the ceremony reminded everyone that violence was the worst way to solve our differences.

Naia walked back to them casually.

"We do this to remember you," a priest said, speaking to the living and the dead. The interfaith clergy lit butter lamps for peace with a flame that had travelled the long distance from Hiroshima to be with them that day.

Sharlet tried to pray for unity and peace, but felt as if the world, specifically Benji and Audra, had undermined her prayer. How could she pray for unity when he was tearing them apart? How could she find peace when her family was being tossed across the solar system?

Then she heard the bell, the bell from Hiroshima that had rung at 4:15 pm, when the bomb dropped. They rang it again here. A clear sound. A sound of going away. Of launching. Of disappearances. Of sudden goodbyes. Of no goodbyes. It startled her, gripped her, as if her son were leaving right then.

They brought out the mandala then—a beautiful sand painting of blue and orange and startling green, fragile, easy to blow away. The monks who had crafted it invited people to come up now and destroy it.

Many walked up, and with a hundred fingers they carved swaths of themselves across the sand, ruining the beautiful design. The destruction of such beauty was supposed to bring home the price of violence, the pledge for peace. Today, though, it felt as if those fingers had pushed into her heart. She could see the back of Naia, her hand enveloped in the bodies of others, her fingers no doubt clawing through the bright sand. Her fawn looked lost without her, backed away from the crowd and looked around.

Looked at Sharlet.

For a moment, this creature, not really there, studied her, with an expression of so much loss that Sharlet wanted to hold it. But she was sure the fawn would shiver, and when her own hands passed through the deer, she might shiver, too.

❧ ❧

After the ceremony was over and the sand mixed together, placed in a bottle, and given to the great, great, great grandson of Sadako's brother, Audra gathered Naia and Benji together.

But Sharlet wanted to see what was left of the mandala. She walked up after the crowds dispersed and saw what remained: tiny grains of green sand; crumbs on a brown board, on a brown table, in the sun. She ran her finger down the front of the board, just in case a bit of sand might have clung to it. *He's taking all the beautiful things with him.*

Her heart felt like it dropped into a well. Her eyes blurred with tears as she looked down at the erased mandala.

Then something flapped in front of her face. She looked up. In the air around her were a thousand paper cranes flying, their bright colours like a reconstructed mandala in the air. They begged for her, it seemed, to come to them.

"I think I got the whole service!" Benji said from way behind her as the cranes rose.

Could he take the service back to where the mandala was whole again? She turned to look at them, across the terra cotta courtyard, a surface the colour of Martian sand. All she'd known was Little Tokyo. Raised here. Married here. Buried her husband here. Her family was all she had left.

The cranes surrounded Naia.

"Naia," Benji called from outside the colourful whirlwind, "don't touch them. I'm trying to capture you for Gramma. So she can have you to play with."

Like a fawn she couldn't touch.

Would she rather have a holographic granddaughter, or a holographic city?

She could hear something like a bell in the distance.

The cranes flew to her now, surrounded her in a breeze.

"And now you, Momma. Hold still," Benji said.

"Non't be scared, Gramma," Naia called.

A whirlwind of origami birds snapping pictures, scanning her, recreating her like the fingers of the crowd to the mandala. *Don't take it all away, all of this.* A flock of paper flew between her and her family, and she tried to stay still, but they were like insects and she raised her hands to swat them away.

"Hold still, Momma. Almost done," Benji said.

Almost *done.*

Back in her apartment, Benji did the unthinkable—at least to Sharlet.

He built the holographic Sharlet in front of her. She watched it come together: first, tiny grains of sand formed a picture of a woman, then the shape of an older woman, some woman from another time, but so obviously from Little Tokyo—an older woman whose family would eventually leave her completely alone. But this woman smiled. This woman who looked like her turned around, walked across the room, leaned down, and silently waved at Naia. Naia giggled.

"She's perfect, Benji!" Audra said. "Oh, that's a riot! That looks just like you, Mama. What do you think? Isn't she the perfect hologram of you?"

Sharlet crossed her arms and walked into the kitchen. She pulled together tea for everyone—the cups, the hot water in the pot, the tea leaves in the floating metal infuser. Out of the corner of her eye, she saw Audra's hand on the counter. She turned—

—but it wasn't Audra. It was the Sharlet hologram, her mouth open and speaking though no sound came out, looking like someone who went through something horrible, who was trying to tell her something but was unable to speak. She looked lonely. She looked lost.

"No," Sharlet said, slicing the air between them. "No." She left the kitchen and went down the hallway to her bedroom.

Benji yelled after her, "I haven't gotten the voice works, Momma, but there's definitely a way to program certain phrases! Momma?"

She shut her door.

She would only get a year. One year, and then they would be up there on some other planet. They would have a Sharlet, a holographic one, to smile and play with. And she would have a holographic Naia.

There was a knock at the door, Audra's voice. "Mama, we're sorry. We didn't mean to frighten you. I know that must be, well, jarring, to be surprised by yourself."

"It's not me," she says.

"I know it's not you. I didn't mean it that way. Can I come in?"

She doesn't answer at first. She looks out the window at the shadows getting longer outside, the darkness climbing the side of the buildings. "Yes."

Audra came in, walked to the window. "It is a beautiful city."

"He has to turn it off."

Audra nodded. "I'll tell him that."

"I don't want it walking through my house like a—a ghost of me."

Audra touched her arm. "I'm sorry, Mama."

The hologram would go with them, would live with them; would get to watch Naia grow up, get to play with her, get to be part of this family.

"You're all I have left."

"You can still come with us," Audra said.

The cars below stuttered and started, streams of people all trying to get home. She could imagine what each of them was seeing from the windows of their cars. She could imagine what the people walking across the street were seeing, which shops, who would be standing in the doorways. She could envision them smiling at her while she walked to greet them at the market. It was her world.

"I don't think there are new worlds for old people."

"There are other older people going. We could work to get a visa for you. I know they'd say yes."

What would she rather have: a holographic family or a holographic city?

"Everything here is so familiar to me. I know all the people I see."

"I know."

"I don't know if I want a new world. I just don't want you to leave mine."

Audra hugged her. "Oh, Mama Sharlet."

They stood there, holding each other as the room darkened. Sharlet felt her world dissolving around her: the deafening silence, the people she knew fading, the buildings growing fainter, an intense darkness surrounding her like space. All of Little Tokyo flickered, and she was frightened—frightened of it disappearing.

New worlds are for the young. They can create their own traditions and history.

She gripped Audra. She needed them here. To never see Naia till she was a woman. She needed Little Tokyo. She knew this place. It had stories around every doorway. There was too much to leave, too much leaving. He didn't even have half of Little Tokyo in those little birds.

She released Audra, searching her eyes.

Sharlet said it out loud. "He doesn't even have half of it." She found herself surprised at what she was saying. A little excited. "He doesn't have half of Little Tokyo yet," she said to Audra. "And Naia won't have any of it."

Audra waited, nodding slowly. "What do you mean, Mama?"

She walked out of the room, down the hallway with inspiration, and stepped into the living room to see Benjirou looking up at the hologram of Sharlet, as if he were adjusting her to make her more perfect. Sharlet stopped at the door. This was what people must see when they were together—and it gave her an eerie out of body feeling, as if she were walking into her own memory.

"Not even half of it," she said, lifting her hand.

Benji turned. "I'm so sorry, Momma."

On the wall behind him was a map of Little Tokyo as seen by the little birds.

"You have the buildings and the streets, and people walking, but you don't have the stories. That's Little Tokyo." She threw up her hands. "You don't know what it all means, how it all connects. No one will up there—"she pointed to her ceiling "—on Mars."

"Maybe you can come with us and tell us those stories."

The hologram Sharlet looked at him so lovingly, Sharlet thought. *I am not afraid of you.*

"I can tell you the stories, and we can take your birds—they can record, too, yes? I'll take the birds to the grocers and the shops and temple, and I'll take them to the Budokan to talk to the young basketball players, the athletes, and we'll fly them into the homes of my friends, and I'll collect all the stories for you to take."

She looked at Sharlet the Hollow. *You are not even the half of me.*

"I don't want to leave here. I have a life here," she turned to Audra, "in this bubble, and this bubble is important to me. All of my stories are here."

"They're not in a place, Momma," Benji said. "They're inside you."

"When you walk through this house, you can see yourself running here as a boy, can't you? You can see your father chase you into the kitchen. I can. When you walk into your bedroom, you can smell the days you were in high school. I can."

Audra laughed.

Sharlet said, "I don't think the holograms will be enough for me. And if I had to make that choice to let you go to Mars or leave Little Tokyo forever—I have to let you go."

She started to cry because it wasn't what she meant. It sounded so much worse saying it out loud. Why did they have to take something away from her?

She trembled when she said, "But I get my one year. I get that year with you," she glanced at Audra, "and my baby," and she looked down at Naia, who was finger-painting the coffee table digitally. "I can teach her all about Little Tokyo, and we can make recordings of stories—and if you want to put them inside this doll of me." She looked at Sharlet the Doll, the one who looked so alone. *I'm not alone*, she thought. *You're alone because you need stories.* "Then you put them inside her."

That Sharlet faded away. Benji said, "I'll work on her later." He looked at his mother, the real one. "You don't have to make your decision today, Momma. And there's no pressure either way."

Sharlet knelt down beside Naia. "You and Mama Sharlet are going to make Little Tokyo more alive, aren't we, Naia? More alive than it's ever been before to you. You can hold a lot more in your head than some birds, can't you?"

She felt stronger saying what she needed. She would concentrate on making the year educational for Naia, recording the stories of her friends and of the people of Little Tokyo. It would be okay. She could do this. She was too old to make a new life. Benjirou and Audra would be so busy in their new lives there—and Naia would make friends—and this would leave her alone on Mars; she would lose her independence, her familiarity, in the latter part of her life. This was the right decision. She would make the most of the fleeting year.

Naia beamed up at her, "Look at what I made! I made the mandala come back," she said. She pointed to the coffee table with its greens and blues and oranges, a rough rendition of the mandala with doves and a fawn.

"Oh my," Audra said.

"It's beautiful," Sharlet said. "Don't—don't touch it. Can you—" she turned to Benji. "Can you freeze this image on the coffee table?"

Benji thought for a moment, "She's just projecting her Playboard. It's virtual. There's no real way to permanently attach it to the table."

Sharlet put her hands around it, trying to hold on to it.

"Now it's time to run our fingers through it!" Naia said.

"No," Sharlet said, "we're going to try and save this one."

Benji explained, "You'd have to leave her Playboard on. You can save an image on it, which we can transfer to a 3D projector—which I can build for you. We may not be able—"

"No, Naia!" Audra shouted.

But Naia was already running her fingers over the board and the mandala smeared, just as it had before in the plaza under the hands of everyone else. She wasn't mean. She was radiant.

"Don't mess it up!" Sharlet cried, holding her hands to her face.

"I *love* mess it up!" Naia said, smearing it all together in bright swirls.

For a moment, Sharlet thought she had conquered her fear of them going away—and with the erasure of the mandala, she saw again something beautiful she would lose and she began to cry.

Naia looked at her. "Non't cry. We can make another one." She laughed. "And another one. A red one now. And then—" her face held such surprise "—one that looks like *stars*."

They sat around Naia that night, as she created. And, tentatively at first, because each mandala was something so beautiful, so unique, the four of them sat around the coffee table making, and destroying, mandalas all night.

~eeeee~ Brazos

I came out to mend a wooden fence. I figured the cows had knocked the rail over. Maybe the wind jimmied it loose. Then again, seeing the man walk out of the caprock, without a car or anything, and no public road for a good ten miles, I could entertain the notion that some god wanted a conference with me.

It was a hot morning in June, the temps already accelerating. I watched him pass head-high mesquite, his grey felt cowboy hat never touching a branch. He had on jeans and a denim work shirt, but his boots were Tony Lama, and his pants weren't even dusted with dirt or mud. The shirt looked pressed. He must have thought this all charming, like he was playing a role. He leaned on my wooden fence. Smiled a lot. We yapped for fifteen minutes about dry West Texas weather, like we were neighbours, except he had a gleam in his eye. I knew I would lose something. With my wife having moved to Indiana, it was just me and Susan now, and a few hired hands. We'd already lost enough around here. So I tried to calculate just what that loss, this time, was going to be.

While we talked, I watched butterflies fly out of his right palm—one after another, each different than the one before. Kinds I'd never seen. He produced them like a nervous tic. I was supposed to be impressed.

He was so busy being *creative*, he hadn't planned on any of these species actually surviving. There weren't any pairs. Each butterfly, wings testing the wind, tossed itself over my fence.

"This all your land?" he asked, as if he didn't notice the butterflies at all.

"I'm just borrowing," I told him with a smile.

"A hundred acres."

I nodded.

I could tell he didn't care by the way he changed the subject. "So, about your daughter . . ."

"Susan's a bright kid. She's going to college," I said.

"My son's got his eye on her," he said. He looked across the fence, staring at my hundred acres.

"Well aware of that," I said. I still held a hammer in my hand, and I tapped it against the wood.

He looked at me, "And what do you think about that?"

"About your son?"

He summed it all up for me. "About my son, a full-fledged river god, being interested in your bright, college-bound daughter."

I took a moment to think. I already knew what I felt about it. Nothing good ever came from the love affairs of gods. Every young girl got turned into something. I imagined a Susan Savane cactus—a new species—somewhere on my land in a few weeks. Or maybe by refusing, I would be turned into something. My family had been marked already.

"Well, it don't please me none."

He acted shocked. "Have you met my boy?"

"Can't say that I have. Heard he's a little trapped by the Brazos."

"He *is* the Brazos," his dad said proudly.

"Yeah, but he can't leave his river, can he?"

"He's eight hundred and forty miles, the longest river in Texas. His reach extends from New Mexico across the middle of the state, all the way down the Gulf Coast. I don't really think that's trapped, do you? Especially when he's a bit more mobile in that area than you are."

I chuckled. I had him running. "But I can take a truck and drive to Oklahoma."

He looked over the fence as if he liked my land. He changed his strategy. "He can give her everything she wants. A hundred acres, a thousand acres. Waco."

"He can have Waco." I smiled.

"She could have a whole city, or more than half the state."

"Hmm," I nodded. "And that would be impressive. It would. But what happens if it don't work out?"

"Don't work out?"

"Divorce is pretty common around here." Unfortunately, I was the poster child—two, so far. They left me. You move on, survive. "You gods don't have the best reputations for leaving your spouses—girlfriends—with much security."

I was hoping he wouldn't strike me down there, figuring he wanted to win my daughter's favour. That wouldn't happen if he killed her dad.

"Transmutations are unfortunate, but very, very rare. Even then, one gets great things by risking greatly."

"You know, you can jump off the canyon thinking you can fly, but that don't mean it's worth the risk. Some great things aren't."

He'd never gone back to leaning on the fence; he pulled it toward him with one hand. "But it's really not up to you."

"Then why are you talking to me?"

He laughed, like, oh goodness, I had done something clever.

"Your customs. Asking the hand of the daughter from the father."

"Usually that's a job for the interested boy. Not his dad."

He looked at me hard. "If you'd come down, I'm sure my son would ask you himself."

"I'm sure he would."

He tried to find something cracking in my eyes, and I wasn't gonna give him anything, especially not my daughter.

❧ ❧

I was *pretty* sure she didn't love him. She came back from a Baylor weekend all flustered by this charming guy she'd met, told her what beautiful skin she had, how he could see that she had a beautiful soul—like an aura around her. He'd appeared beside the suspension bridge, rising on the top of a waterspout, his arms out wide. Asked her if she and her friends from Lamesa High wanted to go swimming. He'd heard them talking on the riverwalk, loved her voice, her laugh. He'd *touched* her, too. In the water, she could feel something warm try to get under her swimsuit, like the water itself was curious. On a calm day, waterspouts danced on the surface of the river, and he picked her up in one and spun her about till she got dizzy. Nearly puked, she said. He was cute, except for that. Golden hair. Wide chin. Muscles. She'd heard stories about him. About a couple of the other gods he hung around with, Whit and Leon, how they partied with naiads.

"Why would he want someone like me?" she asked me over breakfast.

"'Cause you're smart and beautiful, and he can have any naiad he wants, but he wants something he can't get." I stacked pancakes on a plate for her.

"What if he gets me and it turns out . . ." she said, and I looked back at her. She bit her lip. She looked like she was seven all over again.

"That he leaves you?" I said.

She looked away, over into the living room, toward the fireplace where things are burned. "I'm not as strong as you."

"You survived."

"Is *that* what this is?" she said quietly. She didn't mean it as a jab. "I want someone who will stay for sure. Gods are fickle."

I wanted to tell her that everyone was a bet for leaving, that you couldn't tell it in their face, or their laugh, or any moment that you took them to the lake. They could lie there on a blanket and tell you that they couldn't imagine another face next to them but yours. They could rub sunscreen on your shoulders and talk about how full of peculiar habits you both would be when you were old. They could stand in front of a preacher and say the words that they would use on you as a binding contract, but for them it would just be a day's thoughts, as changeable as a sunset sky on a summer evening. To escape you, they could explain all their previous decisions perfectly.

"Honey, I don't want you to give up on regular people because of your mother. I *do* want you to think twice about being the girlfriend of a god. They don't treat us equally. They can run us over. It's not a good spot for anyone." I put the pancakes in front of us and we prayed quickly to the other god, the one who let these lesser ones run amuck; who couldn't control wives and mothers, either, and we doused the pancakes and prayers in syrup.

She said Brazos had kissed her. It was really slobbery. She smiled.

"What do you expect from a river god?" I winked at her.

She had plans to go to Purdue. We'd talked about it. I was going to help pay her first three years. She promised to get a scholarship to help out, and a job in her senior year, and I said that was great. But she glowed when she talked about him.

"He liked me, Dad."

"A lot of guys like you."

"But he's a *god*."

"Which means he's trouble."

"But it means something else, too."

Still, she didn't write him or call his waterproof cell. The last few weeks she wouldn't really leave her room except to go to school. I looked at her face. She was afraid of everything, as if we lived on a frozen lake and every step might cave the whole thing around her. She needed someone. Sure, I wanted to give her a river god. He had the power to protect her if he wanted. But would he protect her from himself?

I remembered all my myths. Nobody came out unchanged.

His dad—and I didn't really know what god he was, except that he could make little lonely butterflies—stood in front of me and gold coins appeared out of his palm, one after another, dropping to the ground on my side of the fence.

"College is expensive these days," he said.

I didn't answer.

"Two good schools on the Brazos: Baylor and Texas A&M. Susan would do well at either—two of the best schools in Texas. I'd make sure she got her medical degree."

"Susan doesn't need your help."

"You do."

The coins slapped each other on the ground.

He said, "You expect to afford a good college on what you're making? You know you can't, that she'll have to take out loans, work when she should be studying. I wish you could see that this is an opportunity. Brazos loves your girl. He's smitten. Just last week, he was so distracted thinking about her, he ran backwards for three hours! She hasn't called him. It's been a whole month and he's just feeling tortured. Some of his forks and bends are drying up. As a father yourself, you must know how hard this is, to watch your kid going through this."

The coins made a pile at my feet. I looked down and back up, and he smiled at me.

"They met for a weekend," I said. "That's puppy love."

"Maybe so. But you could drive Susan down there and meet him for yourself. See if it's a weekend fling—or if it has the potential to be *everlasting*."

Now he offered immortality. He was getting desperate. I knew the stories—and the immortality often ended up being a constellation in the sky, something too far to ever visit. Funny that you have to give up life to become immortal. I look up there and see everything this world has lost. And I don't want to see Susan.

"No. I have a better idea. Why don't your boy come up?"

"He can't—as you've so boldly pointed out."

"Well, let's see. He's a god without the powers to go get the woman he loves. That's pretty tragic. Lowly, powerless humans would sacrifice anything to be with the ones they love. And your kid's a god?"

"Your point?" he asked. The coins had stopped falling from his palms. The sky above us clouded up and it looked like another storm was coming.

I figured this was him.

"When I think of a good match for my daughter, I think of a hardworking boy. Someone willing to stick with her when the going gets rough, not someone who's used to calling in dad for a favour, or turning her into a tree or a rock or the Possum Kingdom Dam."

"That was a journalist."

"It doesn't matter who it was. It's behaviour that I don't think makes for a good husband."

The grass on my side of the fence began to turn brown and wither in a half-circle around his feet. I was playing with fire, I knew it. I remembered Tammy, who became a drive-in theatre, and her family transformed into Dairy Queens all along Interstate 180. They popped up overnight, even as her family disappeared. My daughter needed stability, not power.

A wind kicked up over the caprock, rushed at me.

He opened his arms wide, much like I figured the boy did for Susan when they first met. It was a magnanimous, easy gesture. "Where I come from," he said, "there are whole forests—tall blackjack oaks and willows, bright yellow flowering dogwood, huge pines, and in between, there are secret prairies covered in wildflowers. We got lakes stocked with fish—largemouth bass, crappie, and catfish. You can see chickadees darting from tree to tree, waxwings singing cantatas, whip-poor-wills calling out from the forests of the night. It's beautiful and lush. We're offering the *better* side of the state." He sighed. "Forgive me for being honest, but your side has always seemed like a dirt floor to me, more for sweeping—" He looked through me, behind me, and the vision of West Texas scorching behind me made me turn, just to reassure myself that it wasn't all gone "—than for growing anything."

"It grew the girl your son loves. Now, that's ironic."

He stayed calm. The world around him bubbled and thrashed. He knew I knew where it was all coming from. He smiled, laughed a little. Then he paused and breathed out, reworked his pitch. He opened his palm again and this time water poured out. "Your side is such a dry, dry place. A family married to a river god could pull some weight on Mount Locke. You wouldn't have to bargain with the water-hogs of West Texas, the ones you rent from to irrigate. You know what they say about West Texas—the rich ones are the ones with water, not oil."

I was tired of him. I grabbed his palm, stuck a finger over the stream of water. It splashed against my hand. I was fast. He didn't know what to think; he didn't strike me. "See this palm—it's got no marks on it. Things come out of it, but nothing marks it." I opened my own palm and placed it in his. "Now, mine is different. See the cracks, like a map with rivers in it. I stuck my hand in this land and pulled out what I needed. Wound barbed wire fences. Hauled mesquite. Planted cotton and maize and sorghum. I created these hands, mister, and these hands created life—my life. What have your son's hands done? I'd like to see them. I know he has arms to reach out and grab my daughter, but what do his *hands* look like?"

"My son doesn't need to work with his hands like you do. It is the privilege of being a god that I offer your daughter—and, by association, your family. You won't have to work that hard again."

"That's too easy. I ain't selling my daughter for some time off. Your son's going to have to work harder than that if he wants Susan."

"I can approach Susan, you know."

"You can try." I pulled on one of the boards of the fence, the fence I built, and by moving that particular rail, the one he'd been leaning on fell down, nearly got his foot. It was mechanical magic. I meant to show I was a threat. Even if I ended up being the next strip mall on the Lubbock Highway, I wasn't going to let him near Susan.

Thunder in the distance.

"But," I said firmly, "he can come up and see her."

"He can't do that and still *be* the Brazos."

"So he wants her to do all the sacrifice. If he wants her—if he truly loves her—he'll find whatever way he can. As a god yourself, I'm sure you know of some way."

Clouds swarmed, blanketing us in black.

He said, "To leave the river, he would have to become human."

I nodded. "There are worse fates."

"He was meant to be a god."

"My daughter was meant to have a normal, stable life."

"He loves her."

"How much?"

"You have no right to ask."

I leaned back, made like I was going to my truck. "Maybe you can see this as a window of opportunity. I need some help on the ranch. All we have is irrigation, as you pointed out, but he's welcome to come help out this summer. Let me meet him. Let him get his hands dirty. Dry. He'll learn a lot about Susan seeing her here, seeing where she came from. That should be important to him."

"You would expect him to give up everything on the *chance* that it may work out? What's he supposed to do if it doesn't?"

I got back into my truck, rolled down the window, escaping the raindrops falling around us, a whole sheet of it above me, ready to descend. I rested my hand on the steering wheel, getting ready to start the truck, make a slow getaway. The band of paler flesh around my ring finger was almost the same tan as the rest of my hand.

"Live. He's supposed to live."

Awake, Gryphon!

By candlelight, the monks roused Prince Lha from sleep, slipping on his sandals, even as the palace walls shook around them. They tossed a robe on him; one of the monks had a crown in his hand, another a cylinder of sketchings, and, as a flock of swallows turned in the air, they flew with him out of the prince's bedroom and into the dark marbled hallway.

Blasts rocked the palace; heavy shouts came through every window. The prince could see firelight and smoke ripple the air, climbing and twisting like vines outside the window.

"My father is home?" the prince asked as he ran. He was only nine. Two of the monks flanked him in order to hide him from view, a third followed close behind.

Vedic Buseil told him, his face pitying and long. "Your father is dead. Your brothers and sisters are dead. All of them were killed on the plains of Solobar, by the Horde and the Varidian Army."

The Vedic continued before the boy could react. "We are taking you to the catacombs for safety. The Horde is outside the gates of the city; the Varidian Army is not far behind. When they come together, the city will be taken and sacked, and they must not find you or the Wisdom you now carry," and he looked at the boy again, "O King."

Lha stumbled when he heard the words. "I'm not king." He began to cry. "I'm not king. I have eight brothers and five sisters—" he wept. His palms were cooled touching the marble floor. He laid his forehead against it and cried.

Where was the Wisdom? If his father were truly dead, if all of his brothers and sisters had perished, then the Wisdom would come to him, but he didn't feel it. "You will feel sure about every decision because eight generations of kings' knowledge will be in your head," his father had told him. "But you don't have to worry about this because you will probably never be king."

The monks surrounded him, their dark blue robes like the curtains of his bed, leaning down, perhaps wanting to carry him. The Vedic pushed through them and knelt in front of him, softly cupping his chin and raising it. A tear ran down the Vedic's face. "I know. I know this is hard. But you're the last of the king's children, and we have to get you to safety. We can mourn below. We can't stop now."

They would hide him in the catacombs under the Holy City, catacombs that led back into the mountains behind them. The monks would stay and guard the temple for as long as they could. The boy archers would launch a flurry of arrows, all they had until they were gone.

The Wisdom had not come to him yet.

He was sure of that. He would know more, know what to do *right now*. He wouldn't be frightened. He'd be able to command the armies. Tell people what to defend. What strategies to use. He would lean across a map with little dolls and know where to place them.

"You won't ever have to worry about this," his father had told him. "But if the Wisdom comes to you, you will have the memories of all the kings before you, all their Wisdom in your head. Each king is wiser than the last, and nothing is ever lost. You are suddenly sure—of all decisions."

Lha was not sure of anything.

They raced out into the raucous main courtyard, a brown surge across the stones. Smoke. Fire. Everything became louder.

There, he saw the archers, boys, hurrying into their armour, clanking, scraping. Their thin arms shackled in the metal; faces just waking, wiping sleep from their eyes. Long torches stood around the courtyard, flickering as the boys scattered, unprepared. They yelled to one another. If Lha looked over the wall, would he see a line of fire, the face of the Horde?

A catapulted stone flew over their heads as they ducked, and it smashed into the courtyard, opening it to the floor below. The whole courtyard rumbled and swayed. The Vedic rushed him back into the kitchens, the paths masked in smoke and dirt and debris. He heard the high sharp whine of arrows being released. Would he be able to take a bow as these boys did? One boy turned to fill his quiver, and caught the king's eye. His expression flat, lips set, eyes following the new king, and the king could not break the stare, like a flash of lightning had burned the boy's expression into his eyes. As the sounds of metal arrows rattling in metal buckets receded, and boys' shouts faded, Lha felt separated from his kingdom, headed for safety.

As they entered the hall behind the kitchens, a strong voice called from behind them. "King!" and then, "Lha!" The monks could not stop. It was Kargas, Lha's tutor. He ran after them, catching up to them as they ducked down a stairwell. Lha ran his hand along the stones just to keep his balance.

Vedic Buseil scolded, "Where have you been? He's been *alone*."

Kargas ignored everyone but the young king. At the bottom of the stairs, they ran into a passageway that would lead even further into the catacombs. They stopped to catch their breaths.

Kargas stood, silhouetted, as much shadow as man, his long sword in a sheath on his back, beard masking his face. Lha ran to him and put his arms around him—a boy, really only a boy, not a king, not now. Behind Kargas, Vanel, the boy's nurse, stood in the shadows. She reached out and touched his bare hand, the one wrapped around Kargas. Surely Kargas would know what to do. Surely Vanel would have a plan.

Kargas held him for only a moment. "Your majesty, I had to assess the danger," he said, pulling the boy from him and kneeling to look him in the face. "The Variden and the Horde are attacking together. Our armies were overwhelmed. I'm so sorry about your brothers and your father."

"The king put you in charge of his life!" Buseil roared.

Kargas spoke slowly, without breaking eye contact with Lha. "That king is dead. I am here with the king." And then to Lha, "Do you have a plan?"

Lha could tell that Kargas was searching for the Wisdom in his eyes. Yes, it should have happened while he was still sleeping. The great spiritual consciousness, the Wisdom that his father carried, that had been carried for generations. It should have come to him. He could see they all looked for it. He began to weep again—tried to hold himself back, to be stronger in front of Kargas.

How could he tell them that the Wisdom of his father had not come to him? That he felt no wiser than he did the night before, when he had been drawing images of soldiers in battle, imagining war. Those drawings had come to life, raced now like water across the land.

"We should," the young king began, choking, seeing if he could find the Wisdom, "bring all the people in the Holy City into the catacombs." He remembered the young archers on the wall. "We will save *everyone*."

Kargas looked surprised. "Will you leave no one in the city to defend it?"

"Everyone should be saved." It was a boy's voice that came from his mouth.

Kargas looked at him, then back at Buseil. "Could a brother be alive?"

"No, we know they are—we know. The Wisdom will come to him."

Kargas smiled weakly, brushed back Lha's hair. "You're still asleep. King Lha, let the archers protect the city, the monks defend the kingdom. If we all run, who would save the city?"

The boy looked up at the great orange mosaic that ran the length of the ceiling, down the halls of the Holy City, colour so far out of reach. "The Gryphon," he said suddenly. "The Gryphon will defend the city."

As soon as he said it, he knew it must be the truth. Surely, the Gryphon would choose to help them this time. Was this the Wisdom finally come? Yes. This was the insight that would save his people.

When he thought of the Gryphon, he imagined walking to it, and the great Gryphon would fold his wings around him. He would say, *Nothing will harm you, son.*

Kargas shook him. "No, that is not Wisdom speaking."

Buseil touched Kargas' arm. "Remember, the boy is king. There will come a moment when you have to decide—" The palace shook. Dust came down above their heads.

"Waking the Gryphon is not Wisdom," Kargas told the Vedic. "This city's kings have an *obsession* with that creature. That *corruption* of a holy gryphon! Breathing sunlight, judging souls. You know he can't be trusted." He turned to Lha. "Remember your history, your majesty—all that I taught you about your fathers and grandfathers, the kings of the Holy City. Every time a king tried to rule with the Gryphon at his side has been disastrous. He turns on us in battle. He judges whom he wants to judge. Every king has made that mistake once, but you, you are not going to make that mistake." He touched the boy's face.

Lha trembled. "What if the Wisdom is telling me I should wake the Gryphon?"

Kargas paused, looked at the Vedic. "It doesn't make sense for Wisdom to repeat mistakes—your father would know that."

"We will lose the City!" the king said.

"We may lose the city, yes. But cities can be rebuilt. We cannot lose the Wisdom."

The monks looked at Kargas. He gestured for several of them to leave, and with a thunder of moving robes the monks ran down the hall, their reflections on the marble floor flapping like a flock beneath their feet. With them ran all of Lha's hopes of saving anyone else.

He cried out, "Am I king or *not*?" His voice echoed in the hall.

The monks stopped and turned.

The boy shouted again. "Do you believe I hold the Wisdom or not?"

The king looked at them with his nine-year-old eyes. Kargas pulled him to his side. "Your majesty, they defend the city."

Kargas yelled at the monks to go. Buseil looked torn, as if he fought to stay, as if maybe he was thinking about their options.

Kargas said, "I will take him to the catacombs. Go!"

"The Gryphon has a lot more to offer than his strength," Buseil said.

"There's no time to bribe the Variden. They just want revenge. Once the Gryphon is dead, the Horde will take the gold. We have nothing to offer them, Buseil. Defend the city—while we have it."

Kargas stood facing Buseil for a few moments, neither of them speaking. Buseil looked at Lha. "Long life to you, King Lha," he said, and turned with the monks, running back into the dark passages that led to the wall of the Holy City; until they were absorbed into the dark.

King Lha remembered his brothers and father running off to war. "You're too young to come with us," they had said before they left that night. "We'll come back and see if you've practiced your archery." But Lha never practiced his archery. He drew pictures, hundreds and hundreds of pictures of birds, of plants, of pets, of people. His bow sat in the corner of his room. Instead, there was a growing collection of drawings and paintings waiting for his father to praise, to admire.

"Creator. You are a creator," his father called him, smiling once at his pictures.

Kargas yanked his arm in the dark passageway and Vanel took his other hand, her face turned away, a flicker of firelight curving around her foreign nose. Together they ran as the bells rang above them, and the walls shook, and dust filtered down like snow on their path.

≈ ≈

Vanel and Kargas had encouraged him to follow his art. Kargas found ways to bring him rolls of paper, ink, and brushes. Kargas spoke to the king—"He will astound us all"—and so, fewer war studies, strategy, swordsmanship, and more art and music and philosophy for him. For he was a *ninth* son of the king. Vanel and Kargas were allowed to craft him as they wanted.

"These stairs!" Lha suggested as they ran past another set of stairs. "We can hide down here. I know this place."

"Lha, we're going to run away from the city tonight," Kargas said. "We have horses."

"But the armies—"

"Don't think about them," Kargas said.

"We're going to be a family," Vanel said. She beamed at him.

Lha looked at her, his eyes wide.

Kargas, running beside him, said, "If we escape together, we stay together. We become a family."

"But what of the Holy City?" Lha asked.

"It's lost for now. We'll have to come back."

"Where will we go?"

"We have safe passage," Kargas shot a look at Vanel, "to a neighbouring city."

"To Varid," Vanel said strongly, as if she wanted him to know. "My home city."

"The Variden are at war—with us." Lha stopped running.

Kargas and Vanel stopped running too. "*I'm* not at war with you," Vanel said. "I love you."

"We don't have time to explain," Kargas said, breathing hard. "The armies of the Horde will be inside the gates any moment. Prince Lha, come here now."

The boy stumbled backwards. "I'm—king."

Kargas huffed, looking at Vanel. "Lha. Right now you are King of Nothing. The city is falling. You are half asleep, thinking you can make decisions in this sudden moment. You must listen to me. I've always taught you how to be a better king than any of your brothers could ever be. But you can't be a king here—not yet. You will need to grow into the Wisdom you've acquired. There will be a new Holy City." Kargas looked at him as if there was really no other viable option. "And it will be in Varid."

Something huge welled up inside of Lha and poured out of his mouth. "But—they killed the king and the princes!" His own voice surprised him. He held his head as if it would explode. "You can't live with their killers."

Vanel pleaded with him, "The Horde killed them. The Horde. Please, Lha. Come quickly or we'll all die."

Kargas ran at Lha, his great bulk suddenly in front of him. "If I have to carry the king like a sack of grain to save his life, I will."

Lha ducked away from Kargas' lunge and ran toward the stairs leading to the catacombs. "Lha!" Kargas called, but Lha dove into the darkness as fast as he could.

Lha knew the catacombs and the passageways of the kingdom well. He and his brothers had played in them, hid in them, warred in them. He wiped fresh tears on his sleeve.

He ran the maze of passages in the dark, panicked, letting his fingers trail along the wall, even as he hurried farther away from everyone, to the forbidden passages, to the one that would lead him to some great door, its golden words across the arch: *Let Wisdom Seek Power and Power Seek Wisdom, Else the World is Lost*. Kargas had told him about the door, but not where it was.

He heard distant shouts. He passed by the entrance to Where Kings Sleep, sliding his hands over the dark walls, the grit loosened by his fingers falling like dust behind him. His foot stubbed hard against a rock and he stopped. To his horror, he felt around his feet a mass of rocks. He could tell even in the dark that this passage was closed, that there were rocks from floor to ceiling. No air passed in front of him. The dark gripped him.

They had sealed up this passage with rocks. He imagined a door beyond it with the words above it, and he climbed the rocks on his hands and feet, trying to reach the top, but they were piled deep and he could not get to any door. And what would he do if he got there? He had no way to wake the Gryphon. Could the Gryphon hear someone pleading even if he were asleep?

"Lha!" Kargas bellowed. "*King* Lha, there's no time!" They came closer and closer.

He crawled back down the mound of stones, and ran back to the twisted ironwork gate in front of Where the Kings Sleep, and slipped through its gaps. He could hide here for now.

He'd been here before. King Arund, his father, had brought him here to honour the past kings. *They would know. They would know what he should do.* They were where the Wisdom came from, after all. The unlit torch from the wall was heavy in his hands, like a club, and in grabbing it he dropped the striking stone to light it. He heard Kargas and Vanel just down the hall. He went down the pathway into the darkened crypt, letting his body slide against the wall. When he was far enough away from the door, he turned against the wall and tried to use his crown to spark the torch. Nothing. Probably scratched the crown. He tried his stone necklace instead, scratching the black stone against the wall until—yes—a spark lit the edge of the torch's cloth. But the black stone's edge cracked and crumbled in his hand—pieces falling to the ground. Another kingly thing ruined.

The torch lit the crypt. He walked past the kings of the Holy City—those who had managed to protect their city with armies, and with the Gryphon.

"One with magic, one with gold, one with marriage, one with holiness," Lha repeated.

"These are the ways a king protects his people," his father had said. "You will never have to worry about this. You have eight brothers, after all. But you are a creator, and your methods of being king would be very different." His father smiled at this. "And you helped me once, when the Gryphon was raging, when the Holy City could not appease him. You helped me put him to sleep."

"How did I help you?" Lha had asked.

"You were innocent. And you still are."

In the crypt now, the kings flanked him, their polished crypt doors holding everything and nothing.

"I want to wake the Gryphon," he announced to the room. His voice was small as he addressed the kings. "Is that the right thing to do? Is that your Wisdom speaking to me?" But nothing came to him, and he stifled his tears. "I'm trying. Is that your idea or mine? You were supposed to give something to me."

He went into his father's crypt, the wine-coloured door open. He looked left at where his father would soon lay. A giant marble slab lay there now and he shined the torchlight on it. It reflected like the sun.

The Gryphon is made of sun. Kargas had taught him that. *The Gryphon can sense your heart. He makes his own decisions about who lives and dies. He is unpredictable.* He remembered how Kargas used to tell this story: King Arund faced down a gryphon enraged by the sins of Variden—a city nearly destroyed by the Gryphon's wrath. He took a piece of the Gryphon's gold, putting him to sleep, and won peace for the land.

Then Lha heard the Bells of the South Wall. They were everywhere. He looked up at the ceiling, imagining the boys shooting their arrows, the fire, armies waiting outside the door to come in. He saw the boy's face, *that* boy, firing his arrows into the sheet of men covering the land. He looked down over the table and saw his own face, the face of the king. The face of the boy.

The Gryphon could save that boy.

He whispered to the slab, as if his father already lay there. *Where is the gold you took, father? Where is the gold you took? I need to know where it is. I can save everyone if you can just tell me where the gold is.* He started to cry. *You didn't leave me with enough to save them. You didn't leave me with enough.*

The gate rattled down the corridor. He threw the torch against the wall and quickly stepped on the flames. He crouched in his father's crypt.

He heard Buseil's voice quaver as he spoke to someone. "I need your holy promise. Your holiest promise. All the gold of the Gryphon if you promise no harm to those in the Holy City."

"Vedic, you have our word. We have already stopped. You've proven your wisdom by telling your men to stand down."

"I am not a wise man," Buseil said. "I am trying to save as much of the Holy City as I can."

One of the other men said, "Then you're a saviour."

Buseil sounded flustered. "I—I am just a man." A key in a lock, a heavy door opening, footsteps retreating, the gasping of a dozen men as they stood in the presence of something amazing.

"He's a lot bigger than I remember," said one finally.

"He's a good size."

"He's only good when he's asleep," another soldier said.

"I thought there was a lot more gold than this."

Buseil said, "No one can take the gold without waking the Gryphon. That first piece, the one we were able to get, was an accident. An innocent hand took it. We told the Variden and the Horde that we never took from this gold. It was made by the people of all the cities. What purpose would it suit men devoted to faith?"

"An innocent took it?"

"The Gryphon can search every heart, but the hearts of innocents read pure. You're going to have to kill the Gryphon to get the gold. He's asleep now, so it should be easy."

"Why did you never kill him?"

"What purpose would that serve? We wanted peace, not death."

"There's at least one coin gone," said a soldier.

"Oh, yes, one coin—but that is just to keep the beast asleep. We touched nothing else."

"Sometimes," said another man, one with authority in his voice, "I wish I were the Gryphon, and I could tell who was lying and who was telling the truth." A slippery, whispered scream of metal—a sword unsheathed. "Where's the last piece? Or would it have been safer to keep more pieces out of the pile? The Variden will want to kill the beast themselves. We just want the gold—every single piece. All the gold for the lives of those in this city. Every piece."

Buseil cried out, "The king only kept one piece—we don't know where it is. It's—in his room, maybe. Let's go see." A sharp cry. Something like a soft bag of grain fell to the stone floor.

A man said, "We'll do that. And your room as well. First, though, start bagging up the gold we have."

"What do we do with the beast?"

"The Variden will want him. Even asleep, maybe they can drown him or burn him or crush him. I'm sure they'll try several things."

Was the man right? Lha wondered. Could there be more pieces of gold? Could his brothers have had pieces hidden in their necklaces? If he ran in there now to awaken the Gryphon, he could be killed. The Gryphon may not awaken. Maybe he was wrong—maybe he never received the Wisdom.

He walked outside his father's crypt. The door to King Baruch-Azil, the first king, was open, and he could see the empty balcony, the cave awash with firelight, and the golden words above the door: *Let Wisdom Seek Power and Power*— Of course the door was with the first king. Without Buseil's key, he never would have found it.

"Lha!" He turned and saw Kargas standing in the corridor with Vanel. Several Variden soldiers came up behind them.

Kargas held the soldiers back. "I made them promise that they would protect you, Lha." He walked towards Lha. "The only son who wasn't a warrior. We need you. We need a king who is a creator. A peacemaker. Come with us. You could start a generation of kings that care more for the cities around them than appeasing a wrathful, sun-spitting creature that thinks he's a god. We have a *chance* to try something different this time." Kargas smiled. "We will save your life and the culture and Wisdom you carry," he said. "We can build another Holy City."

Cold crept up the back of his neck as Lha realized the truth. "You wanted me to live—only me?"

"Lha, we couldn't take a chance that the Wisdom would go to any of your brothers. Look at the mess warriors make of life. You can still be trained and mentored in more creative, peaceful ways."

Kargas opened his arms wide; Lha shook.

"There is no *Wisdom*," Lha whispered. "You killed everyone for *nothing*!" The words poured out of him. He threw down his crown, ripped off his necklace and threw them on the floor of the crypt because it was all dead. All dead.

The black stone necklace shattered, revealing the edge of the gold coin, and both he and Kargas seemed to realize it at once. The Variden saw it as well.

"He has the coin!"

Why would he have the coin in his necklace? He'd worn it many times during many ceremonies. Had he held terrible power all his life—the power to wake the Gryphon? Could he have saved his father?

The Variden swept around Kargas like a flood. Lha picked up the coin, turned and ran straight for the balcony. Through the door of King Baruch-Azil's tomb, past the plaques that read of his deeds, past the place where he was buried, sleeping on his side, with his back to the Gryphon he had long ago rescued.

Lha ran past the brown robes of Buseil on the balcony, draped across three steps. Lha glanced at the monk's face, bleeding from the mouth, a tiny smear on the steps.

Lha leapt from the balcony, exhilaration at what he saw. In that moment, it was only the Gryphon, here now, for the first time. Bigger than six or seven horses, it was an eagle sleeping on giant cat's paws, brown and golden feathers covering its sleeping body. It heaved up and down in perfect peace.

For an instant, Lha flew, like the Gryphon must have flown in battle, free of anything that might weigh him down. And then, suddenly, his hand drove like a nail into the pile of gold coins, breaking a finger, scratching his arm; his other hand dropped the coin he'd been holding so that he could find his balance. His legs sunk into the pile till he was on his knees.

The left side of his face slammed into the coins, and yet he looked up and saw, only a few feet away, the Gryphon's eye open.

The Gryphon is made of sun.

"Lha! Don't move!" It was Kargas' voice above him on the balcony.

"Lha!" Vanel screamed. Lha didn't turn around; the eye of the Gryphon did not blink, yet.

"Please help us," Lha spoke a torrent to the Gryphon's eye. "The Holy City is under attack. The people attacking us have black hearts. They are deceptive and want to kill everyone. Protect us! Protect yourself! They're right *here!*"

The Gryphon's great mouth opened. "*Whom* should I kill?" he asked.

"Lha! Be silent!" Kargas raged.

The boy crawled toward the Gryphon. "Everyone who *lies*. Everyone who *deceives*. Everyone who hides the truth away!"

"Oh," the Gryphon breathed in, "everyone."

He lifted his head, stretching his neck as his wings opened, filling the room. The air brushed past Lha's face. The Gryphon looked at the men with bags of gold and he thrust his face toward them, beak wide, eyes glowing. A blast of desert sun came out of his mouth, like molten vomit, and the men dried like husks and crumbled to the ground. The Gryphon turned his mighty head and opened his eyes and mouth at Kargas and Vanel, and the Variden who stood behind him.

"No, not them—I didn't mean—"

"Lha, no!" Kargas yelled.

And the boy yelled, "Noooo, not them!"

Vanel screamed. But the light was blinding, and when it was gone, there wasn't anyone left standing.

And the Gryphon looked at the boy, stretching his wings. "And now, finally, for everyone else."

The boy put his face in his hands, crying. "No! No I said only those with deceiving hearts! Only those who lie!"

The Gryphon looked back at him. "Everyone lies, King Lha."

"No, no. Some are good, some are good." The boy struggled to stand.

"Everyone lies."

"I-I-I don't."

The Gryphon held his gaze. "Has the Wisdom come to you?"

Lha couldn't answer.

"Answer me. Your father is dead. Your brothers are dead. I know this. I know it because you know it. Has the Wisdom come to you as it came to your father? Your tricky, deceitful father . . ."

The Gryphon looked into Lha's soul. He could feel it—hot, searing, judging eyes.

"No," he said, finally.

The Gryphon blinked. "Another lie you've been told. That you would get any Wisdom at all."

"Please, save the city and the people of the Holy City. They protected you."

"They tricked me. They tricked you." The Gryphon's face came down to his own. "*You* tricked me."

"I didn't trick you—"

"Your father *used* you as a baby. He distracted me with chit chat while you crawled on my gold. Your clothes snagged a coin. I could have killed you—he knew that. But he had eight other sons. You were expendable. But I can't read the hearts of babies, and if I did, they would all be the same." He looked away. "None of your people are worth saving. As far as I'm concerned, you were all in on the plot."

The Hundred Bells pealed again. They both looked to the crest of morning above the cave's open crevice. Lha said, "Please save the city! We'll be *better* people."

"Will *all* of you?" The Gryphon pushed his head against the boy, backing him up. "Will everyone be better? Can you vouch for the hearts of every one of your tricky, deceitful holy people?"

Lha stumbled off the pile of gold. "I'll make them." He faltered. "I'm king."

"How will *you* promise that *they* will be perfectly good?"

Lha's back slapped against the cave wall. The Gryphon held him there with his head and a paw, gazing through one slowly brightening eye.

"I can try."

"Whom *can* you vouch for?"

"Me. I can vouch for me."

"You?"

"I won't lie. I won't be bad. Ever. I'll be a good king." He began to cry.

The Gryphon shouted, "You'll never ever make a mistake. Ever?"

"Never! I promise to be good. I'll be good. I'll be *good*." The boy folded like a piece of paper standing against the wall, curled over the Gryphon's paw, and cried deep heaves and tears that wouldn't stop now.

The Gryphon watched him. Listening. Assessing. The boy shook. His fingers held tightly onto the Gryphon's feathered paw.

"You might one day be a good king, but you've had a very bad first night. I'm a benevolent creature, but I've had a very long sleep—nine years too long." He moved his face close to the boy, whispering, "I, too, have been frequently deceived by the hearts of men. I know that these tears are about betrayal, not merely grief. I, too, have been used like this. I'll take your trade. I'll protect your city and your people as long as *you* never make a mistake ever again."

He breathed through the holes on his beak, a mist over the boy's wet face—a thick, musky smell, like spices and death.

King Lha's head became foggy. He could not stand. His legs gave way, and he fell on the gold.

"But you'll pardon me for hedging my bet. Sleep now, King Lha. The innocent are rarely wise, and the wise are rarely innocent. But maybe you made the wisest choice. Maybe the Wisdom did come to you. I, at least, will save the city. But age brings both wisdom and corruption. If I left you awake, you'd betray me. But if you are years asleep, you'll remain pure. I would call this a *just* punishment—but tonight, child of a deceitful father, a deceitful people—" he paused, stretching his wings, preparing for flight, for battle, "it will feel like peace."

ﾟﾟﾟﾟﾟﾟ Bear With Me

Evelyn leaned her suitcase against a camper shell covered in snow. She felt the Yukon burn her cheeks with cold, felt her nose hairs freeze into pins. She savoured what she called "the moment before she met Bear face-to-face," where she was prepared to overlook any minor flaws—lack of flossing, hammertoes, belching. She'd lost ten pounds, had her hair cut, took skiing lessons. She felt amazing and prepared herself not to care if he should back away in fear or hold up the sign of the cross to protect himself—or worse, if he should show the subtle facial signs of disappointment.

The big moment would have happened at the airport, but he'd asked someone else to pick her up. She adjusted for his lack of sensitivity, hoping it was an unavoidable emergency—some salmon at the Fish Ladder needing directions to the sea, perhaps.

His small house had red shingle siding and a blue roof. Had she written this real estate ad, she would have emphasized "comfortable and cozy," evoked fireplace, friends, wine, and photos on the fridge. *Very attractive*. She flexed her gloved fingers twice and knocked.

The door opened slow and creaky, like it did in every horror movie she'd seen. Muddy boots sat against the wall below a blue parka. A set of Christmas lights draped over a kitchen window in the next room, giving the purple walls a lavender glow.

"Come on in. I'm changing," came his familiar voice. Thank God.

Here she was, like women who had come a hundred years ago, lugging their tons of supplies across a snowy pass into a gold-rush town. She hauled her luggage, with no help from the boyfriend, and walked into a potentially heartbreaking house. *Damn, I'm adventurous*. But, with both of them in their thirties, she couldn't afford to be frightened. She'd flown 3,000 miles already; what was one last lug?

Two rooms away, something lumbered into the light of a living room lamp. It was a large brown bear walking on his hind legs. She backed into the door as it closed. She remembered advice she'd read about meeting this kind of bear. *Back away slowly, speaking strongly to the bear. Appear larger with coat and backpack and arms raised. Never run.* Instead, she dropped her luggage. They stood two rooms apart, the ghostly lavender kitchen between them.

Its mouth moved and Bear's voice came out. "You might be startled," it said spreading its arms and claws pleadingly.

She felt a scream falling like sediment into her gut. She could see no lines in the costume; saw the jaw hinge and unhinge. Saliva pearled between his teeth, and she thought she smelled dense fur. No skin between the edge of his eyes and the edge of the mask. Just his eyes, unblinking, wild and pitiful, wider now as he tried to explain himself.

"God," she whispered.

It said, "It's okay. Don't be frightened. I'm not always like this." It spoke slowly. It made no moves, not even to back up. Its tone was serious but casual, as if delivering news that the man she'd come to meet was, unfortunately, dead. "I didn't know how to tell you, Ev."

Her hand found a very heavy vinyl-backed chair and she scraped it between them, ready if the beast should lunge, to protect herself with its metal legs. But the voice said the bear wasn't going to attack.

"How was your flight?" it asked, casually.

It was interested in her flight. She was monitoring her pulse.

"Bear?"

"Not a costume. Real fur. Real me. You might be thinking about the home movies I sent, and those were *me*, but they were me during the day. Night is a whole different creature."

Bear winced at his own words. "If you sit down, we can talk. You can sit in the kitchen, and I'll—" He looked to the couch behind him. "I'll sit here. And I'll explain everything."

He fell into the large, comfy couch. The cushions flattened under his weight; they were clearly worn out. He crossed his legs, as if the normalcy of the gesture might reassure her that she was just chatting in a friend's living room.

She sat down, surprised at herself. She wondered what happened to her boyfriend. She felt like crying for the man she thought was here. She stared at him. *This creature is nothing to me*, she thought.

But he looked very lost. He stared at the ceiling for a moment before beginning. "Okay. It happened like this. I wasn't always a bear. I was human like you. But I—I changed when I was eleven." He sighed. "Not something I did to myself, or some mutant ability that came on at puberty. No. I made a mistake. I looked in the window of a neighbour woman's house, and she was having—well, she was in a very compromising—she was *having sex* with one of the sackers from our grocery store." He looked horribly uncomfortable telling this story, even for a bear. "Red blanket on the carpet. I remember every detail. Burned right into my brain. I was eleven, and I hadn't seen anything like—well, I had seen some things . . . pictures, maybe. Anyway, that doesn't matter. What matters is she saw me. Now, naturally, she got pissed. And well, I'd heard she was a witch, but no one really *believed* that." He swallowed. "No one thought she had any powers or anything. But when she looked at me. I felt so badly. I mean, there she was, naked. Her face so shocked, so horrified seeing me standing there, some person staring at her in—her shame." He seemed to pause, and then said abruptly, "She changed me." He ran his paw across his chest, as if he were trying to wipe something off.

He looked away from her, across the living room. The knock-off cuckoo clock in the corner ticked.

He turned back to her, breathed out. "There's no pressure, Ev. We can have your ticket changed. I just wanted to have the chance to defend—to *present* myself in person." He leaned forward, tucking his enormous claws in his lap. "I hope you remember all the good things." He smiled, but it just showed his teeth. "We have a lot in common, Ev. We like the same music— U2, old Beatles, Coldplay; eight out of each others' top ten movies; we have similar plans for the future. I have a good job at the Fish Ladder." He looked around the room. "I'm not always going to live here. I showed you the house I'm thinking about. You said it was a good buy. *These* are the things to think about. They're what we've built on. They are more our relationship than this small revelation."

The lamplight highlighted a head of dark brown fur. She had expected *some* difference in the man she met online and the real thing—the same you might expect to find when you meet an actor for the first time and they're dressed in everyday clothes, out shopping for melons.

He said, "Are you going to say anything?"

She looked at the kitchen floor. It was spotless. He cleaned well.

"I've had about two minutes."

"Right," he said gruffly. "Understandable. Let's sleep on it."

He stood up suddenly. She jumped.

"I should," she said, "stay in a hotel."

"I have a guest bedroom. I won't hurt you. Please, I don't want to lose you in one night."

She looked him square in his small black eyes, looking for signs of common humanity. "I deserved to know the truth."

The bear looked at the floor. "You think I'm hideous."

"I think you look like a bear."

"I'm not a bear inside—only on the outside. I don't attack people or eat anyone."

"How do I know you aren't lying?"

"I'm telling you I'm not lying."

"But you lied about this."

"I omitted." He looked down, knowing it was a lousy excuse. The walls around him were a trendy orange and yellow, the couch royal blue—dynamic hues; almost comic book colours. And here, a comic book bear stood embarrassed and regretful next to the floor lamp.

"I still deserved to know before now. It's been more than a year."

He didn't answer. He waited as if he hadn't heard her.

"I put fresh sheets on the bed," he said finally.

She picked up her suitcase. Heavier. "A hotel will be no trouble," she said.

He looked agitated. "I promise. I'll be normal in the morning. Different face."

She sniffed back a nervous breakdown. She'd have to call a cab—she'd be alone in a foreign country. She closed her eyes. "Say this to me. Say: 'Evelyn, it's going to be okay.'"

She heard him inhale, and then they were on the phone again. She'd lost her chequebook; her mother had a lump on her breast; she was lonely and making cookies for the office again, because no one else baked and she wanted cookies so badly. In that voice, she heard 430 nights of excitement, patience, frustration, all that she had shared on email and, in moments of desperation, on the phone. This time, as every time, she saw his face, his lips, his eyes as they formed the words, "Evelyn, it's going to be okay." She felt herself relax in the presence of hyperbole.

She kept her eyes squinted, said, "Thank you," and moved toward the bedroom. She heard him walk back into the other bedroom.

Draped over the doorway of the guest room were his thinning He-Man sheets, showing muscled warriors and an evil Skeletor in blue. She could see how he might identify with being a superhero: one part of him normal but powerless, and the other powerful, usually with less clothing, clutching rescued women. Secret identities: your enemies never imagine your vulnerability; your girlfriend never sees your power.

She opened her suitcase on a high bed of three mattresses. He'd placed irises in a clear bowl in her room. Five of them opened like a hand. Her favourite.

He called out from the other bedroom, "I really do love you, Evelyn."

She didn't know how to answer.

She soon climbed into bed and lay there as the night sounds turned to snorting and subdued growling in the other room. On the ceiling above her were glow-in-the-dark stickers of stars in vaguely correct constellations. He snored like an alarm smothered with a pillow—a steady, soft vibration. She wondered if it shook the bed, and whether she could get used to the sound.

In the morning, she saw him pass into the kitchen, and he was a man again, as testified—the same man from the pictures he'd sent, only slightly taller than she was with a thick, red crew cut and pink cheeks.

He poured himself some orange juice, smiling when she walked out of the bedroom. "Did you have a good sleep?"

"I did. I slept long."

"You hibernated. Jetlag and lack of sunlight. It happens."

"You were a bear last night," she said, taking the orange juice from the fridge.

"Yes. You remembered."

She poured herself a glass. "I'm trying not to forget."

"Is it so bad? Is it a terrible handicap?" he asked. "Would you like some eggs?"

She leaned against the counter. She wore her favourite robe over a thin nightgown. Under the covers, she never got cold. The heater kicked in often during the night, a dull roar in the background of her dreams of bears. "I want honesty in our relationship."

"Everyone has secrets."

"Yes, I'll take eggs," she said.

He didn't deserve a second chance, but she really couldn't maintain a state of *furious* for two weeks. They walked through neighbourhoods with flannel-shirted snowmen like real estate agents representing houses with colourful siding—blues, mauves, greens; very few whites. In a place where the ground was white nine months of the year, she guessed no one wanted a house that disappeared. They went to an art gallery. She lingered at soapstone carvings of bears, touching their smooth surfaces with her fingers. She ran her finger down a bear's polished stomach, felt the glassy stone curve under her fingertip. Cold even in the warm shop.

They toured Whitehorse while it was light, shopping, sightseeing, crunching snow with the rest of the crowds. Wherever he went, he was greeted by friends with expectant smiles and glances in her direction. "Oh, so *this* is Evelyn!" And they shook her hand, smiling like they knew more than they were saying.

"I've become a saint," she said.

"They're just being friendly."

"What does 'I'm so glad you're with him' mean to you?" she asked.

He ran off ahead of her to a giant paddlewheeler frozen in a surprise winter. He called back to her. "It means you're *lucky*," he laughed.

They stopped and read the historical markers commemorating pioneers. She'd been doing her own research on women in the Klondike. When women came up in the early days, they traded their homes, countries, lifestyles, peoples, all for adventure, and maybe a husband. She beamed with her connections to these women; she wanted him to see her as risky and hardy. She looked at his face, thinking she might find traces of the bear from the night before, but they had been completely erased by some boy's face. She liked his skin—perhaps more now than before—where it creased when he smiled, where his face smoothed to his ears, the contour of his nose. She watched his lips when he talked, his human, searching green eyes. His cheeks looked pink and vulnerable, like an underbelly.

They walked across the bridge over the Yukon River, stopping to admire the crevice between the ice where water flowed. "In summer it's wide, but as it freezes it slowly closes over until there's just a trickle going through. Just like the light here. In January, we only get four hours of sunlight."

"So you can only look human for four hours," she said, leaning against the bridge railing. "Wouldn't someplace else let you have more of a balance? Like the equator?"

He smiled. "Yeah, like a bear's body would be comfortable there."

"Okay, Texas then." She was thinking practically.

"Here, I can go out at night and everyone knows me. Everyone has a little vice, a little quirk, but we get to be ourselves and no one cares. So I'm the walking bear at night, and everyone just waves and says hi. Where else could I get that kind of acceptance?"

Sea gulls congregated at the bend in the river, laughing at them both. Children tobogganed down the banks and onto the hard river, which otherwise would have swallowed them whole.

"So, here's a hard question," she said. "If everyone's so keen on you being a bear in the dark, why haven't you found someone . . . ?"

"More local?" He seemed to be looking off for the answer. "I've—I've got standards, too, you know? Just 'cause a woman can take the fur and the teeth doesn't mean she's a soul mate."

℮ ℮

He would not let her see him change. He went into his bedroom, slid the sheet of stars, moons, and suns across the doorway. She thought she might be able to hear the change, but she heard nothing but him stripping away his human clothes and putting on his larger bear clothes. He called out from the bedroom, "I tried one year going to Rendezvous parties as a trapper. I dressed in raccoon and rabbit fur, but they really clashed with mine. So, I go very sophisticated now." He came out of the room a decidedly ritzy bear, with dark maroon pleated pants and a matching vest; a gold watch chain stretched over his belly like a rope bridge. "I know. I look like a children's book. But it's better than the alternative."

She complimented him. He blossomed with pride.

As for her outfit, she'd picked up a sexy, dark red velvety dress with a red feather that exposed her luscious shoulders. She was peeling up the long, black gloves when she came out of her room. The bear eyed her up and down.

"Is it tight?" he asked.

She raised her eyebrow. "*Not* a good first comment. I think you should start over with, 'Yes, you look wonderful tonight.'"

He frowned, scrunching his muzzle. Even in all that fur, she could see that he lingered unfavourably on her tastefully exposed chest. "I'm just saying that you're going to be moving around a lot tonight, and I don't want you to be uncomfortable."

"You have failed this test," she said, half-smiling. "I look gorgeous. I am going to find three men who will tell me that this evening."

"The men here are not the kind you want to be flirting with," he said as she put on her coat.

"Because you've done extensive flirting with them?"

He didn't laugh. "People use Rendezvous as an excuse to go out and drink to excess and fondle women, and the women here seem to like that."

"Bear, these are your people. If you want—"

"*My* people? What do you mean by that?"

"We can stay at home. I didn't mean to cause a ruckus."

He had his paws on his hips, his all-black eyes thinking and thinking. He was right about one thing—he looked like a page from Aesop's Fables. "I'm just looking out for you."

She decided she wanted to leave, not argue. "I appreciate that, sir."

He buttoned the top button on her black coat, effectively sealing her in up to her neck. "You look wonderful tonight," he added, grinning, showing those teeth.

"Thank you, Mr. Clapton." Did he mean *now*? Buttoned up to her neck? He walked her out the door. They did not go in his car, but walked the four blocks to Lizard's Lounge. He was too big for the car now, and would have busted the seats, blown the tires. He got heavy as a bear. She hoped that by the time they reached the bar he would be less protective.

The night started anew as they entered the room, as if they were making their way for the first time into other people's stories. It was Rendezvous, as Bear had described, a week when everyone re-enacted the winter gatherings of trappers. Some were in costume—long dresses, men wearing red vests—while others were in regular clothes. She could tell she'd blown several rhythms. A chorus of approval came in a wave from the crowd. Evelyn had never been the centre of so much attention. It was reality tv, where everyone endured thirteen weeks of selection by our lonely hero, until finally, on this night, he brought her to the crowd and revealed his love. Her debut. Great.

The band slammed music into her temples, and she felt suddenly thrown from the very silent world of winter into the rowdy, warm bar. They passed through the crowd to a small booth. Evelyn took off her coat, adjusted her dress. For a moment, she felt naked. Bear looked at her as if she were, and he glanced about the room as if someone might notice her shoulders. She wished she'd brought a shawl.

Greg, the man who'd picked her up at the airport, and his wife April found them. April grabbed her by the arms and said she looked *smashing*. April, however, was not in costume; she had short, messy blonde hair and wore a crinkled, light blue cami under a crème top. She was an ad for the Buckle—how Texan, Evelyn thought, smiling. They joined Bear and Evelyn, set their coats on the booth seats, and ordered drinks. April, diligent in getting to know Evelyn, asked where they'd met. When she heard that Bear had not put up a picture of his more burly side, she leaned back, reached over, and thumped him in the chest. "Bastard!"

She turned to Evelyn. "You have to thump him when he's bad."

They chatted while music played. Evelyn stirred her Caesar—a V8 with a kick. It wasn't so different than the States. Except it was a well-attended costume party in February with no fashion police. Everyone knew everyone else. Ordinary people having a good time. Evelyn relaxed.

Across the table, Bear cleared his throat, scooted carefully out of the booth, and stood beside her, offering his paw. She tried to focus on his eyes alone, but she couldn't help watching everyone watch them as she stood up to dance.

She followed him to a linoleum dance floor, awash in gold light. For the slow song, he took one of her hands and gingerly placed it around his back, then took her other and held it, trying not to scrape it. His pads were soft. Here on the dance floor, he was considerate. He smiled and she looked in his small, dark, inhuman eyes. He asked with those eyes if she was warming up to him. She looked at his wet, black nose. She wasn't sure.

They both warmed to the music and the lights. She felt it pour over her and her shoulders loosened. He shut his eyes, grooved to a bass guitar solo. Flakes of green and pink and gold floated across his Victorian suit, lighting up his watch chain as if he had the sun hooked inside his pocket. She swayed back and forth and put her arms in the air. They rolled the negative space between them back and forth, kneading it with their bodies. He opened his eyes. Perhaps the pink light shone on her cleavage, mesmerizing him. She closed her eyes and pulsated toward him. Then she felt his soft paws on her chest, and when she opened her eyes, it was to wink and smile at him, to suggest that they do some of this in private. But his eyes were suddenly everywhere else, panicky, turning his head, watching who might be watching her. He was not groping her but covering her.

He yanked her close, covered her body with his. She thought he was growling and angry, but he was trembling. Through the rest of the lively rhythm, he held her still against the music. She knew he had his eyes closed now. Did they look in love? Couples whirred around them, and he held her as she tried to break away.

"Bear, I want to dance," she said quietly. "Let go, just a little."

He looked down at her and tried to say something, but she couldn't hear it. The song ended in a blast of drums echoing all over the room. With the last boom, he walked off the dance floor, leaving her to walk herself off. She tried to smile at everyone. She wanted to assure them that they needn't worry—Bear's feelings were being protected, their expectations would all be met.

Immediately Greg thumped him on the chest. Apparently this was the appropriate and usual spot. They pulled back into another corner while Evelyn sat down with April.

"What happened?" April asked.

"I don't know," Evelyn said. "You know him, too. What did you see?"

"He was, like, *diving* for your boobs. You had your eyes closed, but he was hungry, slobbery, and going right down for them. Not like he was a pervert. He's a man and he saw a nice rack, and this is Bear and he doesn't get out much. He spends a lot of time with the fish in the river. Which is kinda ironic, if you think about it. A bear spending time with fish, but not to eat them. And so he's maybe a little un-practiced when it comes to being subtle."

But he was shaking, covering her. Didn't April see his eyes moving all over the place?

"He wanted to see if anyone caught him," April said. "I mean, I saw Greg, and he was looking at your boobs, too, and he didn't need a dance floor."

Evelyn felt exposed. She pulled her bodice up.

"No, girl, it's not you," April said. "Men can be beasts, but we like them like that. And if you can't show some hooters on the dance floor, where are you going to show them? I mean, they only last for a little while, and when they're *gone*, they can't pull a homeless man to his feet."

She watched Greg explain something to Bear in wide, sweeping gestures. She could still feel his trembling body in the hollow of her elbows, where she'd held him. How vulnerable he made himself. He could have brought her up in summer and she wouldn't have known a thing; instead he brought her up in winter, exposing himself on purpose. Winter and summer, like two different places up here. He'd told her that sunlight pulled everyone outside; they shed their coats and then, *bam!* They went biking, canoeing, hiking, swimming. Tourists flocked the streets and the sun never, ever set. Bear looked human for nearly three solid months.

She imagined what it might be like to live here. If not for the women coming up during the gold rush, this place would never have become more than tents. Women settled the miners and gold-rushers down. Evelyn imagined turning her notice in to the real estate agency, telling people that she was going to be a pioneer in the Klondike; she felt the romance of those words. She felt again the tremble of his body.

A lanky man in a red vest with a black garter on his arm came to their table, introducing himself as Terry. April knew him.

He turned to Evelyn. "You look like a girl who hasn't danced enough."

She tried to get Bear's attention, but he was still with Greg. She smiled at Terry, standing up, feeling the pleasant weight of his gaze on her shoulders. Bear was capable of cutting in.

He walked her out to the floor. They took separate grooves and she tried to remember the last time she went dancing. She'd gotten to be such a homebody in the last five years. She spent most of her time with her cat, Sioux, and a rented movie—conditions that propelled her into online dating. She missed going out with friends. She felt like she had inherited good friends from Bear, but they were ones he'd cultivated. While she had turned introverted in a city of hundreds of thousands, *he'd* been a social animal in a small town. Certainly, he made a great host. They'd cross-country skied, dined out, visited museums, watched children throw axes, adults chuck chainsaws, cheered on mushing dogs—all part of this social carnival.

Terry looked to his left and waved to Bear, who was now sitting at the table. Bear didn't wave back; he just stared at them. He leaned forward on the edge of his seat, as if he might get up on the dance floor and maul someone.

Terry grabbed her hands and pulled her into a jitterbug. At their table, Bear stood up to a formidable height. He looked across the expanse of the dance floor. He didn't walk out or demand to cut in; he pulled out his pocket watch casually, like a cartoon bear, and flipped open the casing. It sparked gold. He closed it shut against his chest and placed it back in his pocket. Other couples danced in front of him and still he watched Evelyn.

It's just a dance, she thought.

When she came back to the table, Bear looked away, at his drink. He slurped it through a straw, quickly, noisily, all that vodka going down in one big gulp.

She sat down. "I'm pooped," she said to the table.

Terry followed her to the table, joked with Bear, who grinned with an armada of teeth.

She thought he might say something to Terry. He was obviously feeling possessive, but he just smouldered in polite conversation. She expected him to attack. She expected him to do so many different things with that fur. To be an animal. Instead he seemed pressed into a smaller box. Being a bear did not expand things for him, she thought to herself; it contracted them.

Someone got on stage and announced the entertainment for the evening: Sourdough Sams—eight men in a contest that would make them the soul of the historical trapper. They entertained every night at different bars doing different contests—drinking, eating, singing, dancing. Tonight's was a striptease.

Evelyn and April woo-hoo'd together above the shouts of the crowd. Eight men stripped down to red long johns to "I'm Too Sexy" and then together, like a full-Monty review, down to thongs.

It was so much more than what she was sure Bear could stand. She patted a place next to her, and he obliged. She may have pounded on the table and whistled, but she kept a hand firmly on Bear's thigh. No mixed messages here, she thought. But she wasn't going to shy away from it, either. He stripped the remaining hot wings of meat with fastidious teeth. He did not take her hand or even acknowledge that it was there. He seemed distracted and bored. Every other man in the place looked to be enjoying the spectacle and rooting these men on—they must have been coworkers and friends.

"Do you know any of them?" she asked Bear. She wanted to know who to root for.

"I don't recognize them in their underwear," he said. She couldn't tell if he was being sanctimonious or homophobic. She decided a safe bet would be to root for all of them. When it was over, and the men had swung their last, she put on her coat and told April she was going outside for a breath of fresh air. April said she would join her, but when Evelyn got outside, it was Bear behind her.

"You ready to go?" he asked.

She looked at him. "Now there's the 25,000-dollar question."

"I don't want to fight."

"Me neither. I just want to have a good time."

The cold settled in under her collar, through the threads of her gloves. It came up under her coat to her legs, travelling upwards, leaving a trail of goose bumps.

"Bear, what's with you tonight?" she asked. "Are you embarrassed to be seen with me?"

"No," he rolled his eyes.

"Then what was all that in there?"

He put on his coat. He didn't know what she was talking about. He wasn't much of a dancer in the first place, and naked men weren't his thing. *Good save*, she thought. Besides, the bar was getting too hot for him. He had all that fur, after all.

April came to the door. "Off to get cozy in front of a fire?"

Evelyn smiled and gave her a hug. She didn't think they would make it to the cozy part this week. "We're going to go see if the Northern Lights are out."

"Oh those," she said, waving them away with her hand. "Good luck. I can never find them when I want them. Hey, if you do find them, whistle at them. They say the lights will come down and kidnap you."

"Have you tried it?" Evelyn asked.

"Yeah." But she offered nothing else.

In his emails, he had moved to sex first. She'd tease him along the way, give subtle hints, but he always took the first dive, so to speak. They got explicit; they could overheat a hard drive. Bear had a pretty good vocabulary for sex. She liked that. Oh, she knew he was conservative, but his stories to her were very, very effective. She remembered, though, that he wasn't as good on the phone—a little more embarrassed talking dirty out loud.

She watched this face smile, how the black gums thinned, the pale teeth glistened. She watched the eyes, wet along the rims, slivers of white near the corners. The way the fur moved in tiny waves according to the muscles in his face. He didn't look as frightening, or as foreign, as he had the first night. Still, she couldn't connect the two parts of him; it was as if separate men were tag-team dating her. She had to work harder with the bear than she did the man. She imagined those two conferred on what they thought about her—about love, about passion. Did he even know what he wanted?

They took another route to his house, through a darkened residential area, bordered on one side by steep clay cliffs. He put his arm around her. He tried to be chatty, as if she were upset. Sometimes he would rub his hairy paw against her neck. The city to their left was quiet; no one was out. The streetlights stood majestic in fog. On the way, she shivered, on purpose.

"Cold?" he asked.

"A little," she said.

He took off his coat and put it around her. It was a light trench coat. Not really any help.

She made sure he felt her shiver more as they turned a corner. He asked her again if she were cold and then took off his vest. After all, he said, it was a wool blend. Now he was *bear*-chested in pleated pants.

"You're probably overheating anyway," she said.

He smiled. "I can take it."

"It must be twenty below out here," she said, walking slower.

He thought about it. "At least. But fur is a great insulator." They passed a park with a rock wall frosted by two inches of snow. Evergreens and spruce.

"At least you have the pants," she said. "You need those out here."

He scoffed. "I don't *need* them."

"Course you do, Bear. You don't have *perfect* insulation."

He stopped and looked at her. "You don't know much about bears, do you?" He unzipped his pants without looking around, meeting her eyes with a spark of defiance. She smiled at him and she thought he was finally catching on. He whipped off his pants and threw them over the rock wall of the park behind him.

"Tada!" he said.

She thought he was smiling.

"Satisfied, you little pervert?"

She laughed. "You were too sexy for that vest, and those pants." She took a gloved hand and ran it down his stomach. He had on Snoopy boxer shorts. But she didn't make fun. He was right about one thing: he was putting out heat like a furnace. Her hand was warm on his chest.

"And I'm not satisfied yet, Mr. Boxer Shorts."

She slipped a hand down his shorts, pulled the elastic wide, slipped them down over his legs. "Now you're a naked bear." She tossed those on the wall as well, but he suddenly reached to grab them back.

Behind her, she heard a rush of panting and scuffling, and suddenly two yellow labs passed her, jumped up on Bear, licking and playing. For any other man, this might have been a slightly embarrassing moment, a playful time-out; for Bear it was anything but. He tried to push them down; he reached for the rest of his clothes, yanking them and a pile of snow off the wall. He looked at her, desperate to get away from the dogs. He argued with them, as if they too would speak English. They barked at him. He pulled on his pants. They were soaked in snow. He then strapped on his vest. She took off his coat, knowing that he was coming for it. She watched him stride away from the dogs, moving toward her, talking to them like a master: *Sit* and *No* and *Lay Down*. There was no humour in his voice as he buttoned up his vest, as he fit his arms into the sleeves of the coat. If he'd had gloves, she was sure he would make a point of putting them on over his claws. In minutes he had transformed from a bear back into a children's illustration.

"People just let their dogs run wild," he said, placing his paw on her back and gently pushing her down the street.

Neither one of them spoke all the way to his house. He was stiff and quick in his strides. The northern lights did not come out, but the lamps stayed steady on streets to the left and right of them, and they travelled the dark crevice in between.

One bright afternoon, near the end of her time in the North, they stayed in to watch *The Wolf-Man* at Bear's request. The tv was in his room; they lounged on his bed, snacking popcorn, watching Lon Chaney Jr. struggle.

In the middle of the movie, she felt a surprise: Bear's hand caressing her thigh. She wondered where this would go. After the last couple of days, she wasn't sure if he knew, or what to expect if he got started. She placed her bowl of kernels on the nightstand and turned to kiss him. In the background, you could hear Lon Chaney pleading with his girlfriend not to go out in the night alone. Appropriate dangerous music followed. Bear kissed her with urgency. She lifted his shirt, exposing his pink, human chest, his supple nipples. He pulled off his clothes in advance of her tongue.

She kissed every inch of his body as if they might lose it at any moment. She had the impression she was making love to someone about to go off to war. The sunlight pushed across the room, up their bodies, and lit the wall behind them. His lovemaking surprised her. He held her breasts gently; pressed his palm on her body, firmly, warmly, slowly. He knew what to do with his tongue. Everything he'd written about in emails he could perform, and this bedroom event, his coming out as a sexual man, seemed to insist that he knew what to do with a human body, though he was uncertain about the other one. Moreover, maybe, he knew what to do with *her* body. What surprised her was how badly she needed his human body to tell her that. But this was sex on fast forward. The sunlight faded behind them. He finished just as the hunting dogs started to pursue Lon Chaney through the forest. Their bays signalled a change in him, and she wasn't surprised when he pulled away, covering his face with his hands.

"I need you to go into the other room for a few minutes. I don't want you to see this." He acted like a child hiding himself from her. "I wasn't thinking about the time."

"Bear, it's okay. I *want* to see this. This is a part of you."

He took his hands down, pulled the covers up over his naked body. "No, this isn't okay. You have to go now." She didn't get off the bed. So he jumped up, pulled on her arms, tried to yank her off it.

"No," she said, and dove to the other side of the bed, knocking him off balance, pulling him with her to the bed again. She tried to pin his arms. He was stronger than her, but he was upset, panicked, nearly crying. The same look he'd had on the dance floor. She was going to catch him doing something horrible.

She got right in his face. "It's going to be okay." If he wanted this to work, she had to go back down to Texas knowing everything she was going to be living with. "You closed me out for a year, Bear, but I'm going to see everything."

He pushed her up. He obviously didn't want to hurt her, but the force of his push made her topple into the bookshelf and she steadied herself with her arms. He yelled, "This is my private problem."

"You don't have any *private* problems. You're in a relationship," she yelled back. "That's the whole point."

He got up on his hands and knees on the bed and rushed her, yelling, "You want to see this?"

"Yeah, I want to see this." The glow of light receded from the room, as if they were yelling the light out. After a sudden dramatic crescendo, the tv changed to a blue screen. "You're the same man," she said.

"Watching gets people into *trouble*," he bellowed from the bed, positioned like a dog barking at her to stay out of his yard. "I should know."

"You didn't become a bear because you saw something bad. A bad *woman* cursed you. You were innocent—"

"*You weren't there.*"

Darkness fell hard and sudden. She didn't know what to expect. He shrank. Or, the human part of him shrank, as if he were falling inside of a great pit, covered in hair. His outline was smudged with charcoal fur, darker and darker as he fell backwards into the body of the bear. Suddenly, in a wavy movement of fur, the bear leapt off the bed and crushed her against the books, his terrible teeth revealed, his breath hot.

He yelled, "*Is this what you wanted to see?*"

It was like a Texas wind—like one of those tornadoes that spiral down suddenly in the middle of a street, tossing everything from in front of you. He was every bit a bear at this moment, moaning and roaring at her, but she didn't try to move away. She couldn't really, but she could be terrified if she let herself be. She looked down his throat, past his teeth, to where she thought she might be able to hear the witch telling a boy at his window, "*Is this what you wanted to see? This sex? Didja get a good eyeful?*"

"I am not scared of you," she whispered to him. She said it again, calmly, making it echo off his own throat. He paused for a breath and she repeated herself, firmly. "I am larger than you. You can't hurt me."

His thick hairy body pressed against her. She could feel the shelves across her back.

He stared at her. "I didn't want you to get hurt," he said.

"I didn't. I didn't even change."

He stopped yelling. He eased back a little, though she could still feel his body on her. He looked paralyzed between two actions: holding her and letting her go. She reached around and pulled him closer. She stood in a city where everything changed, everything had cycles, and nothing was in a permanent state. The sun left; it came back again. The river froze; it thawed. Fish swam south; they returned north to spawn. The man in front of her, with tears in his small black eyes, was a bear; tomorrow morning, he would be human; but tomorrow night, he would be a bear again. No escaping that cycle with him. To accept Bear was to never be able to stop the night from changing him. But damned if she wasn't going to show him opportunities from these changes.

She reached down his naked bear body until she had her hand between his hairy thighs. "There is nothing wrong about *this*. This is fantastic. This is good, and you, buddy, are good at it." She looked for some hint of recognition. He blinked; he looked down. "Yes, really." She rubbed his arms. "We're two adults. It's okay to enjoy this. Maybe one day you want to find that witch and sock her in the mouth, but I don't mind the bear part, Bear. You wanted to know that." And it was true. She liked the crazy side of it, the adventure that being in love with a man who became a bear at night presented. "I think you're sexy both ways. But I gotta know one thing: Do you want me?"

He looked up at her. "Yes," he said.

"No, I have to be wanted and valued and respected for all that I am, too—whether I'm conservatively dressed or naked in your arms. Can you do that? Can you love the wild side of *me*?"

He looked puzzled. Maybe he'd never considered that someone else might need the bear side of her loved—but, dammit, she did. And if he wasn't willing to praise that curvy figure she had, well then, she could find another bear to love in a city of a thousand good things.

"You," he said, clearing his throat and looking her in the eye, "look wonderful tonight."

Any woman of the Klondike worth keeping would have pushed the bear back toward the bed. They were not whores, not prostitutes, not gold-diggers. They came up for a new life, whether or not they found bears. These women got something for themselves. Trees and mountains and bars and friendly people and wildness. These women would have climbed under the covers with a bear, and when he suggested they just cuddle, they would have turned and cozied up to the adventure.

"I'm as warm as a furnace, aren't I?" he said behind her, under the covers.

"You're as warm as a house," she told him. And when he pressed his cold nose against her back, it sent a chill that melted halfway to her heart.

The Song of Sasquatch

~1~

Beloved

My lover pursues me through the thicket with an ardent desire of leaves
    opening to the sun. He leaves
    no footprint I give him untouched. Oh brothers,
    awaken not love until it is ready to be
    found. But when it is ready, shake it till it screams.

Friends

We will hide you within the thicket. We will take the lover
    and break him with our hands. No one shall find you!

Beloved

Let him find me in the thicket, with the leaves pressed down in the place
    where I saw him first, when he touched the imprint of my toes
    and gathered the hair pinned to the branch.

Do not hide me, brothers! I want to be seen.

My coat is winter-bound, my eyes hoarfrost hung, my stride brings
    no one chasing, no one speeding through wild rose, where thorns
    cling, except the Lover.
Oh, hurry, Lover, or I will be lost.

Your arms are fragile like the sapling, new to the forest,
 stunted by the shade. Your eyes search for me, like the squirrel
 waits for the sound of wings to come, that last sound. Your glasses
 brass, your instruments brass, and on your wrist, a circle
 of brass. Brass is the sign of my Lover, as he pursues.

Your footfall, your breath—the smell of coffee, and decay,
 the sweat of your excitement.
 You trace my time; I track your love.

Friends

Oh, do not walk on the mud where your feet will be seen. Why do you walk
there?
 Why do you leave him any sign? We will drag the sticks across the
 mud and
 erase you.

Beloved

Do not erase the signs of my love in the thicket, in the mud, in the
 soft places,
 oh, brothers. I beg of you. How long should I run from him? He pursues
 because he seeks the mystery; will I run to keep that mystery, or turn
 to reveal it?

Lover

My lens never captures him, though I have taped his song. Over and over
again,
 I play it. Till I feel I could answer him. The huff and chuff
 and the whistles and growls, and the howl;

How it chills me in the tent of my pursuit; how it coils around me
 with cold
 hands, and promises love and death. And winter.

Friends

He is just a man, smaller than most, a weasel with no brow, built
    more like a bird, hopping along the forest floor, peering down,
    and writing notes—we shall find that notebook! To read him as he
    has read you!

Lover

Oh, beloved, how I have smelled you in the thicket, in the dense
    thicket of noon,
    and your scent to me is like simmering stew in a Coleman stove;
    you are peat, raspberry, smoke, cheddar, and sweat.

I love you with a curious degree-in-large-mammals love,
    with the intricate, discredited studies of cryptozoology,
    and the notes that I take, the notes of notes, the notes of your
    voice, the notes of your love, in the margins of *The Field Guide to*
    Beasts and Myths. Yellow highlighter is a stroke of desire.

Beloved

Let me kiss him with the kisses of my mouth, and bring him the joy of my
song,
    in the thicket when the sun streams through the branches of the pines,
    and the poplars; let us lie down beneath the skirt of the spruce.

I build a bed of spruce boughs. My lover will not be afraid. He has seen me
walk;
    he writes of me that I am a *man of the woods*, that I know the forest,
    that I am
    never lost. I know each tree as if it were my own arm, my own leg, my
    soul
    reaching to heaven.

Let my hand caress his hairless thigh, let his fingers curl around my shaggy
    tresses, a forest of hair for him to hunt me, to search, for clues
    in my chest. Oh, who can find a heart, unless he searches with his?

~2~

Friends

We have seen his camp! Should we, O Brothers, dash his head on a stone?
We see
> his footprints lead to the place of men! Oh, we should seize him, and
> break
> him, rend him and bury him in the thicket! Even now, he rises from
> his tent,
> his eyes search to capture you!

Beloved

Capture me in the coolness of the morning, before you have wearied yourself
> from running. I will slow down. You can find me. My steps closer
> together, my footprints a path to where I am waiting in the thicket.

But I cannot wait forever—the wood rose, the fireweed, the lupine,
> all have their season and they open and then are gone,
> and I cannot wait forever.

Lover

Wait for me. I have measured your stride, the depression of your heel.
> Do not walk so fast, your legs like oak trees uprooted from the
> ground; reveal to me your back, just your back, so that I might see you
> and be encouraged.

Beloved

See me! See me! See me! I am ready to be revealed! I am where the thicket
parts,
> where the field begins. Here I have laid down in the sunshine, to bathe
> in the sunshine, where the hands of the sun run across my chest as
> it does
> the wild barley grass in the meadow, where the wind strokes my
> stomach

like the Lover! See me! See me! It is a time for honesty and
revelation!

Friends

But the Lover will reveal us all! He will bring others to our forests to find us!
 He will take the Beloved from us, and trample our forests
 and unbraid our ways from our hands!

We have seen him in his tent of destruction—we have seen his cooking pots,
 his soap, his toothbrush and camera—they will blaze a swath like fire
 in our forest, a path like flame!

Beloved

How I wish you were like me, so we could walk together
 in the light of the day, past the brothers and the friends, whose eyes
 are haughty now, but who could see you and love you as one of us;
 you could kiss me and they would approve

This is my Lover! This is my Friend! O Brothers of the Woods, do not harm
him!

Lover

On Dezadeash Lake, let me find your footprints;
 on the Tatshenshini River I canoe to find you,
 for your stories linger in Kluane and Pine Lakes
 and up the side of Tachäl Dhäl—I will travel
 the Yukon to find you, Beloved;

I remember, I remember, that night in the woods, when you came to my tent,
 when you stood outside the canvas, the shadow of your body
 like blue water splashed above me; how you listened, with your fingers
 to your mouth; how I listened, how we heard each other's heartbeat
 in the silence. I remember! And pursue your love!

~3~

Friends

Where has your lover gone, most handsome and strong brother? Which way
    did your lover turn—that we may look for him with you?

Beloved

O wretched friends, I had a dream! I heard my lover approach, his hiking boots
    crushing the leaves, he called my name, *Beloved, Beloved, Beloved*

And I rose to greet him, but when I came to his voice, he was not there.
    You crouched there instead, your five voices mimicking his, your smiles
    tore across your faces, your eyes blazing like snickiton fires
    that hold to a single twig, to light a forest;
    your mocking, glibbering howls!

Oh, let not friends rot your love with doubt or shame, even if they threaten
    to leave you; they may spurn you; but alone you choose the hollow
    where
    your heart rests, the stride by your stride, the voice that follows you.
    Bring love to your hiding place.

Let not their fears drive away your love.

Friends

Man is weak and fragile, breaking easy in the wilderness. It is shameful
    to walk with him; disgusting to share his journey; revolting
    to lead him to our places of peace.

Beloved

Oh, under the spruce boughs I shook you, but you would not rouse, Lover.

Friends

It is unnatural to walk with man as one would walk with us; unnatural to seek
   his companionship in the meadow, in the forest, in the hidden places.
   See how he noted you, how he wrote about you, how he wanted to
   photograph you.

Lover

We stand at the edge of meeting; you wait in the brush of almost ready
   You see me with eyes looking to be found; you trust
   with the hand reaching through the willow.

Beloved

Beneath your head I found your notebook, your words, your discoveries,
inked now in red, the pen of your thoughts and desires broken; the ink runs.

My heart sinks like a heavy stone to the bottom of the lake, to the mud;
   There it burns and eats the lake from below, its jaws of flame consume
   the water, the fish and every living thing.

Many waters cannot quench my love; rivers cannot wash it away. It devours
   and drinks and is never satisfied.

Oh, Brothers, the one who pursues you,
   the one who studies you,
   who traces your shadow on the grass you left behind,
   he is the one that loves you.

Love is a hard-fought, hard-run pursuit,
   the sweat of desire,
   the work of the heart.

Lover

I long to walk with you and the night will wrap its stars around us,
   enrobe our souls in mysteries, in mysteries of pursuit, as stars chase stars
   chase

stars. Come, come, come
away with me.

Beloved

Come, come, come back. The night empties its stars into the lake.

ACKNOWLEDGEMENTS

If you look behind this book, you'd see a trail that stretches back, winding through people who encouraged, helped, promoted, taught and pushed me. My trail was EPIC.

Thank you, Brett and Sandra, Sister Sam, and Michael, for believing in me and my writing.

Thank you, Terrence M. Green, who read my work and told me to send "Lemmings" to the editors of *Tesseracts 9*, Nalo Hopkinson and Geoff Ryman, resulting in my first sale. I owe a debt to Brian Hades and Janice Shoults at Edge Science Fiction and Fantasy Publishing for believing and encouraging my writing, editing, and ideas, at an early stage. I want to thank Marcelle Dube and Barb Dunlop for hosting and running some awesome Yukon Writers' Conferences and Workshops for our isolated community of writers up in the far north. Without them, and people like them, writers would have to leave the territory to be trained. Patricia Robertson, Erling Friis-Baastad, Miche Genest, Dianne Homan, Marie Carr, Claire Eamer, Lily Gontard, and Jo Lilley encouraged and advised and wrote alongside me, and damn, I appreciate that. Thank you, Steve Slade, master musician who ran the Arts in the Park for many years, who pushed me to write for performance. Keep all those people who ask you for more. To Bev Brazier and the folks at Whitehorse United Church for being open to love without reservation, and started a writing group in their church. Thank you, Yukon artists Joyce Majiski, Suzanne Paleczny, Neil Graham, Margriet Aasman, Sandra Storey, Jeanine and Paul Baker, and many, many others for helping me develop my art. To the many artists and musicians of the Yukon who are my friends—your inspiration and friendship helps artists in any genre. To Jaime and Dave Strachan, Steve Parker, and David Wesley who read early drafts of many of these stories and offered good advice. Thank you, Susan Zettell for being one of my first writer friends in the Yukon and staying with me even as we both moved around the continent. I would also like to thank the Touring Artist Award administered through Yukon Tourism and Culture and the Yukon Cultural Industries Training Fund for funding writers to leave the Yukon and network with others. (Go to the Yukon—it will love up the artist in you.) And especially Laurel Parry, Michele Emslie, and Ross Burnet: you show the way out and back.

Thank you, Lambda Literary Writers Retreat and Samuel R. Delany who taught me to be fearless in writing LGBT characters. Everywhere. We deserve a little adventure too.

Thank you, Clarion (Greg Frost, Ann and Jeff VanderMeer, Karen Joy Fowler, Cory Doctorow, Ellen Kushner, and Delia Sherman—my teachers—and Kim Stanley Robinson for enjoying Lemmings so much). To Kater Cheek, Justin Whitney, Julie Andrews, and the rest of my Clarion class for being great readers. To editors Cory D and Holly Phillips, Brett Savory and John Robert Colombo, Kevin Chong, Steve Berman, and Nancy Kilpatrick—for choosing some of these stories for anthologizing or publishing. Thank you, Naomi Hirahara for your continued friendship and encouragement to keep submitting work, as well as Virginia Stem Owens, Essie Sappenfield, Bryan Dietrich for the Milton Center and beyond—you took a chance on me that we could talk about faith and speculative literature together. We did.

Thank you, literature teachers and thinkers, in colleges and universities: Arch Mayfield, Geoff Wells, Don Cook, Reta Carter, Christa Smith, Tom Ray, Marti Runnels, Jill Patterson, Stephen Graham Jones, Carol Anshaw. Thank you, Maneater, the newspaper of the University of Missouri-Columbia, for hiring me to write a comic strip about talking bears in the Arctic for $20 a strip. And for Dad who helped me self-publish those strips in a book.

Thank you, Ray Bradbury, who told me it wasn't enough to write stories if you weren't going to send them out, one a week, where the statistics would then be better that you could get something sold. Thank you, Madeleine L'Engle, for giving me your advice and a second interview—delighted that I wasn't one of the Baptists who taunted your early books.

Thank you, Sandra Keith, who offered me in my junior year of high school a directed study class in Creative Writing when all that was offered to juniors and seniors in the whole school was Small Engine Repair. (I went to a high school of twelve people in Bledsoe,

Texas). She also midwifed a tangled novel over two summers after I graduated high school. I used to go to her house and she would critique three chapters at a time. She started this belief that I was a writer. I guess I couldn't shake it. I owe so much to her for changing my life at sixteen.

Finally, thank you, Mom and Dad, for doing so well with a weird science fiction-loving kid. Thank you, Dad, for going with me to the Hollywood Wax Museum and standing with me on either side of Mr. Spock, for buying me subscriptions to *Spider-Man* and *Fantastic Four* comic books, for buying "action figures" of superheroes and *Star Trek*. Thank you, Mom, for reading the Chronicles of Narnia to us in the hallway before bedtime. Thank you for endless Safari Cards, indulging all my reading of gods and goddesses and dinosaurs and wildlife, picking me up when I bombed and bailed the Writer's Digest School of Writing like an asteroid (Mort Castle, I figured it out). Thank you for going to every comic book store and 7-Eleven during our yearly vacations across the United States (sometimes at 6 a.m.), for the heroic church Bible stories and for the weird ones. Thank you for supporting me as my doodles became pictures, and I became a portrait artist in front of Piggly Wiggly's and at festivals. You always believed that somehow I could find a way to put it all together.

Mom and Dad, I put it all together.

AUTHOR BIO

Jerome W. Stueart is a writer, cartoonist and illustrator from the Yukon Territory by way of Missouri and Texas. A Clarion graduate, Lambda Literary fellow, and Milton Fellow, he has had work appear in *Lightspeed, Geist, On Spec, Fantasy, Joyland, Icarus, Geez* and various anthologies, including three from the Tesseracts series. He was co-editor of *Wrestling with Gods (Tesseracts 18)* and *Imaginarium 4*. His novel, *One Nation Under Gods*, is forthcoming from ChiZine in 2017. His work has been runner-up to the Fountain Award and John Haines Poetry Award. He has worked as a vaudevillian, a reporter for the Arctic Institute of North America, a trolley conductor, a tour guide to Theodore Roosevelt's home and has written several successful radio series for CBC North. His heart is still in the Yukon where he lived for nine years, but he now teaches writing, graphic literature, and science fiction at the University of Dayton.

PUBLICATION HISTORY

An earlier version of "For a Look at New Worlds" placed 2nd in the 2015 Little Tokyo Short Story Contest sponsored by the Little Tokyo Historical Society and appeared on the Japanese American National Museum's Discover Nikkei website.

"Sam McGee Argues with His Authentic Box of Ashes" was written and performed as part of the Arts in the Park Heritage sessions, sponsored by Music Yukon, Yukon Historical Society, and Yukon Heritage, Whitehorse, Yukon, August 2014.

"Et tu Bruté" was a finalist to the *Geist* Postcard Story Contest, April 26, 2010 and later appeared in *Geist*, Fall/Winter 2010.

"The Song of Sasquatch," previously appeared in *Joyland*, June, 2010, and then in *Icarus: The Magazine of Gay Speculative Fiction*, Lethe Press, Summer 2010.

"How Magnificent is the Universal Donor" previously appeared in *Evolve: Vampire Stories of the New Undead*, Edge Science Fiction and Fantasy Publishing, March 2010.

"Bondsmen" previously appeared in *Metazen*, October 12, 2009.

"Moon Over Tokyo Through Fall Leaves" previously appeared as "The Moon Over Tokyo Through Leaves in the Fall" in *Fantasy Magazine*, September 2009.

"Bear With Me" previously appeared in *Tesseracts Eleven: Canadian Anthology of Science Fiction and Fantasy*, November 2007.

"Brazos" previously appeared in *Strange Horizons*, July 3, 2007.

"Why the Poets Were Banned from the City" previously appeared in *OnSpec*, Spring 2007.

"Old Lions" previously appeared in Redivider, Spring 2005.

"Lemmings in the Third Year" previously appeared in *Tesseracts 9: Canadian Anthology of Science Fiction and Fantasy*, May 2005, and was runner up to the Fountain Award given by the Speculative Literature Foundation 2005.